High School Super-Star: The Junior Year

Cecil Buffington

iUniverse, Inc.
New York   Bloomington

High School Super-Star: The Junior Year

iUniverse books may be ordered through booksellers or by contacting:

iUniverse
1663 Liberty Drive
Bloomington, IN 47403
www.iuniverse.com
1-800-Authors (1-800-288-4677)

ISBN: 978-0-595-51914-9 (pbk)
ISBN: 978-0-595-62085-2 (ebk)

Printed in the United States of America

iUniverse Rev. 12/23/2008

Buffington BIO

Cecil Buffington was a child of the fifties ------ a teen of the sixties. He was a high school athlete that earned 14 letters while participating in four sports at Jefferson High School in Jefferson, Georgia from 1960-64.

Buffington retired after 35 years as a Management Executive in 2000.

He is the author of *The Chicken Plant* published in 2007. The most detailed account of poultry processing ever written.

He currently resides in Jefferson, Georgia with his wife of over 40 years, Betty.

High School Super-Star: The Junior Year~ A novel by Cecil Buffington

Coach Thomas Shaw was the head football coach and athletic director at Salem High School in Ridgeview, Maryland. The huge AAAA high school had a traditionally strong athletic program.

A knock on his door one mid-August day changed high possibilities to high probabilities for state high school sports supremacy. Coach Shaw quickly discovered that transfer-student Kyle Morgan was not a normal 16-year-old high school junior. Things are about to get exciting around the old school house when;

- **Morgan meets Misty Porter, a beautiful basketball playing cheerleader.**
- **Morgan's CIA Agent father is sent to Vietnam.**
- **The high school super-star signs a recording contract.**
- **Exciting play-by-play sports puts you in the stands at Salem Memorial Stadium and the Eagles Nest Gymnasium.**
- **The dramatic conclusion will both shock you and thrill you!**

High School Super-star: The Junior Year can finally be told.

Contents

Special dedications to the memory of my parents ~ Lucille and Hoyt Buffington, my Grand-mother Emma Bennett, my sister ~ Dianne Buffington, Coach John Davis, Mrs. Mabel Potter, Mrs. Stella Ash and my childhood best friend, Johnny Pruitt. These wonderful people will never be forgotten.

Disclaimer:

No similarity between any of the names, characters, persons, places, and/or institutions in this book with those of any living/dead person, school or University or company/institution is intended. Any such similarity which may exist is purely coincidental . . . .

Chapter One
A Tall, Good Looking Guy!

It was a hot, humid day in early August of 1962 when Kyle Morgan approached the white colonial-style house on South-eighteenth Street. He walked up the steps, grasped the gold knocker on the front door, and proceeded to rap several times on the door.

It was just a moment before a young lady opened the door. She asked, "Yes, may I help you?"

The young man told her that he wanted to speak with Coach Tom Shaw. He had been told this was the residence of the Salem High School football coach.

The young lady smiled as she said, "Coach Shaw is my father. I'll tell him you're here. Please have a seat." She motioned toward the velvet couch in front of a console television. It was tuned to what appeared to be the local news.

Jennifer (Jen) Shaw went into the study where her father was also watching the evening news. She said, "Dad, there's someone here to see you."

Coach Shaw asked, "Who is it?"

Jen answered quickly, "I don't know, but he's a tall, good-looking guy."

Her father was amused at the description. His daughter had just turned fifteen. She would arguably have some well-established opinions on what might constitute a tall, good-looking guy.

As the coach made his way toward the living room, he thought about the first day of football practice slated to begin the next day. His thoughts were that the young man in his living room could very well be some youngster wanting to talk with him about playing football. He could be a transfer in from another school somewhere. The coach mused that every summer there would be transfers in from out of town that usually didn't make much of an impact on the overall success of his football program. He had long ago given up on his early career fantasy that a super-star player would transfer into his high school. A tall guy, he thought, might make us a good receiver.

Upon entering the room he saw a thin, wiry youngster fidgeting in the chair in front of the television. "Hello son , I'm Coach Shaw." ---- "What can I do for you?"

The young man rose to his feet and introduced himself to the coach.

"My name is Kyle Morgan, Sir. I've just moved into Ridgeview from Georgia. I want to try out for your football team."

The coach moved his eyes from head to toe of the tall youngster as he remembered his daughter's description of a tall, good-looking guy. Well, she was certainly right about the tall aspect of the description. The coach inquired, "Have you played much football?"

Morgan went on to tell the coach he had played wide receiver for his high school team in Georgia. He made it clear he wanted to try out for the quarterback position. "I was a backup quarterback for the starting quarterback at Central Jackson last season. He was a senior All-State quarterback. He was really a great football player. He's currently a freshman at Benton State University." Young Morgan went on to tell the coach that while he didn't get the opportunity to play much quarterback, he had learned a great deal in his backup role.

Coach Shaw told the young man, "Son, we have someone in mind for our quarterback ----- a senior to be ----- but we will give you every opportunity to compete for the job. Our first football meeting is at 6:00 p.m. tomorrow evening at the high school gym. Just follow the mob." As an after-thought, he said, "You don't need to be late."

It seemed like the following afternoon came quickly to Morgan. At 5:15 p.m., he walked up the gym steps at William Edward Salem High School. There were already sixty-five or so boys inside waiting for the meeting to start with another fifteen to twenty milling around outside waiting to enter the building. There were several nods and greetings from members of the assembled group. He made his way to an empty chair and took a seat. Now it was just wait for the coach to arrive.

His mind went back to the first time he had ever went out for organized football. He had played on his junior-high squad as a seventh grader. He had been fairly successful. Even with this success he had always considered himself more of a basketball player than a football player. He had not really liked the hitting. He also found himself bored with the practice sessions. He had played two seasons of high school football back in Georgia and found himself liking the game better as time went on. His improvements in the game were extraordinary over the last two years. He now considered himself to be a capable high school football player. He had also grown a full two inches since the past football season. It did not appear he had lost any speed, quickness or agility with the additional height.

Promptly at 6:00 p.m., Coach Shaw stepped to the front of the group. He went into the Salem tradition on the gridiron in great detail. His presentation went over some of the highs and lows of the program over the last five years. He mentioned that 12 former Salem players were now playing football at NCAA Division 1-A schools across the nation with another 25 or so playing at Jr. Colleges or NAIA schools. He made it clear to the assembled group that he fully expected this years team to be a strong contender for the region championship. The meeting concluded with the coach going over the practice schedule for the first week, saying that it would be a full week of non-contact drills in shorts and helmets. The second week would begin full dressed contact practice to get ready for the September the second home opener against Rock-Hill High School. There was about a month to get ready for the first game.

After signing all the appropriate papers and liability releases, Morgan started the walk to his home. He lived about two miles from the high school. He had just left the school premises when a burgundy-colored, 1959 Plymouth --- Chrysler automobile stopped beside him.

The driver asked, "You need a lift?"

At first thought, Morgan didn't mind the short walk to his home, but he also saw this as an opportunity to meet and possibly make a new friend in this strange new surrounding. " Sure, thanks," he answered as he opened the car door.

The driver introduced himself. "My name is Butch Cobb. I've seen you walk by the house several times over the last few days. I live about six houses down from you." After all the introductions and small talk, the conversation turned to football.

Cobb explained that last years team had won eight games with only two losses, but had not won the region. Both losses were to region foes, West Ridgeview and District-Heights. These schools were again thought to be extremely strong this year. Both were rated in the state AAAA Top 10 preseason rankings. He concluded the discussion by saying he played end on the team for the last two seasons, was a junior, played basketball, and participated in track.

As the car pulled into his drive, Kyle Morgan and Butch Cobb had started to develop a friendship. Cobb said, "If you want a lift to practice, I'll be happy to stop by and pick you up."

Morgan replied, "That would be great, I'd appreciate it." He watched as his new-found friend backed out of the driveway and went back down the street.

The Morgan's had been in Ridgeview for less than two weeks. They really had not had much time to meet the neighbors or any other people for that matter. Mr. Morgan had researched all the Ridgeview schools before helping his son decide that W.E. Salem would be a good match for his academic and athletic talents.

They had also considered West Ridgeview High School very seriously.

The family had heard nothing but good things about Salem High School from everyone they had talked with. Young Morgan was comfortable with the decision to attend Salem. He looked forward to starting his Salem years and directing his considerable athletic talents toward their success.

Morgan was soon to turn sixteen. His birthday was September the sixteenth. His father had promised him an automobile for his sixteenth birthday. That was the most distant thought in his mind as he entered into the two-story brick house on Dixon Avenue. His mind was on playing high school football.

Chapter Two
Enter Morgan and Mentz

There were 124 potential players out for football at Salem High School. About sixty of those would be assigned to varsity status. The balance would draw B-team and ninth grade team assignments.

Salem had a reputation of having a strong football program. Every year they felt they should contend for a region championship.

Coach Shaw was a former college halfback at Huntington State College in Virginia. He had been a four-sport athlete in high school where he held all the Virginia state high and low hurdle records upon his graduation. After college he had played two years of professional football with the Cleveland Stallions of the National Football League. After being cut from the team he had married his high school sweetheart ~ Martha Loggins ~ and started his high school teaching and coaching career. His first job was as a physical education teacher and assistant football coach at Mt. Lacy High School in Dunbar, Maryland.

He had been at Salem High School for eight years.

He previously served as the head coach at Wayne County High school in Lower Maryland for 16 years before taking the Salem job as head football coach, track coach and athletic director. He had won 142 games at the AA Wayne County school during his tenure with two state football championships and four state titles in track.

Shaw had been hand-picked by the Salem school board, chaired by Mr. William Edward Salem, to guide the schools athletic fortunes. At Salem, he found great success at winning football games, but the state championship had proven to be extremely elusive. His teams had won 66 games with 20 defeats. Twice the Eagles had won the region 8-AAAA title. They had never been able to advance beyond the second round of the state playoffs. The last two years they had finished third in the region behind West Ridgeview and District-Heights. These were the only regular season losses for the Eagles during this time. Since only two teams from a region advanced to state play, they had not made the state football playoffs since second-place region finishes in 1957 and 1958. The Eagle fans were getting edgy.

There was even some grumbling by some extreme Salem loyalists of maybe needing a new head coach. Some were wondering if he could ever bring home that elusive state championship. His stereotype seemed to be that of a nice guy who couldn't win the big game.

Kyle Morgan was six-feet-five-inches tall. He weighed 178 pounds. His frail appearance was deceiving in that he had zero body fat with strong, sinewy muscle. He had started taking karate and tae-kwon-do lessons at the age of six. He had achieved black-belt status by the age of ten.

His academic status was a source of pride to the Morgan family that consisted of young Morgan, his father --- Kenneth and his mother --- Lucille.

The family had found out early in Kyle's childhood that he was somewhat different from most other children his age. By the age of four he could read fluently and perform math at a high school junior level. He was discovered to have an IQ of over 250 at age eight. The kid phenomenon started school at age four with advanced education classes. He also had started taking college-prep classes at age nine in the fifth grade. He had a photographic memory with amazing ability to read a novel and repeat it back to you in almost exact detail.

His life had been a challenge to find a challenge. He had found that challenge in athletics. He lived for and thrived on competition. His accomplishments at his former North Georgia High School had been extraordinary. Now he was in a new school with new challenges. There was a new exuberance that would present him with the self-motivation to move forward toward his goal of being a professional athlete.

There were a lot of curious glares from his fellow team members as the prospective players took their warm-up laps around the practice field. Butch Cobb fell in beside Morgan and they completed their warm-ups as a tandem.

Coach Shaw began the division of the players into position work with Morgan being directed to the quarterback coach. It was an interested ensemble of coaches and players as they watched the newcomer take snaps and throw to receivers downfield. "Pretty good toss," said Assistant Coach Will Powers after a 30-yard bullet to a streaking receiver found its mark. By the end of the first workout it was evident that transfer-student Morgan had some unique and outstanding talents.

"Coach, you need to look at this guy throw the ball!" exclaimed an excited Coach Powers to Coach Shaw.

"I've been watching him," replied the eagle-eyed head coach..

As they were going home, Butch Cobb said to Kyle, "Man, you can really throw a football. Where did you learn to throw a ball like that?"

He answered, "It's just something I learned coming up through the youth leagues."

Cobb slowly shook his head as he said, "You sure do throw a good ball to catch. It's always right on the money." He would say some years later that on that very first day he knew that Morgan was an exceptional high school football player.

It was evident after that first day that the new boy was far above the other quarterbacks on the team as far as throwing the ball.

Another transfer student was creating some conversation himself with a strong performance at the quarterback position. James Mentz was another pleasant surprise to the coaching staff. He stood six-foot-six-inches, had a strong arm and fairly consistent accuracy.

The projected starting quarterback ~ before Morgan and Mentz arrived on the scene ~ was a senior that had been the backup the previous season. Tommy Carter had seen a lot of action the previous season. He had started two games when the starting quarterback went down with a leg injury. The Eagles had won both games. He was a steady, if not spectacular quarterback. He was strong on leadership and well respected by his teammates. It was evident early on he was not in the league with Morgan or Mentz as a passer.

Returning to the team was All-State halfback Bobby Winkler --- a four-year starter. He was the state 100-yard dash champion the last two years in track. He had finished second in the 220-yard dash the previous year and was the anchor leg on the state runner-up 440-yard relay team and the third place mile-relay team. His speed gave him the ability to score from anywhere on the field at any time. He had scored 31 touchdowns for the Eagles the previous year.

Another potential all-star for the Eagles was the 245 pound, six-foot-eight-inch tight end and defensive stalwart Cobb. He was named to the All-State second team as a sophomore. His father was a world class slow-pitch softball player. He was an avid weight lifter. Young Cobb had started lifting weights at the age of 12 and could bench press almost 400 pounds. He was tremendously strong and could literally throw blockers aside to get at the quarterback or ball carrier.

The biggest problem confronting the Eagles was that both West Ridgeview and District-Heights returned most of their better players from the previous year. Both had experienced signal callers back to lead their offense.

The Eagle defense, would be led by Cobb with senior linebackers Randal Hinsley and Daniel North providing strong run-defense support.

Normally, a Monday practice would consist of reviewing the past weeks game, viewing the game film and looking at a film of the upcoming opponent. Since this was not an available option before the first game, Coach Shaw chose to go over all the various offensive sets and defensive schemes he wanted to use during the season.

Morgan listened intently as he explained the backfield designation system. The number "1" would be the quarterback; number "2" would be the right halfback/wingback; number "3" would be the left halfback/tailback; and number "4" would be the fullback. Holes from left of the center position were; 1, 3, 5, 7, and 9. From the right of the center the holes were; 2, 4, 6, 8, and 10. The zero hole was right behind the center. If the quarterback wanted the tailback to run a play into the "4" hole he would call "34" and give the cadence count, which would be; hut 1, hut 2 or hut 3.

He also drew up four primary pass routes on the board. On all but one route, Cobb would run either a buttonhook or a comeback route. Coach Shaw didn't send the big guy long. While Cobb was an excellent possession receiver, he was not blessed with great downfield speed.

The second day in shorts was primarily working on conditioning with a lot of wind sprints and   reaction drills including fumble recoveries, tip drills and defensive personnel placement.

The third day of practice was of an offensive theme with passing drills and plays ran from the various offensive sets. The primary offense Coach Shaw wanted to run was a power-I formation with the quarterback under center, the fullback directly behind the quarterback and the tailback to the left or right of the fullback. The wingback would go in motion from the weak side and reset in the gap between the strong-side tackle and the tight end.

Cobb would set up on the strong side every play with the other end moving to the weak side. It was evident that he was a primary blocker on every running play.

It was also very evident that the coach preferred to run the ball. He had great speed in Winkler and wingback Tim Shealey. There was also sheer power with fullback North and second-team fullback Van Greer.

Greer was only a sophomore, but you could see he was a very good prospect at 190 pounds.

Morgan worked every third series with Carter and Mentz running ahead of him at this point.

Thursday was a combination of conditioning, offensive and defensive work with a strong emphasis on timing and sustaining blocking assignments through the end of the play. In only four days Morgan could see that Coach Shaw was a sound fundamentals coach that would have the team ready to play the game. He addressed every mistake. It seemed he never overlooked or forgot a mistake. He would recall and mention them to make certain points as the practice moved forward.

At the end of practice Thursday, as Morgan and Cobb were going home, the big- redheaded end started talking about the past year and what they needed to do to improve over that year. "We just couldn't get over the District-Heights and West Ridgeview hump last year," recalled Cobb. "We played good football most of the game, but a little breakdown here or there gave up points that we just couldn't get back." He continued, "We lost two fumbles in the second half against District-Heights that gave them two touchdowns. We tried to catch up by passing and had a big interception that led to another score. We were snake-bitten in that game. Man, I sure would like to beat them this season."

Morgan calmly asked, "What about Rock-Hill?"

Cobb gazed at Morgan and answered, "They won three games last year. We beat them 45 - 0 in last years season opener. I think we are something like fourteen wins and no losses against them over the years. They just aren't very strong. Coach will play everybody and use the game as a good scrimmage."

Morgan asked Cobb, "Do you think I'll get to play quarterback on the team?"

He immediately answered, "Carter is a good guy. We all have a lot of faith in him. We really respect him. He doesn't make many mistakes. Mentz really looks good, but I've never seen anybody throw the ball better than you in practice. My guess is that you'll be called on in most passing situations."

That night while watching television, Mr. Morgan asked his son how practice was going?

"I think it's going all right, Dad, but I'll be glad when we start to mix it up."

Mr. Morgan asked, "Have you turned it up yet?"

Kyle answered emphatically, "No sir!" ---- I haven't had the chance to really go wide open without it looking like showboating." He continued, "Dad, they have a guy that was All-State last year in track who can run a 9.8 ~ 100-yard dash. He's awfully fast."

Mr. Morgan smiled as he said, "You're pretty fast yourself ------ you'll hold your own ---- I'm sure of that."

Ken Morgan had always been a strong supporter of his son's athletic participation. He had coached him all through the baseball little leagues and had worked with other community coaches while Kyle was coming up through the peewee football leagues. At this time, anything his son might accomplish on an athletic venue would not be a surprise to his father.

The Friday practice would be under the lights with a flag-ball scrimmage between the team. The coach wanted to try out the arms of all three of his quarterbacks. He wanted to see who was the best bet to provide positive results for a passing game.

Coach Shaw stood before the team on the sideline of Salem Memorial Stadium and gave them their final instructions. "We will play fifteen-minute quarters with the clock stopping only on incomplete passes, out of bounds and timeouts. You younger players can greatly improve your potential for playing time with a strong performance in all the skill areas. This is a time for me to see who can throw the football, who can catch the football and who can defend the pass in the secondary. Go wide open at all times."

He continued, "All backs, receivers and defensive secondary players will have a flag on each side. These flags will be at least two feet in length. Instead of a tackle, the defensive player will pull the flag from the ball carrier stopping his progress at that point."

Morgan looked around the stadium and was shocked to see it was almost full. He mentioned to Cobb, "Look at the people here to see a flag-football game. This is amazing."

Cobb said, "Salem is a football school. The stadium is always packed. We really have great support from our families, teachers and the community."

The scrimmage started with Carter quarterbacking the "red" first team. Mentz and Morgan were on the "gold" second team. The red team received the ball and immediately moved it into gold territory.

Even in flag ball, it was obvious that Bobby Winkler was an excellent runner. He darted about, zipped, zagged and just outran everyone as they yanked and tugged to try and pull out the flag. On a second-and-three yards needed for a first down from the 28, Carter went back to throw the ball. James Mentz, who was playing weak-side cornerback stepped in front of end Hal Devers and intercepted the ball on the 17-yard line.

Coach Dills turned to Morgan and told him to go in at quarterback. Coach Shaw was in both huddles to call plays. He called for a quick-slant pass to wingback Bradley Snyder. Morgan called the play, "30-slant on one." He took three steps back and fired a tight spiral at the target. The ball hit the receiver on the numbers for a 16-yard gain and a first down. Two running plays gained four yards. Coach Shaw instructed Morgan, "Call the "banana-three pass." Throw to the split end on the sideline. Try to pick up the first down." This was a play that had the flanked-out wingback run a banana or curved route long down the field. A second receiver – the split end – would go down 10 yards and angle sharply to the sideline. The tight end would go down 15 yards and quickly buttonhook back about three-or-four yards. The ball would be thrown low and hard right at the numbers.

Morgan took the snap and dropped back three steps, then stepping toward the receiver, he let the ball go in a tight spiral that slammed into receiver Joey Bales' chest. The ball popped out and fell to the ground. Morgan just smiled. He thought to himself that Cobb probably would never have dropped that ball. He continued to be impressed with the good hands of the big tight end. "Good effort," he said, as Bales came back into the huddle. Coach Shaw slapped the 6-foot sophomore receiver on his helmet and told him to "hold onto the ball."

It was obvious that the coach was not going to open up the game. He called running plays and short passes that moved the ball slowly down the field. From the 12-yard line on a fourth-and-three yards for the first down, he brought in junior-kicker Gerald Campbell to try the 29-yard field goal. It was wide right. Late in the quarter Winkler took a pitch, turned the corner and ran 65 yards for the first score. Morgan thought to himself, "That's one fast football player." James Mentz at safety had given chase, but the All-State back just continued to widened the gap.

It was about midway of the second quarter when Morgan got back in at quarterback. He threw the ball well, but was plagued by several drops. With less than two minutes left in the half – Coach Shaw sent quarterback Tommy Carter in at flanker. He had worked at wide receiver most of the week when he was not at the quarterback position. The coach called the banana route with Carter going long.

He instructed Carter, "Go straight at the cornerback, fake hard to the sideline, then get back into the route."

With the ball at the 30-yard line, Morgan dropped back. He watched as Carter feinted toward the sideline then turned it up field. Defensive-back Billy Smith, a 5-foot-11-inch junior took the fake and allowed a small separation. From his own 20-yard line Morgan threw the ball down field. The pass hit Carter in full stride at the gold 35-yard line and he ran in for the score.

Morgan has been designated as the second-team kicker after kicking tryouts earlier in the week. He walked over to Coach Shaw and asked if he wanted him to kick the extra point. The coach nodded and sent Campbell back to the sideline. Carter set the ball down and Morgan kicked it between the uprights. With the score tied at 7 - 7 at halftime, both teams kneeled in the endzone together for a critique on the first-half performance from the coaching staff.

Mentz started at quarterback for the gold team the second half. On his first drive he moved the team 45 yards before a fourth-down pass was dropped stopping the drive.

Coach Shaw told Morgan to go in at safety on defense. On a third-and-five from the 32-yard line, Carter threw to Winkler in the flat and he was off to the races. Suddenly, all eyes were on the streaking halfback as Morgan began chase at midfield. Winkler was clearly in front of him. To catch him would depend on sheer speed. Morgan closed the gap. Dove for the flag on the speedy backs left side and pulled it at the 12-yard line. Coach Shaw walked up to the red huddle and strongly emphasized to Winkler in no uncertain terms, "Son, don't you ever let up."

Winkler came back quickly with, "I didn't let up coach, he just caught me!"

There was a buzz around the stadium. All his teammates --- those on both teams --- were glancing in Morgan's direction.

Two plays later Winkler scored from the seven-yard line to put the red team up 13 - 7. Campbell kicked the PAT.

With Morgan at quarterback ~ the gold team marched down the field. Primary plays were short passes and an occasional running play ------ usually to Bates or fullback Greer on screens. With less than a minute left in the third quarter, Morgan threw to Walter Deaton from the 18-yard line for the touchdown. The PAT kick by Morgan was good to tie the score at 14 - 14.

The game settled down into a defensive struggle for the early part of the fourth quarter.

Mentz was unable to get the gold team moving during his quarterback series. Carter continued to struggle at moving the red-team offense. He was just not a consistently good passing quarterback. Carter punted to the gold 25 with 6:17 remaining in the game. Again, Mentz failed to move the gold-team offense. Morgan punted to Shealey, who ran out of bounds at the   red team 31-yard line. On second down, Carter threw to Shealey on a slant pass that Morgan stepped in front of for the interception. He returned the ball to the red team 44-yard line.

Coach Shaw walked up to the huddle and told Morgan, "You're at quarterback, call your own plays for the rest of the series.'

On first down Morgan threw a sideline pass to Snyder for nine yards. A quick pass on a slant to Bales netted seven more yards to the 28.   A buttonhook pass to Greer carried to the 18. With 1:07 left in the game, Morgan called for a "110 rollout on 2." This would be a quarterback carry wide into the 10 hole on the right side. Winkler was on the other side of the field. Morgan felt that he could get around the corner without the speed of Winkler to get to him. Cobb was on that side of the field, but his foot speed would not allow him to   interrupt the play. With 0.42 left in the game, he took the snap and rolled right. A sharp cut from left to right toward the goal line at the 10 freed him to zip across the goal with 0:38 left on the clock. His extra point made the score 21 - 14 for the gold team. Suddenly all the stadium was aware that the second team was going to "upset" the first team.

A lot of shocked fans walked out of Memorial Stadium that night. They had witnessed the coming out of Kyle Morgan. He had thrown 23 passes with 16 completions for 223 yards. Winkler had 126 yards rushing. Mentz had completed 8 of 15 for 92 yards. It suddenly appeared that the Eagles had the potential to develop a strong air attack.

Coach Shaw spoke briefly to the team after the game. He told them he was pleasantly surprised at the outcome. He reminded the team that next week would be the start of two-a-days for the week. The early practice would be in pads starting at 8:00 a.m. until 10:00 a.m. The second practice would be from 6:00 p.m. until 8:00 p.m.

~ culminating with a full scale scrimmage the following Friday night. Between practices every day would be spent resting in the gym as possible on mats or attending offensive, defensive, play-calling and other classes in mid-afternoon. Players would leave the sessions each night around 9:00 p.m. Lunch would be served promptly at noon until 1:00 p.m. It would consist of cold cuts, a beverage and a desert. The supper meal would be a hot meal prepared by the parents in the booster club consisting of whatever the parents wanted to provide. It would be from 4:00 p.m. until 5:30 p.m. Meetings would be from 1:00 p.m. until around 3:00 p.m.

Morgan grinned at Cobb on the way home and said, "It sounds like next week will be a killer."

Cobb replied, "You just can't imagine. Coach Shaw puts on a tough camp. He'll work us hard all week. He sort of slacks off the hard hitting during the regular season practice except for a little knocking on Tuesdays, but he nearly kills us in the two-a-day camp." Cobb paused and then said, "You know everyone is still talking about you catching Winkler on that long run. We have never seen anyone that could do that before tonight."

Morgan never answered. He didn't want to dwell on that particular subject. His mind was on the football camp slated for the next week.

The thought running through Cobb's mind as he pulled into the Morgan driveway was, "How can a guy as tall as Morgan be so fast? The shorter guys were usually the sprinters." As he drove toward his home that night, he wondered aloud, "Just what other amazing things can this guy do?"

Kyle Morgan sat in his room that night thinking about his personal goals at his new high school for the upcoming season. He wanted to earn first-team quarterback. He also wanted to fit in with the other boys on the team. Pretty soon it would become noticeable that he was far advanced in most of the football functions at the high school level. He knew he would run faster, throw the ball more accurately, kick the ball farther and straighter and ~ even with all the good players on the Salem team ~ he would standout. He wanted to have a strong positive impact on the team. He needed acceptance as a person as well as a player to accomplish his objective of making high school football a positive experience for him. He looked forward to the beginning of the grueling week of football camp starting the following Monday.

Chapter Three
Who Is That Guy ?

Jen Shaw walked into the den where her father was studying the statistic sheet from the Friday scrimmage. She broke the silence. "Dad, they really look good! This could be our year. They were quite a surprise with all the passing."

Coach Shaw smiled and replied, "Jen, we may be able to put together an unbelievable passing attack this season. What did you think of those two boys throwing the ball?"

She answered, "They look good, Dad. I also saw how fast that Morgan boy is." She asked, "Does he run track?"

Coach Shaw answered, "You know ----- I don't really know!"

After a pause for thought he said, "I'm going to find out next week just what that boy is capable of."

Jen Shaw thought to herself, "There's going to be a lot of interest in Mr. Morgan from a lot of people." Then as an after-thought she mused, "and it won't just be from the football coaches."

The Monday morning, first practice in full pads, went by quickly. It consisted of a lot of running and various drills to get the players used to the full-dress uniform.

It was two weeks before school opened. The administrative staff and teachers were currently working on student scheduling and making preparations for the upcoming year. Coach Shaw walked into the high school administration office around noon and asked Ms. Stella Dingler, the office secretary, "Do you have the transcript in yet for Kyle Morgan?"

"I believe we do Coach," answered Ms. Dingler, "but there is some kind of problem with it."

The coach quickly asked, "What kind of problem?"

"I don't know," answered the secretary, "but there's a note on it to call the school for confirmation on some issues in the file."

Coach Shaw said, "Let me see the file." After the file was handed to him, he opened it and scanned the freshman and sophomore grades for the quickly becoming mysterious Kyle Morgan. He couldn't believe what he was seeing. His grade-point average for 12 earned units over the past two years was 100 percent. There had to be an error. He handed the file back to Ms. Dingler and told her, "You need to move on this at once. I don't want to get this boy entrenched on the football team and find out later he has transcript problems. Find out if this is somehow correct, and if not, get his actual grade-point average on the record. If for some reason this kid is ineligible, we need to know it now. I don't want to spend a great deal of time working with him if he is not eligible to play with us." He reminded her she needed to move on this quickly.

She assured the coach she would take care of it before leaving school for the day.

The transcript was from Central Jackson High school in Rawlings, Georgia. The coach had scribbled down the school phone number. Now he sat down and dialed that number. He had a quarterback meeting scheduled for 2:00 p.m., so he wanted to get this particular call out of the way. When the call was answered he asked to speak with the head football coach. He didn't have a name to go with the individual.

The lady on the other end of the phone told him that would be Coach Travis. She said he was teaching a class at the time and had left instructions not to disturb him for phone calls unless it was an emergency.

Coach Shaw assured her it was not an emergency, but he did need to talk with the coach.

She said, "I'll leave word for him to return the call after class around 1:00 p.m."

Coach Shaw was again looking over the scrimmage statistics when the phone rang. He glanced at the clock. It was 12:59 p.m. If it was the expected call, the coach was certainly punctual.

It was Coach Travis.

"Hello Coach Travis. My name is Coach Thomas Shaw of Salem High School in Ridgeview, Maryland. I have a former student and player from your school on my football team. I want to ask you a few questions about him. I'd appreciate it if you would be completely candid with me. What can you tell me about Kyle Morgan?"

There was a chuckle from Coach Travis as he asked, "What do you want to know about him?"

Coach Shaw replied, " He told me he played some backup quarterback for you."

Coach Travis answered, "Yes, he did start out the season as our backup quarterback."

Coach Shaw quickly asked, "What do you mean ---- started?"

The revelation forthcoming from Coach Travis was indeed remarkable. "Well, we jumped out front of the first couple of teams we were playing by big margins and then put Kyle in the game at quarterback. He was our starting wide receiver. He had eighteen touchdown receptions, ran three kickoffs and four punts back for touchdowns and scored twice on reverse plays. He was first-team All-State."

The coach then returned to his quarterback story. "He would go in at quarterback and on every possession take the team to a score. We were trying to hold down the score , but they couldn't stop him from putting the ball in the endzone. We finally decided that we would let him play defense --- he played safety, for much of the game and not use him at quarterback. We were blessed with an All-State quarterback. Morgan had twelve interceptions last year. He was just so fast he would outrun the ball to the receiver. You have got yourself some kind of football player."

Coach Shaw sat somewhat stunned at what he was hearing. "You mentioned fast," interjected Coach Shaw, "just how fast is he?"

Coach Travis said, "He won the All-State decathlon last spring with a 9.2 ~ 100-yard dash time. He wasn't pushed. We never knew just how fast in the 100 he might be if someone pushed him. He ran both high and low hurdles on our track team. He won the state high hurdles with a time of 13.12 ~ and the low hurdles with a time of 18.62. Both were the best times in the nation. He also won the state pole vault championship with a 15-foot-3-inch vault. In that decathlon --- he high jumped 6-foot-10-inches and ran a 4.15.0 mile. He is an unbelievable track athlete."

Coach Shaw could not believe what he was hearing. He could not picture in his mind this unassuming, quiet youngster doing these amazing things. The coach asked, "Is there anything else about this boy that I might want to know?"

Coach Travis answered, "Well, he was All-State in basketball. We also won the state title. He averaged over 31 points per game. Finally, you might be interested in the fact that he is the best baseball player I have ever seen. He throws a 100-mile per hour fastball, has an unbelievable breaking ball and hit over 30 home runs. He batted .770. We won the state title in everything he was associated with. He is an extraordinary young man."

The somewhat amazed coach thought about the strange report card. "We have a transcript that shows him with a 100 percent grade-point-average for his two years at the school. Can that be true?"

"Yes, that is probably correct!" Exclaimed Coach Travis. "He has an IQ of genius in just about any subject. He has what they call a photographic memory. He never forgets anything he reads. I was told he made a perfect score on his Scholastic Aptitude Test last spring."

"One other thing you might want to know," volunteered the coach. "He was started on martial-arts training when he was very young and holds a black belt in four or five different skills. I always felt this was where he developed that amazing quickness and unbelievable coolness under fire. I wish he was still with us. I had planned on just putting him back there in a shot-gun formation and letting him throw on almost every down."

"Why did his family relocate?" inquired Coach Shaw.

Coach Travis answered, "From what I heard, his dad was relocated to the Washington area. No one knows exactly what he does, but it is rumored he is employed with the Central Intelligence Agency. Mind you, that is just a rumor. He does own a string of restaurant franchises around the Southeast. He has always hired people to run them for him."

Coach Shaw just gazed at the wall as he sat stunned while still holding the phone.

Coach Travis spoke loudly, "Hello, Coach Shaw, are you still on the line?"

"Yes, I'm sorry," Coach Shaw said, "I was just digesting what you have told me. Thank you for talking with me. What you have told me about Morgan will help me a lot in getting him indoctrinated into our program."

"That's fine, coach, I wish Kyle well," said Coach Travis. "You're going to find that you have a young man in your program that can make you competitive with any program anywhere in the country from what I've seen. I'll be interested in keeping up with your programs to see the impact he provides."

For several more moments the two coaches chatted, then Coach Shaw hung up the phone. He could see why Morgan was so close-mouthed about everything he could do. If he had told anyone, who would have believed him? For several moments the coach sat and pondered upon the good fortune that had suddenly been thrust upon the Salem athletic program.

The afternoon practice session went quickly. Some special-team drills and situation offense was the theme of the day. Morgan spent most of the time at quarterback with Mentz taking some snaps in special-situation plays. Tommy Carter worked at split end and flanker on all primary pass plays. In the punting, kickoff, point-after-touchdown conversions and field goals ---- it was evident that Morgan was easily going to assume those duties.

Coach Shaw --- now that he knew what to look for, could see the abilities of Morgan coming more to the front. The coach had decided not to pass on his knowledge of Morgan's talents to the other coaches at this time. He also would not inform the basketball coach or baseball coach of what they had to look forward to when their season rolled around. His thoughts were to limit expectations up front and let the results on the field tell the story of the talent level of Kyle Morgan.

At home that night, Coach Shaw made plans to change the offense to accommodate the immense talent of his new quarterback. He was going to go with multiple formations from a pro-set offense. On many occasions there would be five receivers running routes with an empty backfield. Winkler would become the safety-valve receiver to the outside when he was not specifically running a planned route. A shot-gun formation would be implemented with a one-back and a two-back set. Morgan would have the ability to audible at the line as he desired and as the defense would dictate.

He carefully worked out an audible system for his quarterbacks. Most coaches have their own system for calling an audible at the line of scrimmage. Coach Shaw had never had anyone he felt good about allowing this particular freedom. He also had never had a quarterback with total recall before Morgan.

Before retiring that night he worked out the system he planned to implement. He would use a three-number system. The last number of the first double number would be the primary receiver. All receivers would be numbered 1 through 5 from left to right in the direction the offense was moving. The second set of numbers would be the zone the quarterback would throw the ball into. The final set of numbers would be the yards to go downfield for that primary receiver in that particular zone. An example would be a quick slant to the right side by the number 4 receiver in the set. The zone may be number eight with the final designation being 12 yards down the field. The cadence would remain the same as called in the huddle. An example of this play being called at the line would be; 44-68-12 ~ hut 1, hut 2. In the first two numbers the first number would be thrown away.

Running play changes would be a color to designate a running play. It could be any color. An example might be the number 4 back into the number 8 hole. The call would be : Green - 54 - 38 - 73. The first number in both double first numbers would be thrown away as would the last two numbers called. They meant nothing. The cadence would remain the same as called in the huddle. The call at the line of scrimmage for this play would be; Green - 54 - 38 - 73 ~ hut 1, hut 2. If players were not in a position to run the play they would quickly shift into the needed set.

It was after midnight when the coach finally turned in for the night.

At 9:00 a.m. on Tuesday morning, the team met in a group for pre-practice instructions. Coach Shaw had been gathered with his coaches for over an hour explaining what he wanted to do offensively starting today. The day would be devoted to offense as would Wednesday.

The coaches met with their quarterbacks before formal practice that Tuesday and installed the audible system without a great deal of comment from the players. They proceeded to go over it with all the team during the course of practice. Coach Shaw's mindset was, "I have a genius quarterback. Why not provide him with all the tools available to allow him to be successful."

Thursday, both practices would be devoted to defense with Friday morning work on special-team play and the kicking game. Friday night would see a game-type scrimmage at the stadium.

An inquisitive look was the norm as the team watched the birth of the shot-gun formation with receivers spread out all over the field. Morgan would rollout right and throw the ball back across the field to a receiver on the opposite sideline. He would tuck the ball in and dart by astonished defensive backs that had not witnessed the kind of blazing speed he was displaying.

One other thing was quickly becoming evident. James Mentz was by far the most accomplished defensive back on the field. Several times he made leaping one-hand interceptions on bullets thrown down the middle.

By the end of the days passing drill it was pretty much accepted by all that Kyle Morgan would be the starting quarterback and James Mentz would be the starting strong safety. Tommy Carter appeared to be the most reliable receiver and deep threat. He would move in at flanker in the Eagle offensive set.

With the threat of the passing attack, it would become almost unfair to give the ball to Winkler. During the passing drill, Morgan would see the linebackers dropping back and make an audible call to run the 32-blast or 35-pitch and Winkler would be off to an almost sure score. Many times without a hand being laid on him.

Coach Shaw thought to himself, "We are going to have some kind of amazing offense."

On Friday morning, Morgan was kicking field goals from 40 yards with amazing consistency. He would put the ball in the endzone on all kickoffs and his punts were usually well over 50 yards in the air. A dress rehearsal of the game-type scrimmage was completed by about 11:30 a.m.

Bobby Winkler walked over to Morgan as he sat on the gym steps. "Kyle, you can fly," he said, "how fast can you run the 100?"

Morgan answered," I don't run the 100, Bobby, I run the hurdles and pole vault."

Winkler had not heard any times on Morgan's hurdle exploits, but he was almost willing to bet he would be virtually unbeatable. He had competed against the best sprinters the state had to offer, but he had never seen anyone as fast as his new teammate.

The Friday game-type scrimmage was a high-scoring affair with Morgan completing 22 of 26 passes for 296 yards and four touchdowns. He ran 63 yards for another touchdown and kicked a 41-yard field goal.

Winkler had an 89-yard run for a touchdown and gained over 225-yards rushing. He also caught four passes out of the backfield.

Cobb had sacked a scrambling Morgan on one occasion and put pressure on him on several others. Even after the ball was thrown he usually hit the quarterback. It was not a dirty tactic. It was just the way Coach Shaw had taught defensive end play. He believed in punishing the quarterback.

The first-team offense consisted of quarterback Morgan, halfback Winkler, Shealey at split end and Carter at flanker with the second-team line. Every first-team defensive player possible was sent against Morgan that night to try and slow down his passing and running threat.

Mentz directed the second-team offense and completed 11 of 18 passes for 141 yards.

Cobb was on the receiving end of three of the passes.

Morgan was not used on defense. The coach had decided that with his special team duties, he would use him only in special circumstances on defense.

After the scrimmage, Coach Shaw met with the team under the flag pole. He told them, "I am well pleased with the effort I am seeing.

We are going to be a strong contender for the region championship." He went over the following weeks practice schedule and concluded the meeting with a prayer thanking the Lord that they had completed two weeks without any serious injuries.

After the team started for the locker room, a tall stranger approached Coach Shaw. It was Kenneth Morgan. He extended his hand and spoke to the coach, "Hello, Coach Shaw, I'm Kyle Morgan's father. The team really looks good."

Coach Shaw carried on a brief conversation with the elder Morgan and then moved toward the locker room. It was 11:30 p.m. when he opened the car door and climbed in beside his daughter, Jen.

"Boy! Pop!" she beamed, "that's the most unbelievable thing I have ever seen. How can anyone be as good as that Morgan boy?"

Coach Shaw could only smile as he thought, "If you just knew how good that kid really is!"

Chapter Four
Salem High School

It was now just one week before the opening of the new high school year. Registration and presentation of schedules for students was slated for all day Tuesday.

Football practice for the week would consist of hitting and getting hit. Monday saw full emphasis on form tackling with players forming two lines facing each other and practicing correct tackling form. Each player hit the other five times. Morgan's tackling partner was Mentz. He packed quite a wallop.

The highlight of the tackling session was watching Cobb and linebacker/fullback Daniel North go at it. It was like they were trying to break each other apart. These were two young men that were the very best of friends until they put on pads. Suddenly, they were mortal enemies when blocking or tackling each other. There were moans and groans as these huge young men slammed each other into the ground. After the drill, blood trickled from the chin of North and from the ground-scraped elbows and forehead of Cobb. No one present wanted to get into this drill with either of these players.

North had been the backup fullback the previous year, but was a starter on defense. He led the team in tackles. He was the monster in the Salem 53 defense. Two ends, two tackles and a nose guard made up the frontline with three linebackers. The monster would move to the strong side on every play. The secondary had two cornerbacks and a safety. On obvious passing situations an adjustment might be to go to a four-man front and bring in a free safety to help on pass defense. There was a blitz package with the extra safety and with all the linebackers.

Then of course, there was Cobb. He was the prototype tight end on offense. Good hands, above-average speed, tremendous strength and excellent quickness for a 245-pound behemoth. On the defensive front he was relentless. He worked so hard on defense that he was often rested on offense although he was obviously the teams best receiver. He had 21 sacks the previous year. Most teams didn't try to run a play to his side of the field unless he was double blocked.

There were five players that started both ways for the Eagles. - Cobb, North, Winkler, Rudy Doyle at guard on offense and nose guard on defense, and Hinsley at center/linebacker. The ingredients were there for a very good defense.

The practice continued with a two-on-one drill where two linemen would attempt to block one player with a back running into the hole. This was a killer drill that would always leave a lot of bumps and bruises after its completion.

Bobby Winkler excelled at this drill. He would hit the hole and spin away from the tackle. He was not what you would call a power runner, but he would run tough.

Morgan ran the ball twice in the drill and went down quickly both times ----- brought down once by Cobb. On his second running attempt he was hit hard by tackle Billy Wright. Morgan attributed his lack of success in the drill to the fact he had absolutely no room to maneuver. He ran into the 245 pound Cobb and the 255 pound Wright head-on. It was a no-contest. Coach Shaw saw what he wanted to see from Morgan in the drill. The speed merchant could run hard inside if needed. He never backed down from the violent contact with his two heavier teammates.

After the two-on-one drill it was running plays with live tackling in the secondary on completed passes. On most plays Morgan and Mentz would hit their receivers behind the defense and the coaches would whistle the play dead. The best receivers were Carter; Shealey; Devers; Cobb; Bales; Winkler; and fullback Vann Greer.

Greer was only a sophomore, but it was evident he was pushing North for playing time on offense. He ran hard and was an excellent blocker. He was also an excellent broad jumper and 440-yard dash athlete in track. He had been the star of the B-team the past season with over 1,000-yards rushing in five games. He was also an excellent young linebacker that would provide excellent backup for the starter during the course of the season.

Morgan continued to be amazed by the play of James Mentz at safety. He was always close to the ball and would pick off at least two-or-three passes every practice session.

James Mentz had transferred to Salem from Youngstown High School in Virginia. His family had purchased a pharmacy in town. At Youngstown he had been their starting quarterback as a sophomore. He had thrown for over 2,000 yards as his team made it to the state semi-finals. He had also played safety with 14 interceptions for the season. He had made All-Region and honorable mention All-State. He had grown from six-foot as a freshman to six-foot-five-inches as a sophomore and now stood an inch taller at six-foot-six-inches. His prowess in basketball, baseball and track would leap out at the Salem program later in the school year.   Mentz had firmly entrenched himself as the starter at safety and backup at quarterback.

Coach Shaw continued to refine his new pro-formation offense all week with some single and double-reverse plays ~ along with a "flea-flicker" or the old "hook and ladder" as some still called it ~ to Cobb where the big end would catch the ball and then flip it back to Winkler trailing the play. Goal-line situations and special plays to use inside the 10-yard line were implemented. Most of these plays were play-action with the quarterback under the center.

Morgan was given a free hand at calling his own number on bootlegs, rollouts and scramble situations as desired.

It was about 11:00 a.m. on Tuesday when Morgan walked into Salem High School for the first time. The school had been built in 1954. It was one of six schools in the city of Ridgeview and one of fourteen in the county. It was the second largest school in the county behind only West Ridgeview. Over 1,200 students attended the big Class AAAA school. There were three AAAA schools in Ridgeview with

East Ridgeview joining Salem and West Ridgeview with membership in their same athletic region.

He asked where the administrative office was located and made his way in that direction. He ran into teammate (halfback) Bradley Snyder and they made their way to the office.

In his previous two high school years Morgan had taken six units per year giving him twelve for the two years. To meet academic requirements for graduation --- four units were needed in English; four in math; four in history/civics/geography; and two in a foreign language on the College-Prep Program. This left room for various electives that were worth only one-half unit each. Morgan had never taken an elective. He had taken six units each year because early on there was talk of him completing high school in three years and going on to college. When he had gotten so involved in high school sports he had decided that he wanted to stay in high school all four years.

His parents were supportive in all his wishes on this matter. They were more than happy that their son could enjoy all four years of the high school experience. They also enjoyed watching him perform his miraculous feats in the various high school sports.

This year he had submitted a schedule request that included his first elective. He wanted to take P.E. for the third year.

As he entered the office, he was approached by a gentleman he had seen watching practice on several occasions. The man walked over to him and said, "Hello Kyle, I'm Principle Bill Collins. It's great to have you attending Salem."

Morgan answered, "Thank you, Sir. I'm glad to be at Salem."

The principal continued, "You're doing a great job on the field. I know you will do the same in the classroom. We have your schedule complete. Please look it over and we'll discuss it if there are any questions."

Later, Morgan looked over his schedule. It had him taking English Literature under Mrs. Mabry in first period. Second period was World History and Civics taught by Mr. Aldridge. Third period listed him with College Chemistry and Geometry taught by Mr. Fielding. Fourth period had him taking Spanish 2 under Mrs. Chance. He smiled as he saw his fifth period with Physical Education (P.E.) under Coach Shaw. His final period was a study hall under Mrs. Buntin. This schedule had him with four and one-half units, meaning he would need only two units, one in English and one in math to complete his graduation requirements in his senior year. He was very satisfied with the schedule.

When he left the office he walked toward the gym and into the office of Coach Shaw. "Hello, Kyle, " greeted the coach, "did you receive your schedule yet?"

"Yes Sir," answered Morgan, "it looks good."

Coach Shaw turned extremely serious as he asked, "Kyle, what do you think of our team. I know you played on a state championship team just last year. Are we progressing like you think we should?"

Morgan smiled as he answered the question, "Coach, we have a chance to be a very good team. There are some really good players on this team. It would beat my team from last year by three touchdowns."

Coach Shaw laughed as he asked, "Are you talking about that probability with you at quarterback for us or them?"

Morgan scratched his head and smiled.

The afternoon practice was brutal. Every day now there was a scrimmage with practices moved to Memorial Stadium where every play was almost like a game-type situation.

On Wednesday, a two-minute drill was installed along with situational punt-return blocking and increased play calling at the line. A "goosum" or quick-snap play was installed where the quarterback would pat the center on the inside of his leg, take a quick snap and run the ball into the zero hole. This would be when there was not a nose guard and it looked like there might be an opportunity for the speedy quarterback to get into the secondary.

Live pass blocking drills would abound with Morgan continually demonstrating uncanny speed to the outside in scramble situations. By now it looked like the chosen offense was a shot-gun formation with Winkler beside the quarterback. Morgan was deadly from the shot-gun formation. He would be about five yards directly behind the center. The extra time for him to pick out a receiver instead of retreating made him almost unstoppable on the short routes. One thing that did not make Coach Shaw happy was the inordinate amount of passes his receivers dropped. While Morgan did throw a howitzer at times, he could adjust the touch on the ball to the coverage situation as needed.

There were still too many dropped balls from the receivers. The coach decided he would start emphasizing no drops from this point on by starting some punitive running for those players dropping dead-on-target passes. He felt this would increase concentration on catching the ball.

The coach decided that while there would be a Friday night practice, it was not to be a scrimmage. The practice would be closed with a dress rehearsal for the opening game. Rock-Hill had a game-type scrimmage the previous week that was scouted by baseball Coach Chandler. The Eagles would work their offense and defense against the opponents defense and offense. Rock-Hill was primarily a running team with a good tailback and a 220 pound fullback that carried the ball on about fifty percent of their plays. Their offensive philosophy was the old "three yards and a cloud of dust." They liked to grind it out and try to hold onto the ball. They threw the ball only on occasion with short, quick passes as their main forte in the passing game. The halfback was a 185 pound junior named Sammie Kellar and the big fullback was a senior named Les Wilkes.

Salem had beaten Rock-Hill 41 - 7 the previous season. Winkler had scored three touchdowns and rushed for over 240 yards. It was evident that Coach Shaw didn't think they could stop the Eagle ground game. He was certain they could not stop the Salem passing game.

Much of the game Salem would have seven men in the box, ~ that being down linemen ~ to stop the running game. They were determined to run the ball, so the Salem defense would be determined to stop the run.

Coach Shaw felt good about his squads ability to move the ball. His plans were not to turn up the juice offensively for the first two games of the season with twice defending state champion District-Heights coming up the third game of the season.

Chapter Five
Opening Game Week

The Monday practice was divided into group practice. The quarterbacks and receivers ~ other than running backs ~ worked out with the defensive secondary. Coach Shaw worked with the group. It was live tackling and blocking until the whistle.

The offensive and defensive lines worked together on blocking, pulling the guards and pass rush. After about ten passes, Morgan left to work on punting, kickoffs, point after touchdowns (PAT's) and field goals.

It was nearing the end of practice when all eyes turned toward the kicking area. Morgan was kicking field goals steadily from the 20-yard line on out. Now he stood beyond the forty-yard line preparing to kick a 50-yard field goal. Even the professional's didn't kick 50-yard field goals in 1962. The holder was Carter. The ball was placed down. He came forward with the strange side-winder, soccer-style kick he had learned as a small boy in his North Georgia back yard. When he first started using this kicking method many of his teammates laughed at him. No one was laughing now! The ball rose quickly, arched gracefully end over end, straight toward the goal posts. It cleared the crossbar with room to spare. Four more kicks out of five from that distance parted the uprights.

Coach Shaw watched in amazement as he pondered what such a weapon might mean with a game on the line. It was an awesome sight to watch the talented youngster kick a football. He was so accurate it was almost unfair to the opposition to send him into a field- goal kicking situation. Coach Shaw had never had or even seen anyone that would even attempt a 50-yard field goal. Now he stood and watched it as commonplace on his Eagle squad. He decided he would not hesitate to attempt the long field goal if over 50 yards and less than 60 yards.

Tuesday was spent on offense. About thirty minutes was devoted to the two-minute drill. Morgan would call two-or-three plays at once in the huddle. Many times he would audible into another play as he saw a weakness in the defense. A play was put in for botched extra points or field goals. Coach Shaw had decided that in the event of a bad snap or busted play on place-kicking situations the holder was to toss the ball to Morgan and let him ad-lib the play.

Cobb at right end on the kicking team would sneak a look back after initial contact and if needed run toward the corner of the endzone for a fade pass.

The holder, Tommy Carter, would then move out into the flat as a safety valve. Of course, the primary objective was to get the ball in the hands of the speedy Morgan and let him finish the play. They ran the play eight times and scored the conversion on every play.

Several reverses were installed with Carter and Shealey carrying the ball. A tight- end reverse was put in with Cobb carrying the ball. Screen-pass plays were to the fullback left or right, a tight-end screen and a Utah/shovel pass to the halfback lined up beside the quarterback.

A play was also installed where Morgan would simply line up wide at flanker and Mentz would air it out. The objective was to allow Morgan to out run the defensive player and get behind him for the long pass. The play was ran four times and every time Morgan was at least five yards behind the defensive back. He scored easily on every occasion. The defense knew what was coming, they just could not match the sprinter speed of the junior athlete.

By the end of practice, a play had been installed for just about every situation. Morgan was calling 90 percent of the plays with an audible on about 50 percent of them. The team had accepted the new man as their leader and had total confidence in his play-calling ability --- as did his coach.

The first 10 plays were scripted for the opening game. The first play would be a toss to the halfback, with the second a dive to the fullback. If the ground game was moving the ball, the team would continue to pound the ball.

If a passing situation arose after second down, the call was up the quarterback. He could call a running play and then audible into a pass if the defense dictated it as a better opportunity to get the first down or gain big yardage.

Tommy Carter, the former quarterback, was continuing to impress as a receiver. He had better than average speed and ran his routes to perfection. On most throws the ball was in the air to him before he even turned around. Morgan and Mentz had developed this type of confidence in him.

Cobb was just Cobb. Throw the ball anywhere close to him and if he could get a touch on the ball ------- he would catch it.

Shealey, Devers, and Sophomore Joey Bates were the other primary receivers. Bobby Winkler was just like Cobb when it came to catching the ball. Very dependable. Daniel North and Van Greer at fullback were dependable receivers on the screen pass or as safety valves on some particular plays.

Coach Shaw liked what he saw in his passing game and he knew with Winkler and Morgan carrying the ball, the running game was going to be very formidable.

As the Tuesday session closed, the coaching staff was eagerly anticipating the opening game . They rated the Eagles offense a strong A-plus as to readiness to play.

Wednesday was defense all the way through the session. North would call the defensive signals from his monster-man position. He was probably the most consistent tackler on the team, with Randal Hinsley a close second. North liked to hit a runner about belt high, lock his arms and literally drive him into the ground.

Cobb was an excellent tackler also, but he would just manhandle the ball carrier with his massive size. He could grab a ball carrier by the jersey or shoulder pads, or even by an ankle and bring them down. He had developed several spin moves and feints that allowed him to get by that initial block and make the tackle. Nobody worked harder to get to the quarterback or ball carrier than Butch Cobb.

The interior line had Boyd Massingale and Donald Walters at tackles with Howard Seeley at the nose guard. Mike Struthers was the other defensive end at about 195 pounds. In the secondary, Bobby Winkler played strong-side cornerback. Tim Shealey was at weak-side corner and Mentz was at safety. There was good speed in the secondary.

Coach Shaw had decided to use Morgan at free safety on some obvious passing situations and just let him follow the quarterbacks eyes and try to outrun the ball to the receiver.

Blitz situations were covered in minute detail as were goal-line situations and kick-blocking formations. On the PAT-kicking situations, Mentz, with his great height and leaping ability was to line up directly in front of the kicker. He would jump as high as possible on foot contact, trying to block the kick. He had done this several times over the last few weeks in practice.

The session was closed with punt coverage and punt returns, kickoffs and kickoff returns. Everything had been covered. Now it was close to being put into practice. One more day until the opening game.

Thursday was a practice in shorts and helmets. It was a relatively short practice with emphasis on running plays and short route passing drills.

After about an hour the coach called the team together. He spoke slowly and deliberately as he said, "Fellows, we have worked hard for this opening night. Tomorrow night, you will see the result of that hard work." There was applause from the players. He continued, "We have the opportunity to be a very good football team, it begins with this game." More scattered applause. "When you step out on that field tomorrow night representing Salem High School, I want to see good, hard, clean, competitiveness. I want to see you busting your tail to make the play and win the game. I believe you will do that. As a matter of fact, I'm know you will do that." Applause came from all the team. The coach issued instructions for everyone to be at the gym at 5:00 p.m. the following day for taping and coaches pre-game instructions.

After getting dressed Cobb walked over to Morgan and said, "Kyle, I'm not going straight home. My parents won't be in until late, so I'm going over to the Mentz Pharmacy for supper. Want to come?" Since he was riding with Cobb it was go with him or walk home, the quarterback decided to go with him.

Upon arrival at the downtown pharmacy, he was quick to notice the throng of teens gathered outside the store. There were several of his teammates present. He also recognized several girls he had seen practicing cheerleading outside the gym during football practice.

As they entered the building, James Mentz saw them enter and walked over. "Good to see you, guys. Mom has something special for tonight. She's prepared some pizza and set up a salad bar. It's all on me for tonight, so dig in."

Morgan looked around the drug store. He immediately liked it. He glanced at the menu above the snack bar. There were grilled cheese and other sandwiches; hot dogs; hamburgers; and all flavors of ice cream listed. Various soft drinks; chips; and candies were also available. The prices were low enough to be attractive to a high-school student or just an around-the-town citizen.

It was obvious the snack bar was not a super-profitable venture from the prices. There were tables and booths with red-and-white checkered coverings and an area cleared out for a small dance floor. A Rock-Ola juke box blared out rock n' roll music as several couples danced in the middle of the floor.

Morgan was not aware of the teen-gathering place. He was not much of a mixer, so he had not been invited over.

A young lady walked over and asked him if he wanted to dance. Since he was snacking on a piece of pizza, he raised it toward his mouth, and smiled as he told her, "Not right now, let me get with you later."

She smiled and walked away.

Her name was Misty Porter. She was a football cheerleader and the leading scorer on the girls basketball team.

Cobb came over with a very lovely young lady at his side. "Kyle, said Cobb, I want to introduce you to Cindy Gray. She and I have sort of dated since the ninth grade. Her father is our School Superintendent ~ Richard Gray. She is really anxious to see you play football."

"That's right," said Cindy, "Butch has told us so much about you."

By now there were five or six young ladies around the serving bar. Porter chimed in, "We're going to win them all, aren't we, Kyle?"

Morgan smiled as he answered her, "We sure are going to try."

For the next hour there was dancing and more eating of pizza.

Morgan finally approached the young lady that had approached him earlier and asked her to dance with him.

Misty Porter was a very nice young lady. She was extremely outgoing and cheerful. As a matter of fact, she never seemed to stop talking about her school, the football team and anything else that popped into her mind. As Morgan and Cobb parted company with their schoolmates, he wondered what kind of impression he had made on her. One thing was for certain. She had certainly made a very positive impression on him.

As he and Cobb were heading home, Cobb said, "We go there a lot and just snack and listen to the music. Mr. Mentz and his wife opened that little snack bar up shortly after their arrival in Ridgeview. All the guys' and gals' go there. It stays open until 9:00 p.m. on Saturday and from 1:00 p.m. until 5:00 p.m. on Sundays."

Morgan smiled at his big friend and said, "Thanks, Butch. I'm not a big social butterfly, but I want you to know I did enjoy the fellowship tonight."

Cobb answered, "I think everyone enjoyed meeting you. I know Misty Porter did!"

Morgan smiled sheepishly and asked, "You really think so?"

Cobb countered with, "I know so!"

Upon his arrival at his home, he met his mother as she entered the den. She told him dinner would be ready in about fifteen minutes. When he told her he had already eaten some pizza and the details about the snack shop, she smiled and said, "Well, I'm glad to see you getting out with your friends for something other than football practice."

He replied, "I did enjoy it, Mom. It was a lot of fun."

She said, "Well, from now on give me a call before you go over there and I won't prepare as much dinner if you snack out."

When Mr. Morgan entered the room he wanted to know about the team outlook. Kyle and his father talked for almost an hour as he went over all the various things he was doing on the team. The elder Morgan started for the door, turned and said, "Son, you're home now. Salem is your school until graduation. Give them your best."

Kyle replied, "You can be assured Dad, I'll leave it all on the field."

Friday evening arrived quickly. Morgan found himself extremely excited during the school day. He was restless, wanting to get the game underway.

His mother and father were going over to the Westside Restaurant for dinner, then attend the game.

At 4:30 p.m., Butch Cobb pulled up in the driveway.

On the way to the gym, Cobb asked Kyle, "Are you nervous?"

Morgan answered, "I was more nervous dancing with Misty Porter than I am right now." Almost as an after-thought he continued, "but I am anxious to get this first game out of the way."

Cobb replied, "From what I've seen you do on a football field, I can't wait to play the game. Throw to me when you can. I'll catch the ball."

Morgan smiled at him and said, "I know you will, Butch."

At around 5:30 p.m., Morgan sat on a table in the locker room as Coach Powers wrapped his ankles with athletic tape. All the backs, ends and linebackers would have their ankles wrapped. Several of the interior linemen were also taped. By 6:15 p.m. the team boarded the two school buses' for the two-mile trip over to Memorial Stadium.

Upon their arrival at the stadium, the coach went over the starting lineup on offense and defense. He also told the team that if they won the toss they would always take the football. His philosophy was that quick points on the board were always a positive and could in some instances even break down a teams confidence. He told North he would decide penalty acceptance or decline the penalty on defense and the quarterback would make the decision on offense. He instructed his team to relax for the next fifteen minutes before taking the field for pre-game warm-up.

At 7:00 p.m., the call came for the team to take to the field.

Once on the field the linemen would get with Coach Powers on one side of the field and Coach Dills would have the backs and receivers running drills on the other side of the field.

A little later Morgan would step to the side of the field and launch several practice punts. At 7:30 p.m. the team was called off the field. They took off their helmets, took a knee in the endzone underneath the flag pole and waited.

The coaches huddled for several moments, then told the captains, Winkler, Hinsley and North to leave for the coin-toss. The team waited on the goal line as the coin was tossed. A load roar came from the stands. The Eagles would get the ball first.

Sixty-eight Salem Eagle football players ran onto the field that night toward their destiny.

Bobby Winkler was the deep back on the kickoff return team at the 10-yard line. Tim Shealy and Bradley Snyder were up about 15 yards at the 25.

The Rock-Hill Stallions kicker stepped into the ball and sent it toward the 15-yard line where Winkler took it on a high hop and cut to his left. He juked by one tackler, brushed off another tackler at the 30 and cut back to his right before bolting down the sideline. As he raced across the mid-field stripe there was only one tackler between him and the goal. The speedy senior turned on the speed as he cut back toward the center of the field and darted into the endzone. It was an 85-yard touchdown run. A Morgan PAT kick made it 7 - 0 with only 0.14 seconds gone off the clock.

The kickoff from Morgan was taken on the four-yard line and brought back out to the 23. A first down sweep netted a two-yard gain before the Rock-Hill quarterback ---- a junior named Zach Peevy ----- dropped back to pass.

A toss down the middle was intercepted by Mentz on the 40-yard line and returned to the Rock-Hill 28.

On first down, Morgan called the scripted play, a toss to Winkler. The All-State tailback took the ball in stride at the 30-yard line and cut off tackle before veering toward the far sideline. It was now a footrace between the ball carrier and two defensive backs. They never stood a chance. With only 2:22 minutes gone in the game, Salem led 14 - 0.

On the next series Rock-Hill ground out one first down, had a penalty for motion, and stalled with a fourth-and-eight at the 34-yard line.

Winkler went back to return the punt. The Stallion punter got the kick off to him at the Salem 35-yard line. He fielded the ball and again turned on the speed. He was tripped up at the Stallion 39 after a 27-yard return with 4:31 left in the first quarter.

Morgan and the offense huddled back at the 46-yard line. The quarterback gave the play to the two-rows-of-five players that formed the typewriter-type huddle that Coach Shaw favored. His call was a "39-pitch." Winkler wide. Again the pitch was perfect as the Eagle tailback caught the ball at the 42 and sped toward the sideline. He cut back against the grain and suddenly found himself with a huge hole in the middle of the field. It was Katy-bar-the-door as he raced the final 25 yards untouched for the score. A key downfield block by Carter had helped him avoid a possible tackle on the 20-yard line. A Morgan PAT kick made it 21 - 0 with 2:04 left in the first quarter. The stands were buzzing.

The Stallions were trying to mount an attack. Their inability to get outside made it a tough job to mount any sustained drives. The start of the second quarter saw the stallions pick up a first down and again stall at their own 40-yard line, so another punt was called. This time the punter made sure to angle the ball to the sideline away from Winkler. It went out of bounds on the Eagle 44-yard line.

North crashed the middle for three yards, then bulled for six more. On a third-and- one, Morgan ran a sneak for four yards and the first down at the 41 of Rock-Hill. On first down a holding penalty wiped out a 15-yard gain by Winkler and placed the ball back on the Eagle 45. Another toss to Winkler picked up nine yards leaving it second-and-16 for the first down. Shealey replaced Winkler and ran for five yards. From the 41-yard line on a third and 10, Morgan called the buttonhook to Cobb. The big end caught the ball, but was hit immediately. He failed to make the first down by three yards. With 3:34 left on the clock in the first half, the Eagles called time out.

Coach Shaw motioned for Winkler to return to the huddle and called a 39-pitch. Winkler took the toss and swung wide. He saw the end blocking his path, so he cut back toward the inside of the playing field. A crunching block on the outside corner by Carter sprung him into the secondary. Now it was one-on-one with the Stallion safety. Again, the defensive back was seriously overmatched. Winkler raced in for his fourth touchdown of the first half.   Morgan kicked the PAT. With 1:51 left before intermission, it was the Eagles - 28 and Rock-Hill - 0.

At halftime the talk was on what the team wanted to do as to offense the second half. Coach Shaw walked over and said to Morgan, "We'll probably play you about two series in the second half on offense."

Morgan acknowledged with a brief nod.

Coach Shaw then raised his arms for quiet. He told the team, "You have played well, but we haven't had a great deal of competition thus far. Keep working on defense. Try and get the shutout. On offense, we'll keep it pretty much on the ground. We're not out there to try and humiliate anyone. Morgan, you and Mentz can call the plays the second half, but keep them pretty much basic." He then turned to Winkler and told him he wouldn't be playing much offense the second half. The team returned to the field to a thunderous roar from the Salem faithful.

Rock-Hill could not mount a drive against the Eagles on their first drive of the second half. On a third-and-12 situation ~ Cobb broke through and sacked their quarterback for an eight-yard loss. Another punt directed away from Winkler went out of bounds on the Eagle 24-yard line.

Bobby Winkler had not ran much inside up to this point. Morgan called a 32-blast. Winkler took the handoff and broke out the backside of the defensive line. He cut between two linebackers and ran 66 yards for his fifth touchdown of the night. The PAT kick made it 35 - 0 with 4:06 left in the third quarter.

The kickoff went to the Stallion return man on the 16-yard line. He brought it out to the 26. Two wildly thrown passes fell incomplete. On third down the stallion quarterback tried to reach for a receiver on the 33-yard line. Mentz stepped between the quarterback and the receiver and intercepted his second pass of the night. This time he didn't stop running until he was standing in the endzone for a 32-yard interception-return touchdown. Morgan kicked the PAT. It was Salem 42 and Rock-Hill 0 with 2:17 left in the third quarter.

Rock-Hill managed their best drive of the night down to the Eagle 35-yard line. It stalled out on a botched fourth-down handoff three yards short of a first down with 10:02 left in the game.

James Mentz was now at quarterback for the Eagles. He had Greer and Shealey in the backfield with him. On second down from his 41, Greer fumbled and Rock-Hill recovered.

Coach Shaw motioned to Morgan and told him to go in at free safety.

Morgan grabbed his helmet off the ground in front of him and ran onto the field. Four passes later he intercepted a pass on the far sideline and ran it back 43 yards for a score. His first touchdown as an Eagle. His PAT kick made it 49 - 0 with 4:01 left in the game.

Again the Stallions tried to pass their way to a score. Again it was intercepted. This time by cornerback Billy Smith. He carried the ball to the Stallion 21-yard line. On a third- and-six from the 17 with 1:23 left in the game, sophomore fullback Adrian Devers took a handoff and raced in for a touchdown. The PAT kick from Morgan made the final score, 56 - 0.

Coach Shaw didn't fill good about that score, but the youngster was a sophomore that would play mostly B-team during the year. He thought maybe he should have had the team take a knee and just run out the clock. After the game he apologized to Coach Almond from Rock-Hill.

The opposing coach told him, "I know you were not trying to run the score up on us. Don't worry about it."

Never the less, Coach Shaw filed the incident away in the back of his mind. He was aware he had the kind of team with a skill level that could literally embarrass an opponent if he did not keep the situation totally under control.

In the locker room back at the Salem gym, Coach Shaw spoke to his team. "I don't have to tell you we were head and shoulders above the team we played tonight. They tried hard, but could not approach our athleticism and skill level. We will play much better teams in the coming weeks. We stayed pretty much generic on offense. I promise you that won't become the norm as the season progresses. We will throw the ball. We can throw the ball! We had four interceptions on defense. I felt we could exploit them in that area with the speed of our secondary. Winkler, you played your normal game against Rock-Hill. You ran for over 200 yards each of the last two years against them. I don't know what your final total was in this game at this point, but with kick returns it was probably over 200 yards again." He looked at Winkler and smiled as he said, "I'll bet they're going to miss you."

He told everyone to be in the film review room at 3:45 p.m. Monday to review this game and start preparations for West Calvert. He closed out the meeting with a prayer.

When he walked in his house that night Mrs. Shaw smiled and said, "The team really looks wonderful, Tom.   It could have really, really been bad, couldn't it?"

He nodded his head as he answered, "It was worse than I wanted it to be." Then he thought to himself, "If I had turned loose the passing game on this team ~ It could have been 100 to 0."

Chapter Six
The First Day of School

At 8:00 a.m. on Monday, September five, 1962, Kyle Morgan walked into Salem High School to start his junior year. The names of all the students were posted on the door of their homeroom. He found his name on room 306. His homeroom teacher was Coach Powers.

He took a seat behind a football teammate, Mike Struthers, and waited for the home-room teacher to arrive.

School started at 8:30 a.m. with first period slated to start at 8:45 a.m. You had five minutes to move from class to class between periods. His homeroom was quite a distance from the English class he had in his first period. He finally made his way into Mrs. Mabry's classroom and prepared for his first class session at his new school.

Mrs. Mabry was a nice lady. She had a daughter named Ann. She would become a good friend of Morgan as their year moved along. Ann was a member of the basketball team. She was also on the football cheerleading squad. She was an honor student that served as the president of the Beta Club. The Beta club was an activity that featured straight A students only. Morgan would be invited into ~ and join the club ~ after the first quarter report cards came out. Ann Mabry was a junior. She was also a most impressive young lady.

As the day moved forward, Morgan ran into many of his teammates and made new friends in all his classes. Many of the students had seen the game the previous Friday night. They knew he was a football player, but knew very little about him other than that.

In fourth period he was chatting with his teacher, Mrs. Chance, when she asked him how far along in Spanish he was after taking Spanish I the previous year. He started to converse with her in fluent Spanish.

At that point, Mrs. Chance sensed something different about Kyle Morgan. She would find out later that he spoke five languages. American; French; Spanish; Italian and German. He had studied these foreign languages and mastered them in his eighth and ninth grade summers as a means of relieving summertime boredom.

In fifth period, he had physical education under Coach Shaw. In this class you would dress for activities three days each week and have a classroom health session every Tuesday and Thursday. On this day no one was required to dress. It was just find you a locker, go to the classroom and listen to Coach Shaw as he explained what he would expect from the class in the upcoming months.

His final period of the day was a study hall under Mrs. Buntin. Later, Coach Shaw would give him a letter that allowed him to be excused from study hall and workout for track when he would be playing or practicing baseball later in the day.

It almost seemed that his schedule was designed to free him up the final two periods of the day.

Coach Shaw had not played a part in the scheduling. It was just a coincidence, but it would turn into a great asset later in his high school year.

The school day ended at 3:15 p.m. Morgan made his way to the gym to dress for football practice.

The review of Friday nights game consisted of viewing a film of the game and going over all the weak points. The film was backed up to allow emphasis on various points and to grade out individual performance.

The coach would grade the film on Sunday and have everything ready for presentation to the squad on Monday evening.

The past Friday night it was the Bobby Winkler show. The speedy senior tailback had rushed the ball only five times for 176 yards and four touchdowns. He had ran a kickoff back 85 yards for a score and also had a 27-yard punt return. His total yardage for the game was 288 yards. Next there would be a film of the next opponent for viewing and familiarization.

Morgan would learn that high school game films from all over the state were rushed to Mt. Evans, about 65 miles from Ridgeview, on Saturday morning. They would be processed by the following Sunday at noon. Two copies were always made. One for the team and one for the next team you were scheduled to play. A signed agreement allowed the following weeks opponent to pick up their copy of the film. It cost over $150 to get both films expedited and out on time. The film company would work all night Friday through Saturday night to get the film ready. Many schools would get their film to the shop on late Friday night or during the course of the night. It was a sophisticated system that was a big part of high school football.

When watching the game film of West Calvert going up against Carlyle High School, it was evident that the Calvert squad was a better team than Rock-Hill. It was also evident they would not present a great challenge as far as beating the Eagles. West Calvert had won the game 14 - 7. Their greatest threat was a smallish, quick running back that had ran for 145 yards and scored both their touchdowns. His name was Mark Hollinger.

The Monday practice was all business. Coach Shaw went immediately into working up a defense to stop their key plays. He wanted to blitz their quarterback on almost every play and try to knock down their backs before they could get underway. The coach felt they would not be any type of passing threat and only the one back, Hollinger, was a threat offensively.

It was after practice that Coach Shaw asked Morgan and Mentz to come into his office. Since Cobb was with Morgan and providing him a ride home, the coach told Cobb he could come into the office, also. The coach began, "We have looked at the West Calvert film extensively over the weekend and we do not feel they will provide us with strong resistance. We want to keep the offense as bland as possible in this game. We won't show District-Heights any long passing, any wide sweeps other than Winkler ---- whom they already know very well. We won't use any gadget plays under any circumstances. We want to throw the book at District-Heights the following week. Keep the plays inside the tackles for the most part and all passes at about ten yards or so. Do you think we can do this?"

Morgan smiled and answered, "Coach, we'll wear Winkler out on them."

There were scattered laughs as the coach and players departed the office.

That night Morgan ran the plan by his father at the dinner table. Mr. Morgan said, "Your coach must really want to beat District-Heights."

Morgan answered , "I think we're already getting ready for them now."

The next two days of practice were spent on passing drills and blitzing defense. On the Thursday practice in shorts the emphasis was on defending the West Calvert Power-I attack.

The team was informed that they would leave the school parking lot at 3:00 p.m. on Friday afternoon. A short trip to a Morgan Cafeteria for the pre-game meal would be at 3:30 p.m.   It was about a 40-minute trip to West Calvert.

Ankle taping would be from 5:30 p.m. until around 6:30 p.m. Plans were to take the field at 7:00 p.m.

A student bus would leave for the game from the parking lot at 6:00 p.m.

Ken Morgan had mentioned that he had received a call from Coach Shaw about having the pre-game meal at one of the two Morgan Cafeteria's in Ridgeview earlier in the week. The younger Morgan had not heard whether or not a deal had been struck until informed of it by the coach.

That night Cobb and Morgan again went over to the Mentz pharmacy snack shop and had a light supper.   Around 8:00 p.m., Cobb dropped Morgan off in his driveway. "See you tomorrow," said Cobb.

Morgan nodded, waved goodbye and went into the house. With his father out of town on business for the next two weeks, he completed his studies and went to bed around 9:30 p.m.

Mr. Morgan had made it clear he would be back for all the football games, then return to his business assignment.

At the Friday P.E. class Morgan and any one on the football team did not dress out for class. They just tossed a football around in the gym.

The Friday pre-game plan went well. The food at the cafeteria was good and all the team agreed it was a great place for pre-game meals.

Morgan's mother had been a hostess for the event and sat at the table with the coaches.

Coach Shaw mentioned to her that she had a remarkable son.

She replied, "Thank you, coach. As almost an after-thought she said, "Coach, it just absolutely amazes me when I see some of the things he does on a football field." It was not a bragging type comment. It was just a matter-of-fact statement.

Lucille Morgan had watched her son as he participated in sports his entire life. She continued to be amazed at the unbelievable things he was able to do. And one thing was assured to her at this stage --- anything he might do on an athletic field or in academic accomplishment did not surprise her anymore. However, she did feel that he had some kind of destiny to accomplish greater things in later life.

She thought about her husband, Ken. He had been a high school athlete when they started dating many years earlier. This had led to a college scholarship to a major university and eight years as a professional baseball player with the Bison organization. After an injury to his knee he had went to work with the Justice Department. It was true that Ken Morgan was with the Central Intelligence Agency. He was one of their better agents and spent much of his time in various assignments around the country and even out of the country at times. He had started up a restaurant business simply to serve as a front for the family as his son was found to be exceptional in virtually all athletic endeavors. He never wanted to have to explain any of his national security job to anyone or have questions on his employment asked of his son or wife.

Now that one cafeteria had grown to 46 in six states, with at least ten more planned over the next two years. The Morgan family had become very wealthy.

It was just about 7:00 p.m. when the coach sent the team on the field. The Eagles were dressed in their road uniforms with white shirts, navy-blue numbers, gold helmets and gold pants with a white stripe trimmed-in-black down the side. At 7:55 p.m. ~ Hinsley, North and

Winkler walked to the center of the field for the coin-toss. The West Calvert Trojans won the toss and elected to receive.

Morgan kicked the ball in the endzone so the Trojans started play on the 20-yard line. Tailback Hollinger ground out a first down in two carries to the 34. A quick pass to Harris netted nine more yards before Hollinger broke off the right side for 14 yards. A motion penalty moved the ball back to the 48 with first-and-15. As the Trojan quarterback Cassidy dropped back to pass, Cobb crashed through the blocking back and dropped him for an eight-yard loss. An incomplete pass and a draw to Hollinger netted six yards to the 42-yard line. On fourth-and-nine the Trojan punter kicked out of bounds on the Eagle 23-yard line. It was evident Winkler was not going to be allowed to field the punt. They were kicking away from him in all instances.

Morgan brought the offense onto the field. On first down North crashed off tackle for five yards. Winkler burst for 6 more yards. A wingback misdirection play with Shealey went for five yards. The Eagles stayed on the ground for the next four plays before a holding penalty by Shealey moved the ball back to the Eagle 37-yard line. On a second-and- 23, Morgan threw a swing pass to Winkler for nine yards. A third-down pass to Carter on a quick slant netted 12 more yards to the Trojan 42. Coach Shaw called for the punting team. He sent Carter on to punt instead of Morgan. West Calvert fair caught the punt at their own 17-yard line.

Again they tried to get the running game going, but a penalty and a fumbled snap resulted in a fourth-and-nine yards from the 18-yard line. The Trojan punter stood at the goal line and kicked the ball on a low trajectory away from Winkler at the Eagle 49-yard line. A 33-yard punt.

Mentz was in at quarterback on the series. Winkler darted for four yards, then ran a sweep for 11 to the Trojan 36. Greer powered off tackle for six yards. A power sweep by Winkler almost broke for a touchdown as he was brought down after a 21-yard gallop to the Trojan nine-yard line. In two plays Winkler crossed the goal line from the four-yard line. A Morgan kick made the score 7 - 0 with 1:26 left in the first quarter.

West Calvert started a drive from their 26-yard line that featured the talents of their senior tailback ~ Hollinger. He continuously ripped at the line gaining positive yardage as the Trojans moved the ball over 50 yards to the Eagle 21-yard line. On first down the speedy back broke off tackle and ran for a touchdown. It was nullified by a holding penalty by their left end on Cobb. A 15-yard penalty moved the ball back to the 36-yard line. The Trojan quarterback threw a screen-pass to Hollinger that was stopped at the 25. A reverse was sniffed out by Mentz, who came up to hit the ball carrier for a three-yard loss. From the 28-yard line the Trojan quarterback again tried the screen to Hollinger, who was closely covered by linebacker Hinsley. The pass fell incomplete. On fourth down a quick pass on a slant to Hollinger was complete for 14 yards, but was three yards short of a first down on the Eagle 14-yard line. There was only 3:28 left on the clock in the first half.

The Eagles stayed on the ground with power plays into the one and two holes. Winkler carried five times for 26 yards. No one else touched the ball. As the first half wound down, the Eagles looked like everything but a high school super-power.

At intermission - Coach Shaw worked on defense. Primarily stopping tailback Hollinger. He told Mentz and Morgan to, "stay on the ground as possible." He stopped Morgan as he went out the door and again affirmed that he wanted to showcase Winkler in the second half. Coach Shaw was doing everything in his power to convince District-Heights scouts in the stands that this was a one-dimensional team with the All-State tailback Winkler as their primary threat.

The Eagles received the ball to start the second half and again moved the ball on the ground. After moving to the 44-yard line, a motion penalty followed by a mouth-piece penalty (Flanker Carter had not put his mouth protector in his mouth. It was left dangling from his helmet) moved the Eagles back to the 25. Again, Morgan did not throw the ball, but continued to feed Winkler, North and Greer for inside tackle running plays. Coach Shaw would later say this was the most boring game he had ever coached. A Carter punt rolled dead on the Trojan 34 with 6:37 left in the third quarter. Hollinger gained the first down on two carries. Cobb sacked the quarterback for a six-yard loss on a rollout and two passes fell short of their target forcing another Trojan punt to the Eagle 31-yard line. Winkler went wide for 11 yards to the 42-yard line before North plowed the middle for eight more yards to the mid-field stripe. A buttonhook pass to Devers netted seven yards. With 2:34 left in the third quarter Winkler took a toss from Morgan, went wide toward the sideline, cut back against the grain and broke free at the 35-yard line. The inevitable had happened. If you just kept pounding his tremendous speed at the defense, eventually he was going to break one. The 43-yard touchdown run and subsequent PAT kick from Morgan made it a 14 - 0, Eagle lead.

The West Calvert coaches reacted expectedly on their next series. They opened up the offense. Coach Shaw told Morgan to go in at free safety. He wanted a five-man front with two linebackers, and four in the secondary, including his three defensive burners, Morgan, Mentz and Winkler.

Morgan kicked the ball to the six-yard line. It was returned to the 29. A quick toss was complete for eight yards. A pass down the middle was deflected and almost intercepted by cornerback Carter. On third down a draw to Hollinger gained yardage for the first down to the 44-yard line. A down and out pass was complete for 11 yards to the Eagle 43. Hollinger ripped for eight yards ~ then got the first down at the 27-yard line. On first down the Trojan quarterback went back to pass and was blitzed from two linebacker slots and Cobb on the corner. It was the big defensive end that got to him. The loss was for eight yards back to the 35-yard line. On a second-and-18 for the first down, a pass intended for Hollinger on a fly route was intercepted by Morgan as he went high above the intended receiver for the catch. Salem had the ball at the 12-yard line with 3:54 left on the game clock.

The Eagles were not in any hurry as they watched the clock wind down. After grounding out two first downs out to the 40-yard line, the Trojans began to use their timeouts. After a Greer first down run to the Trojan 41-yard line with 1:54 left, they were out of timeouts. Mentz came in at quarterback and took three drops to his knee as the game ended with Salem winning a hard fought 14 - 0 battle.

The Eagles had rushed for over 280 yards and the Trojans had ran for 148 yards. Hollinger had rushed for 116 yards to lead the Trojans.

On the Salem side it was Winkler with 164 yards rushing and Greer with 41 yards. It was not a pretty win, but Coach Tom Shaw was sure that District-Heights did not know about Morgan's passing and running abilities and the explosiveness of the Salem offense.

In the locker room Coach Shaw told his team, "You did what I wanted you to do. You won the game and showed District-Heights nothing. Next week we are going to turn you loose and go after the twice defending state champions and their 30 game winning streak." He concluded with, "Have a safe weekend and get your thoughts on District-Heights. We intend to win that game."

When the coach arrived home that night, his wife and daughter, Jen, were watching television in the living room. Jen said, "Really Dad, we stunk it up!   I know we can throw the ball better than that. We should have beaten that team by forty points."

The coach smiled and asked, "Did we really look that bad?"

They both nodded, "yes."

There was a puzzled expression on their face when the coach smiled back at them and said, "I am really proud of the way we played tonight."

Chapter Seven
The Big Game

Coach Shaw didn't even bother to review the West Calvert game with the team. He went right into the game tape of the District-Heights game with Ashbury-Central. District-Heights had won the game 44 - 7. Ashbury- Central was a class AAA school that was usually a contender for their region title.

The focus of the Cougars team was their outstanding senior quarterback Billy Raymond and two tremendous running backs, Will Thurmond and Hal Damons. They also had a defensive line that featured two All-State performers in Richard Clinton and Marcus Fitzpatrick. Their offensive line averaged 240 pounds and their defensive line averaged 230 pounds. They averaged over 45 points per game the past season and were on that same path so far this season. They would give up less than six points per game in 14 games. They had now won 31 games in succession and were ranked number two in the United States.

They had won the state track title the previous year with the Eagles finishing second. While Winkler had won the 100-yard dash, Thurmond had finished second. He had beaten Winkler in the 220-yard dash in a photo finish. Clinton and Fitzpatrick were weight men on the track team and both had beaten Cobb in the Shot put. He had managed to beat Clinton in the discus.

They were a very good football team.

Almost two hours were spent viewing the tape. Coach Shaw went over the various tendencies of the team to run a certain play in certain situations. The outside practice was primarily just a loosening up session with about 45 minutes of throwing, receiving and blocking assignments against the Cougar defense.

As they pulled into the Morgan driveway that evening, Butch Cobb said, "Kyle, I want to ask you something."

"Sure, go ahead," replied Morgan.

Cobb said, "You saw the film, do you think we can we play with District-Heights?"

Morgan laughed and answered, "Butch, there is absolutely no doubt in my mind we can play with that team. Why do you ask this?"

Cobb answered, "We just haven't been able to beat that crowd. One year we won the region and they had beaten us bad during the season. They are just so intimidating."

Morgan said, "Butch, we will find a way to beat them. I promise you that."

Cobb grinned and nodded his head, "I believe you, Kyle. I can't wait to play them." Butch Cobb thought to himself as he drove home that night, "It's a new era, they just don't know what they're up against."

At home that night Mr. Morgan and his son discussed the upcoming game. "How do you feel about it, Kyle?" Mr. Morgan asked.

"I feel good about it, Dad." Kyle said. "If the coach will turn us loose, I think we have enough speed, players and skills to beat them or anyone else we might play."

"I agree," said Mr. Morgan. "Son, what you did the last two games was remarkable. You could have ran or passed for score after score in either of those games, but you worked with your coach to keep the advantage of surprise for this big game. I'm proud of you!"

Kyle said, "Dad, that is going to be one surprised team when the real Eagle team shows up on Friday night!"

The excitement around the school was unbelievable. The cheerleaders had signs hung up everywhere.

A sock-hop dance was planned for after the game at the high school gymnasium. Laura Billups was the girlfriend of Bobby Winkler. She approached Morgan as he was having lunch and asked if she could talk with him. He followed her over to another table where she said, "Kyle, I have a friend that really thinks you are a great looking guy. She would like for you to ask her to go to the dance this Friday night after the game. It would be a big favor to me if you would ask her."

Kyle smiled as he replied, "Laura, I appreciate your letting me know about this, but I don't have plans to attend the dance. Tell your friend maybe we can get together some other time." It was obvious that Laura Billups did not like the outcome of that conversation. Morgan would find out later from Winkler the girl was senior cheerleader Connie Hollis. She was a very pretty and popular young lady.

The state rankings came out in the newspaper on Tuesday afternoon. In Class AAAA the District-Heights Cougars were a unanimous number one. West Ridgeview was number four. Salem was not ranked, even in honorable mention.

The Tuesday afternoon practice was intense. You could see the look of anticipation on the face of all the players. The game didn't seem to be causing much of a stir on a statewide basis. The Cougars would be at least a three touchdown favorite by all the high school newspaper prognosticators.

Kyle Morgan could see it coming together. He and his receivers were almost as one on all the pass routes. He had learned where to throw the ball for the best chance of a completion and he knew where his receivers would struggle on certain passes to make the reception.

After the Thursday practice, Coach Shaw had another meeting with Morgan and Mentz. He told them he appreciated the job they had done in the previous two games of keeping the big-play potential of the Eagle team hidden.

He told them they could open up the game tomorrow night. "You two will call your plays tomorrow night and have full option to audible as needed on anything I may send in. The ball game will be in your hands when you are in the game under center." Both players thanked the coach and walked out of the office.

James Mentz placed his hand on the shoulder of Morgan and said, "Kyle, I just want you to know, I don't care if I get in at quarterback tomorrow night. I know what a threat you are on every play and I respect that. I just want to do what it takes to win the game."

Morgan answered, "Thanks James, I know you mean that. It means a lot to me in that you have that much confidence in me. I do appreciate it."

By 6:30 p.m., all the parking spaces around Memorial Stadium were full. Cars were parking a mile or so away. District-Heights fans had been in town since noon and many had come to the stadium and formed a line at the ticket booth by 3:00 p.m.

Right after school many Salem students had started a line at another ticket booth on the home side of the field. It was an amazing sight to say the least.

Coach Shaw completed his final pre-game instructions. The team dropped to their knees for a short prayer before trudging out to the field. The Eagles were dressed in their home-blue jerseys, white numbers with gold pants and gold helmet. This was the same colors the team had worn since the first Eagle game back in 1948.

A load roar went up when the Eagles won the coin-toss and elected to receive. Winkler took the opening kickoff on his seven-yard line and ran it back to the Eagle 22. Morgan talked to his typewriter huddle, called the play, slapped his hands together, and brought them to the line. On first down from the I-formation he gave the ball to fullback North on the 41-blast. The bullish runner crashed to the 24-yard line where he was hit hard. As he was going down the Cougars All-State linebacker Fitzpatrick ripped the ball from his arms. District-Heights had recovered the fumble at the 21-yard line. A major point of emphasis all week had been to secure the ball on interior running plays. The Cougar players were continuously ripping at the ball trying to cause the fumble. Now the defense had created a major opportunity for their offense early in the game.

Quarterback Raymond brought his team to the line and used the speed of his two All-State halfbacks to drive the ball to the goal with runs of seven, five and eight yards. On a second down from the one-yard line, Thurmond crashed off tackle for the score. A PAT kick made it 7 - 0 Cougars with only 2:07 elapsed from the game clock.

It was an anxious crowd as the Eagles prepared to receive the kickoff.

Again Winkler took the kickoff and was hit hard on the Eagle 31-yard line. One of the things you always want to do as the quarterback is lift a teammate up after a mistake. In the huddle, Morgan again called a middle run with North carrying the ball. The fullback was hit hard at his 35 by the blitzing Clinton and, amazingly, again the ball was ripped out of his hands by the Cougar defense as he fought for yardage. After digging through the pile the referees ruled that District-Heights had again recovered the football at the Eagle 29-yard line. A deathly silence fell over the stadium when Thurmond took a pitch wide and ran almost untouched into the endzone with only 2:52 off the clock. A PAT kick made it 14 - 0 for the Cougars.

Daniel North had been a dependable player for Coach Tom Shaw on offense and defense for three years. He had fumbled twice his sophomore year, but had not lost one since that time. He was an honor student with the second highest grade-point average on the squad. He had already accepted an academic scholarship to Harbor City College where he planned to study pre-med. His father was a doctor. Now he was about as down as a football player could be. The tears flowed from his eyes as he came off the field. The pats on the back and kind words from his teammates did nothing to ease the pain the Eagle captain was feeling at the time.

The kickoff came to Winkler at the seven-yard line. He broke off to the outside at the 20 and was finally knocked out of bounds at the Salem 42-yard line.

Morgan and the offense ran onto the field. On first down a quick pass to Devers went for six yards. On second-and-four for the first down, he threw an out pattern to Carter. The ball was perfectly thrown, but bounced off the receivers pads and, unbelievably, directly into the hands of Cougar side back Danny Whitman. Was Cobb right? Were the Eagles "snake-bit" when they played the Cougars? As Morgan moved into position to make the tackle the lights suddenly went out. He was hit from the blind side by a Cougar blocker and went down hard. Whitman ran untouched into the endzone for the touchdown. On the extra-point attempt, Cobb and Mentz lined up directly in front of the kicker. Mentz managed to get a hand on the low-trajectory kick and deflect it off course. With 8:12 left in the first quarter District-Heights led 20 - 0.

A shaken Eagle quarterback was receiving care on the sideline.

The Cougars could smell blood at this point. Their coach called for an onside kick that barely made it the required ten yards before tackle Donald Walters managed to fall on the bouncing ball at the Eagle 47-yard line.

A stunned Eagle coaching staff called the Eagle offensive team together and made it clear that they had to move the ball on this series.

Coach Shaw asked Morgan, "Are you good to go, son?"

He nodded his head, grabbed his helmet off the ground, and said, "Let's do it, gang!"

A still somewhat woozy Morgan and the offense ran on the field in the almost silent stadium.

Mr. Morgan had moved down to the track behind the team bench to see how his son was faring after his injury. He decided to watch the game from behind the bench for awhile.

Meanwhile, Morgan looked at his huddled teammates and said very calmly, "It's time to go to work, guys. We have to score here!" He called a "30-screen." He retreated as the defense came at him. At the last second he looped the ball to Winkler at the Eagle 40- yard line. Twenty-two yards later Winkler was pulled down at the Cougar 31. After an overthrow incompletion on first down, a pass to Cobb went for eight yards. On third down, Morgan had again called North's number, but changed it to a buttonhook pass to Cobb when he saw the Cougars nine-man line set to blitz on the play. Cobb pulled in the quick toss for seven yards and a first down on the Cougar 16-yard line. A pitch to Winkler went for four yards. On second-and-six for the first down, a pass play had been called. When Morgan saw a four-man secondary and the linebackers close to the line, he changed the play to a "39-pitch" to Winkler. The speedy tailback turned the corner and went in for a touchdown with 3:09 left in the first quarter. A Morgan PAT kick made it 20 - 7, Cougars leading.

The kickoff from Morgan was through the endzone. The Cougars started from the 20-yard line. Thurmond and Damons alternated carries from their split back veer offense for two first downs as the first quarter ended. District-Heights, 20 and Salem, 7.

The second quarter saw the constant battering of the Eagle defense continue as the cougars moved toward the goal line. A six-yard run,

10-yard pass and eight-yard run placed the ball at the Eagle four-yard line. Thurmond crashed into the endzone for the score and an eventual 27 - 7 lead.

Coach Shaw spoke in a firm, positive tone to his team as he awaited the kickoff. He told them the game was a long way from being over. He told Morgan that "an answer to the District-Heights score on this series is crucial." Morgan just nodded his head. Coach Shaw could not detect the slightest hint of negativity as to getting back in the game from his quarterback.

Winkler returned the kickoff to the 28-yard line.

Morgan trotted onto the field. He looked over the huddle and said, "That's enough, guys, it's time for us to take over."

A sideline pass to Carter went for 12 yards. A sweep by Winkler gained eight more yards. On first down from the Eagle 48-yard line ~ Morgan called "banana-pass five." This would place all receivers --- two ends and three backs --- into pass routes. The backfield was empty for the first time in the game. The Cougars had not seen this formation and quickly called timeout.

When play resumed Morgan changed the play to a "banana one" from play-action. A fake to fullback North and a rollout to the right with a fake reverse to Shealey from the left side set up the pass play to a streaking Carter at the Cougar 20-yard line. Morgan stopped at the Eagle 40 and fired the ball down the field. The ball was slightly over thrown and fell incomplete. Back in the huddle he said directly to Carter, "You were open, buddy, my fault. I'll get it right this time." He then called the play. "Same play to the opposite side of the field. He looked directly at Carter and said, "I'll get you the ball this time if you can get open." Morgan again faked the handoff to a reversing Shealey and rolled out to the left. He made it look like a quarterback rollout until the last second. Suddenly he squared up and fired to his flanker as he ran wide open at the Cougars 25-yard line. Carter caught the ball without breaking stride and raced into the endzone for the score with 3:31 left in the first half. A Morgan PAT kick made it 27 - 14.

Coach Shaw thought about an onside kick, but decided not to risk leaving the Cougars with a short field this close to halftime. Morgan drilled the kickoff into the endzone.

A first down pass fell incomplete. Damons ran for seven yards and then got the first down at the 32-yard line. On first down quarterback Raymond threw to Thurmond for 22 yards. There was a flag on the play. After a 15-yard penalty placed the ball at the 17-yard line the Cougars kept the ball on the ground as the first half came to a close.

In the locker room at halftime very little discussion was focused on the offense. The coach had decided that he wanted Morgan in on defense on any potential passing situations. He also wanted more blitzing to give his secondary a better opportunity to intercept the pass. The Cougars were double-teaming Cobb every play on defense. He wanted Hinsley to cheat toward the big end and hit the gap created when a double team was being executed.

As the team left the room Coach Shaw called Morgan over and said, "Go in as you see fit on defense. Read that quarterbacks eyes. We need the ball every chance we get the second half. I'm not concerned that we're not going to score, I'm concerned with stopping them from scoring."

Morgan nodded that he understood and ran toward the field.

To start the second half - Morgan again kicked the ball out of the endzone. From the 20-yard line, Damons ran for four yards then Thurmond drove for five yards. On a third-and-three for the first down the Cougar coaching staff tried to cross up the Eagle defense. The call was for a pass in the middle to get the first down. Morgan had noticed the excitement as the player brought the play into quarterback Raymond. He was guessing a pass for the first down. He also guessed a quick pass to the tight end just a few yards off the line. He slid toward the weak side end and never took his eyes off the quarterback. The play developed with the quarterback raising up and firing the ball to the tight end just as Morgan had guessed. It was not a good pass and Morgan could not get to it for an interception, but he had managed to knock it down. On fourth down the Cougars reluctantly punted to Shealey, who fair caught the ball on the Eagle 38-yard line.

The next series for the Eagles started as a series of blunders with offside and motion penalties moving them back to the 27-yard line. On first-and-20 for the first down - Morgan fired to Carter for 12 yards. A sweep by Winkler went for two yards and a quick pass to Cobb made it third-and-two for a first down from the 35-yard line.

Morgan called the "goosum play." He lunged forward for a first down on the 39. A quick hitter to Shealey picked up nine yards and a swing pass to Winkler went for 14 yards to the Cougar 38-yard line. An out pattern to Carter was good for five yards. Two incomplete passes brought up a third-and-five yards for the first down from the 33-yard line. Morgan faced his huddle and called the play, "110 rollout on two." At the line, "hut one, hut 2," he barked. The ball was snapped and the quarterback stepped to his right toward the 10 hole. After two steps he was going wide open. He sped by the stunned secondary of the Cougars and was untouched as he crossed the goal line. A PAT kick made it 27 - 21, District-Heights with 4:02 left in the third period.

The Cougars started from their 20-yard line after a Morgan endzone kickoff. They went on a 12-play drive that culminated with Damons ripping off the final 16 yards for a 34 - 21 lead with 0:06 left in the third quarter. The Salem fans were deathly quiet.

Carter took the short kickoff and returned it to the 34-yard line as the third quarter ended.

On first down to start the fourth quarter, Morgan passed to Cobb on the quick slant. The tight end rumbled 24 yards before three defenders were able to get him to the ground. Winkler ran for six yards, before an incomplete pass brought up a third-and-four for the first down. Again the lanky quarterback called his own number and slashed to the 12-yard line ----- a 24-yard run. On first down a pass to Carter carried out of bounds on the one-yard line. As Morgan looked at his huddle, he suddenly called a time out with 9:04 left in the fourth quarter.

Morgan had noticed that fullback Daniel North was not in the lineup. When he approached Coach Shaw he was asked, "What's the problem. Kyle?"

Morgan answered, "We need North in the game, Coach."

The coach nodded his head in agreement. He called over to North to get into the game. In the huddle Morgan calmly called a "41-blast." There were grins all around the huddle as they came to the line. On this play there was not to be a fumble or any hopes of stopping the big fullback from crossing the goal line. With 8:32 left in the game - North burst across the goal line to score for the Eagles. A PAT kick by Morgan made it Cougars - 34, Eagles 28.

This time coach Shaw rolled the dice. He went for an onside kick. It was to no avail. The Cougars fell on the bounding ball at the Eagle 47-yard line. Several moments later it would seem to be a major mistake.

On first down, Damons took a pitch and broke it down the sideline for 36 yards to the Eagle 11-yard line. Three plays later Thurmond exploded into the endzone to make it 40 - 28 ---- 41-28 after the successful PAT ---- with 6:34 left in the game.

Morgan walked over to Coach Shaw and said, "Coach, let me move to flanker with Winkler and have Mentz throw it to me. I can get behind their secondary. We need a quick score."

Coach Shaw nodded his approval. He grabbed Mentz by a shoulder pad and said, "Let Morgan call the play, but you're the quarterback on this series."

It was easy to see that the Cougars were pumped up. Their kicker boomed the ball eight-yards deep in the endzone. The Eagles would start at their own 20-yard line.

Morgan called the play. He directed Winkler to go wide left while he would go wide right. The call was "banana four" with North left in the backfield to block for Mentz. His final comment to Mentz was, "Get the ball over the secondary, lead me, don't throw it short."

Mentz nodded. He knew exactly what he had to do.

On the snap, Morgan ran directly at the cornerback and then sped by him. It was obvious he had not had to defense the blazing speed Morgan was capable of achieving.

Suddenly, Mentz from in the pocket could see separation between the speedy receiver and the Cougar defensive back. He concentrated as he made the throw. It had to be out in front of the receiver due to the tremendous rate of speed in which he was moving.

At the 35-yard line of District-Heights ~ Morgan caught up to the ball. He cradled it in his right arm as he raced toward the endzone. He was 10 yards in front of the defender when he crossed the goal line. The roar from the home crowd was deafening. A Morgan kick made it 41 - 35 with 5:28 left in the game.

Coach Shaw looked at the scoreboard. He implored his defense, "We have to have a stop here. We need that ball."

The Morgan kick went deep into the endzone, so the Cougars would start the series at their own 20-yard line.

Damons ran for three yards, then nine yards and a first down. Thurmond broke loose for 10 yards and another first down.

The clock continued to run off the precious seconds.

Morgan ran onto the field. He went over to Hinsley and told him to go to a 54 defense and crash the corners. Morgan was at free safety with Winkler and Mentz on the corners.

From the 40-yard line, Damons was stopped for a yard gain. Thurmond hit the middle for four yards. It was third-and-five yards needed for the first down. The quarterback took the snap and dropped back. He was going to try a screen pass to Damons. Cobb leaped as the ball was released and batted it to the ground. The clock showed 1:32 when Dowis dropped back to punt for the Cougars. When the coach of the Cougars saw Morgan and Winkler back to return the punt he quickly called timeout.

When play resumed it was obvious what they had discussed. The punter angled the ball out of bounds at the Eagle 36-yard line with 1:18 left in the game.

Morgan moved in at quarterback. A quick out to Carter was good for 12 yards. An incomplete pass was followed by a 16-yard toss to Shealey, who stepped out of bounds at the Cougar 36-yard line with 0:57 left in the game. In the huddle Morgan called for the "flea-flicker" play. A quick pass to Cobb, who would then toss the ball back to Winkler as he came by him. It worked to perfection. Cobb caught the ball at the 32 and Winkler pulled in his backward pitch at the Cougar 35-yard line. He was dragged down at the 12-yard line with 0:43 left in the game. Morgan threw out of bounds to stop the clock with 0:39 on the clock.

The Eagles had one timeout left. Morgan Looked at his huddle and called the play. "39-pitch on one." Winkler took the toss and swept wide. He received a beautiful block from Carter at the six-yard line and scored standing up ---- then they saw the yellow flag. Carter had been called for a clip. The ball would be placed 15 yards from the infraction spot. It was still first down, but the Eagles had to go to the two-yard line for a first down. The ball was spotted on the 19-yard line with 0:31 left on the game clock. Morgan threw wide of Shealey on the five-yard line. He then connected with Carter on a down-and-out pass to the eight-yard line with 0:18 seconds showing on the clock.

Morgan called time out.

As Morgan and Coach Shaw talked on the side line, the team kneeled at the 15-yard line. There was no panic. It had been a roller coaster of emotions throughout this game. Now it was do-or-die time. The team was thinking do all the way.

Morgan returned to the huddle. He looked at his teammates, then at tight end Cobb. He said calmly, "We're going to make you a hero Mr. Cobb, get just inside the endzone, drop to both knees and the ball will be about a foot off the ground. Catch it!" There was a slight smile from most team members as they came to the line. The team confidence in their amazing quarterback was overwhelming to say the least. The ball was snapped, Morgan dropped back two steps and moved slightly to his right to find a passing lane. There was Cobb dropping to his knees just inside the endzone. The pass was a bullet between two defensive players ~ the ball hit him directly in his chest. He squeezed the ball and was immediately piled upon by four-or-five defensive players. The referee's arms went up signaling a touchdown.

It was bedlam in Memorial Stadium that night.

Eagles Touchdown!

As the team lined up for the all-important PAT kick by Morgan, the scoreboard clock showed 0:12 seconds left in the game. The ball was snapped, Morgan swung his foot and the score was suddenly Salem 42 ~ District-Heights 41.

On the sideline Coach Shaw looked into the stands at the hysterical Eagle supporters. There were tears in the eyes of the coach as he watched Morgan tee the ball up for the ensuing kickoff. He had waited eight years for the chance to beat District-Heights. Could they hang on for another 12 seconds? Could they possibly beat the number two rated team in the United States? He quickly answered both questions in his mind as he thought, "With Morgan in the lineup ~ anything is possible."

Number 20 (Morgan) kicked the ball into the endzone.

District-Heights lined up and threw the ball far down the field where a leaping Mentz pulled in the ball for an interception at the

Eagle 41-yard line. The clock showed 0:06 seconds left in the game. As Mentz and Morgan trotted toward the sideline ~ Morgan told Mentz, "Take the knee and finish them off, Jamie."

Mentz smiled as he ran back on the field. All the Salem people in the stands had gathered on the track and it was a mass of humanity waiting to rush onto the field after Mentz closed out the game with his kneel down.

The ball was snapped --- Mentz dropped to one knee --- and the game was officially over. Several thousand Salem students and fans ran onto the field. Kyle Morgan was hit harder than he had been hit the entire game as he scrambled to avoid the hugs and kisses from everyone that could get close to him.

He looked up to see Misty Porter with her arms around his neck.

He gently removed them as the opposing coach walked up to him. "Great game Morgan, congratulations," said the coach. "You guys deserved to win the game. You played a magnificent game. I hope you win them all, unless we get to meet again down the road."

Morgan shook his hand, thanked him and turned to see his father and mother standing nearby. He walked over to them and after congratulatory hugs he said, "Well, Dad, what do you think? Can we win this thing or what?"

Mr. Morgan smiled as he said, "I think this team has a very good chance of winning it all."

On the bus ride back to the dressing room just about everyone that could get on the bus did. Principal Collins and Superintendent Gray were on the bus. The mayor of the town, Mr. Brady, was on one of the buses'. There were at least three-or-four more teachers that rode back to the school with the team. Several parents and teachers had to be asked to step off the bus due to lack of room. Upon the teams arrival back at the school, it was like a madhouse.

In the dressing room, Coach Shaw asked the team to kneel with him in prayer. Afterward, he spoke to the team. "I have been a high school coach for 25 years. This was the finest performance I have ever seen. You over came more adversity than anyone would have thought humanly possible. Your parents, your community, your school and I could not be more proud of you. Celebrate this win this weekend. We'll start getting ready for Galveston on Monday."

It was after 11:30 p.m. when Morgan walked out of the locker room back at the gym. His mother and father met him as he came down the steps. As they walked toward the parking lot he looked around for the family car. It was nowhere to be found.

His father walked over to a beautiful blue 1963, Ford Thunderbird. He asked his son, "how do you like it?" He then handed the keys to his son and said, "Happy birthday, Kyle."

Kyle Morgan had not given much thought to this being his birthday. His dad had promised him an automobile on his sixteenth birthday. As he looked at the beautiful car and thought about the fabulous football game he had just been a part of --- he just couldn't imagine a better birthday.

On Saturday morning Kyle Morgan slept late. He was tired from the previous nights game. His father was going to take him to get his drivers license later in the morning. Later on in the day, he planned on going over to the Mentz Pharmacy snack bar and just hang out awhile.

The family planned on attending their third church on Sunday in the hunt for a regular place of worship. The church had been recommended to Mrs. Morgan by the mother of one of the Salem students she had sat near at the ball game the past Friday night. It was the mother of Misty Porter.

He kept replaying the game over and over in his mind. He remembered every play and every high and low associated with the game. He thought to himself, "Monday will be a fun day at Salem High School."

Chapter Eight
The Guidance Counselor!

When Butch Cobb pulled into the driveway that Monday morning he quickly noticed the new automobile. When Morgan told him it was his, he said, "Man, every girl in the school will be after you with wheels like that."

Morgan just grinned and joked, "Well, I guess I should learn to drive that thing then." Morgan would continue to ride with Cobb for the next several days until he received his on-campus parking permit from the school.

Upon their arrival at school the hysterics had already begun. The cheerleaders had placed more signs up during the weekend praising their victory over District-Heights and proclaiming an easy victory over Galveston the following Friday.

As he walked into homeroom he was met by Coach Powers at the door. "Good morning, Kyle," said the coach. "I haven't told you personally, but you played a great game Friday night."

Morgan thanked the coach and moved to his desk.

Throughout the day there were proclamations from all the teachers praising the team for their big win the previous Friday night. Mrs. Mabry in first period English spent about half the class time talking about the game with anybody that wanted to discuss it. She looked at

Kyle on several occasions and smiled at him. He quickly looked down at his text book and stayed out of the discussion.

Mr. Fielding ~ in third period chemistry and biology ~ went to the extreme with a rolled out red carpet he said was for all the football players in his class. Morgan reluctantly stepped onto the rug at the prodding of the teacher and several of his classmates as he proceeded to his desk.

Principal Collins congratulated the team over the load speaker and singled out Morgan, Hinsley, Winkler and Cobb for making the Baltimore Sun high school performance honor roll in the Sunday edition.

That afternoon at practice the team viewed the film of the District-Heights game and Coach Dills went over the stats. The Eagles had gained 508 yards rushing and passing. Winkler had ran for 168 yards and returned kicks for 112 more. He had scored four touchdowns on runs of 28 yards; 39 yards; 34 yards; and 66 yards. He also ran a kickoff back 85 yards for a fifth score. Morgan had thrown the ball 23 times, completing 17 for 228 yards. He had scored on an 80-yard pass from Mentz. Defensive ace Mentz had intercepted two passes. Hinsley had 12 tackles and Cobb had 10 with three sacks of the quarterback. It was in the words of Coach Dills, "a remarkable game."

Coach Shaw then took the floor. He complimented the team on its ability to come back after an interception and early fumbles put the team in a hole to begin the game. He then told the team the book was closed on District-Heights. The Galveston Hawks were waiting for their shot. They were unbeaten and ranked number six in the class AAA polls. They had beaten Calumet County this past Friday by a 39 - 14 score. They were probably going to move as high as fourth in state rankings this week since several teams ranked above them had lost their games. He went on to say that this week there would be several changes in the offense to provide more of a quick-strike opportunity to put points on the board. He made it clear he believed the Eagle team had the ability to score from anywhere at anytime.

After viewing the film of the Galveston team, the Eagles moved to the dressing room. Outside the gym there were two buses' to take the team over to the stadium for practice. Coach Shaw explained that they were going to need the lights since he planned on a practice until about 8:00 p.m. that night.

The entire practice was on offense with more pass routes added and an offensive scheme that would prove to be about 25 years ahead of its time. The basic offensive set was a shot-gun formation with Winkler moved out to a flanker with either North or Greer in the backfield. On most plays the set back would go in motion emptying the backfield and making five receivers available for Morgan to throw to. On several plays there were three deep receivers with one running a fly route toward the corner of the endzone, another crossing to the other endzone corner and the flanker or motion man streaking straight down the middle.   Usually Cobb and Devers at end would break the play off short to serve as safety valves. A quick shovel pass was installed to the back after a play-action fake.   Screen passes were practiced for about 20 minutes. It was evident that Coach Shaw believed the Eagles could move the ball through the air almost at will.

On the way home, Cobb said to Morgan, "It looks like the coach is going to air it out Friday night."

Morgan answered, "It sure does look like it."

Cobb then said, "Kyle, I appreciate your throwing to me on that last play Friday night."

Morgan smiled as he replied, "Butch, I have more faith in you catching the ball than anyone we have. You were the only choice in that circumstance."

Cobb countered, "Well, I still appreciate it. I'll never forget it."

Tuesday and Wednesday practice was devoted to pass offense and pass defense with a lot of work on the deep passing game. At times both Winkler and Morgan would line up at receiver and go long. It was a mismatch when they did. The only time the pass fell incomplete was when Mentz missed them, which was not very often.

On Thursday morning at 9:00 a.m., Morgan was to meet with Mrs. Rollins. She was the high school guidance counselor. He was scheduled to spend two hours with her doing a psychological profile to assist the teachers in their everyday dealing with their students. She was later to comment that she had never talked with anyone like Kyle Morgan before.

Morgan was greeted at the door of the guidance counselor office by the teacher and Superintendent Richard Gray. He was going to sit in on the first part of the session. After a few moments of conversation --- mostly about football --- Mrs. Rollins started the probing questions.

She mentioned to Morgan that she noticed he was on the College-Preparatory Program. She inquired as to whether he had decided on a career at this time?

He told her he had not decided on what he would do at this point as far as a career, but he wanted to acquire a law degree at some point in the future.

She asked, "Why do you say that?"

Morgan answered, "It's just something I would like to have."

She asked, "Do you want to be a lawyer?"

He answered back, "Not necessarily, but I want the degree and what it represents for my personal satisfaction."

Now the teacher was getting curious. She asked Morgan what were his favorite school subjects.

He answered without hesitation, "I really don't have a favorite per se. I like them all about equal."

She then asked him, "What is your most difficult subject?"

Morgan answered, "They're all the same to me."

She noted the 100 percent grade-point average on his records. She asked, "How do you accomplish this?"

Morgan answered, "I just do my assignments and take the tests."

She asked, "Do you remember everything you read?"

He nodded that he did and answered her question. "Yes, I can remember almost verbatim all the novels and text books I have ever read. I have read all the encyclopedias and dictionaries in their entirety and remember them completely."

She got up and walked over to the bookcase. Picking up a copy of the M-N-O encyclopedia she randomly opened it to a page and asked him to read it to himself.

He glanced over the page and handed it back to the counselor. He then proceeded to recite back to her the exact text that was written on the page.

Superintendent Gray and Mrs. Rollins excused themselves and stepped into the outer office.

"His transcript said he could do that, but it is somewhat unbelievable." Mrs. Rollins told Gray, "He appears to have a photographic memory that absorbs everything he reads and stores it in his brain. He certainly appears to have total recall."

Superintendent Gray said, "I've never seen anything like that." He turned and left the office.

Mrs. Rollins went back into the room and continued to ask the junior numerous questions about his amazing and unique abilities.

He told her that he would make up his mind about attending a traditional college sometime during his senior year. He definitely had plans on some type of professional sports, but had not decided just what that sport would be at this time. He continued, saying that he lived for the challenge of participating in high school athletics. Sports was about the only thing he had found that he actually had to work hard at to be successful.

The session closed with a 200 question test that was designed to show the student strengths and weaknesses' as to subjects and grade placements. Morgan's score was literally off the board. His answers were the ideal for every question and concluded that he was suited for all courses. His grade placement was primarily master's degree in about 10 different arts and sciences.

After the session, Mrs. Rollins would state for the record that Kyle Morgan was at the genius level on all the provided high school courses and would probably max all tests and reports required in his college-prep curriculum.

By the end of the week, Morgan's mental capabilities would be known to all of the school faculty. There would be no more astonishment at his string of 100 percent homework grades or his perfect scores on all tests and reports. The capabilities of Morgan the scholar was to become as evident as the capabilities of Morgan the athlete.

Friday arrived with a coolness in the air. The trip over to Galveston was about 30 miles. The pre-game meal would be at 4:30 p.m. at the Morgan Cafeteria East Side. All the cheerleaders were invited to the meal this time. Morgan found himself sitting by Misty Porter and across from Butch Cobb and Cindy Gray. It seemed that he often found himself around the hyper junior cheerleader and female athlete.

He really did enjoy her company. She was a sweet ~ down to earth young lady ~ that was always laughing and having a good time.

By game time the temperature was around thirty degrees. By far the coldest it had been for any game this season. As the team made its way to the field, Coach Shaw stopped Morgan and told him, "Make sure you concentrate hard with the cold temperature. You'll call the plays as you see fit."

Morgan nodded and trudged onto the field.

The Baltimore Sun newspaper had moved Salem High school to the number five ranking in Class AAAA. Galveston was currently at number four in AAA.

When the game was completed there were not any doubts left that the Eagles were at least that good. The team struck early with their new offense as Morgan threw time and time again to Cobb, Winkler, Carter, Devers and Shealey for short to medium-yardage gains. Winkler threw in 106 yards rushing on only 12 carries including a 35-yard touchdown run in the third period. The half time score was 27 - 3 with Morgan kicking two field goals of 43 and 42 yards and completing three touchdown passes to Winkler for 33, 38 and 36 yards. Winkler would catch seven passes for 188 yards. Cobb had eight receptions for 79 yards. Tommy Carter had four catches for 77 yards including a 22-yard touchdown in the fourth quarter. The final score was Salem 41 and Galveston 10. The Eagles had ran up over 580 yards of offense with Morgan completing 29 passes out of 35 thrown for 440 yards. It was an awesome performance that had everyone shaking their head in amazement as they left the stadium.

The ride home from Galveston was subdued that night. It was just a matter-of-fact victory that was expected. The calmness and maturity that their sixteen-year-old quarterback ~ going on twenty-five-years-old ~ continually displayed had settled in on everyone.

That night upon his arrival home, Coach Shaw's wife Martha waited as he entered the den. She looked at her husband and asked, "Tom, What are you doing? Those aren't normal plays you are using out there. Where in the world are you coming up with those things?"

Coach Shaw looked at her and smiled, then he answered, "A coach works all his life trying to develop a player like Kyle Morgan. Someone that can just about do anything on a football field. Then when you find him, you almost feel embarrassed when he does what he does on that field."

He told his wife there were four films sent to him from Morgan's high school coach of last year. "You should see him play in those games. They put in these type plays just to get him the ball and he scored eighteen times on receptions. He is just so blamed fast and smart that no one can stay with him."

Mrs. Shaw asked, "Tom, is Bobby happy with becoming a flanker after being a featured running back for you for three years?"

Coach Shaw answered, "Bobby will still get his carries and yards. Plus, he will dominate on the outside catching the ball with his speed. If he gets open, Morgan will hit him. I'll guarantee it."

Coach Shaw then told his wife something he had not told anyone. "We're going to win the state this year if we can keep everyone healthy. I honestly believe that if I was to put Morgan at tailback he would score on two of every three plays he touched the ball. The kid is that much better than his peers at the high school level."

Martha Shaw looked at her husband of 25 years and asked, "Tom, is it fair to use someone like Morgan against average kids?"

The coach answered without hesitation, "Regardless of these amazing attributes he has, he is still only a 16-year-old boy. We have to remember that."

He proceeded to show her the report that had been submitted to all the teachers by Mrs. Rollins. Martha Shaw shook her head and spoke softly to the coach. "Tom, they say that madness lies just around the corner from genius. Be careful with how you handle that boy. You probably have more influence with him now than anyone at the school and as much as anyone with him other than his parents." Tom Shaw paused for thought, then replied, "Mott, I'll watch him like an Eagle. Now lets get some rest."

Chapter Nine
The Bully !

The Sunday High School Sports News had moved the Eagles to the number three spot in the Class AAAA rankings.

Monday was an uneventful day with rain through most of the day. The coach decided that he would have a run through of plays in the gym in shorts after the game-tape review. The Mitchell County Ravens were a region rival that had beaten Rock-Hill by one point the past Friday night. The 14 - 13 game was won on a touchdown by the Ravens with less than a minute left in the game.

Coach Shaw tried to impress upon his team that the best way for them to get beat was to become cocky and complacent with their current success.

Mentz received a lot of work at quarterback with Morgan lining up at flanker on several occasions.

It was Tuesday in sixth period study hall. Morgan was working on his geometry assignment for the next day when he heard a commotion from the other side of the class room. He looked up and saw some sort of altercation going on between a large boy and the football team student-manager Riley Gates. Gates suffered from Down Syndrome. He was involved in virtually all school activities as either a manager or ball boy.

On the track team, he ran the mile, usually finishing about a lap behind the other contestants.   He often was the butt of insensitive jokes by some of the less-sensitive students around school.

The other boy involved was named Danny Adams. He was six-feet-four-inches tall and weighed well over 280 pounds. Adams had been an above-average football player until midway through his sophomore year when he was caught shoplifting from the town hardware store. He, along with a couple of buddies were stealing everything from frog gigs to fountain pens. Coach Shaw had kicked him off the football squad and would not allow him to return. He now spent most of his time in after-school detention or undergoing some type of disciplinary action.   He was a senior that ~ despite all his disciplinary baggage ~ was still on course to graduate.

He had the smallish Riley by the shirt collar. He slapped him twice and was about to slap him again when Morgan grabbed his arm. "That's enough," said Morgan.

Adams turned and asked angrily, "Who do you think you are to tell me what to do?"

Morgan answered with a question, "Why don't you leave him alone?"

Adams ranted for a moment ~ then challenged Morgan to step outside, and, "as he put it ---- settle the issue!"

"You don't want to do that!" said Morgan. "That'll just get us both suspended or expelled. I'll tell you what I will do. Coach Shaw has some boxing gloves in the gym. I'll put them on with you and you can take out some of your frustrations on me. That is of course, if you can hit me."

Adams said, "I can hit you. After class, moron, I'll meet you in the gym."

Danny Adams did not know the full extent of what could have happened to him that afternoon.

As a part of his Central Intelligent Agency qualifications, Ken Morgan had been required to take various courses on self-defense when he joined the agency. While taking various karate, kung-fu and tae-kwon-do classes around the country, he had started his young son on the same training. By the age of 10, young Morgan was black belt in all the marital-arts with the exception of a green belt in ju-jitsu. He was capable of holding his own with virtually any age or weight class by the time he was 12. Often he and his father would work out together and more often than not would battle to a standstill.

When Morgan entered the gym he saw Adams standing in the middle of the floor with several of his rowdy buddies. He proceeded to the office and told Coach Shaw he needed the boxing gloves for a few moments.

The coach reached inside his bottom drawer, picked up the gloves and walked toward the gym floor. When he saw Adams, he wasn't overly surprised. He asked Morgan, "You sure you want to do this?"

Morgan answered, "It needs to be done Coach, he won't hurt me."

Coach Shaw said, "I'm not worried about him hurting you, son, ~ I'm worried about you hurting him."

Morgan replied, "I'll take it easy on him." He smiled as they walked to the center of the gym.

When both combatants were gloved and ready to go, Coach Shaw went over the rules. "Anybody can quit at any time they choose to do so. When a participant goes to the floor and can't get back up the fight is over. After the fight both fighters will shake hands and the issue will be closed." Both nodded in agreement.

Morgan stood toe to toe with his large opponent and dodged several wild swings as he danced from side to side. At that point he began to pepper the larger boy with short jabs to the nose and mouth. Adams tried to get in some hard rights as he created clinch situations. He was trying to get his speedy, dancing opponent to stand still long enough for him to get a glove on him. By now, Morgan was pouring it on. He jabbed, threw stinging rights to Adams' body and taunted him with left-hand flicks to the face.

After several moments, Morgan decided he had humiliated his opponent enough. He decided to end it. A couple of quick left-right combinations and a hard stomach punch put Adams on the floor. He tried to rise, but groggily fell back to the floor.

Coach Shaw walked over and flashed some ammonia smelling salts under his nose and he quickly came out of it.

The fight was gone from Danny Adams by now. He saw that he could not hit the quicker Morgan and he could not keep his opponent from hitting him. It was over. As Morgan extended his hand ~ the big boy glared at him ~ and reluctantly accepted it. He turned and walked away, shedding his gloves as he went.

Coach Shaw retrieved the gloves from the floor. He and Morgan walked back toward the office. He stopped and asked Cobb, standing nearby, what it was all about. When Cobb told him what had happened, he again was not surprised. He felt there would be quite a few extraordinary occasions while dealing with Kyle Morgan as the school year continued.

The Mitchell County Ravens were not much of a test for the Eagles on a cold, Friday night in September. Morgan threw only 12 times with 10 completions for over 240 yards. Two touchdown passes were to Carter for 65 yards and 25 yards. It was on the long touchdown pass to Carter that had seen the Eagle quarterback accomplish another of his amazing feats on the field. The play started out as a quarterback rollout to the left. Before crossing the line of scrimmage, Morgan was hit by the Ravens defensive end. The amazing quarterback raised his left arm and threw to a streaking Carter over 40 yards downfield for the easy score. The team had seen Morgan throw with his left hand on many occasions in practice, but never for over 10 to 15 yards. He had thrown the ball over 40 yards in the air with velocity and touch. A 61-yard bomb to Winkler closed out his quarterback duties for the night. There were 1:16 seconds left in the first half. He also ran 75 yards on a rollout for one score and returned a punt 73 yards for another score. The score at the intermission was 35 - 0, Eagles.

Mentz played all the second half at quarterback and threw two touchdown passes of 28 yards to Cobb and 17 yards to Joey Bates. He finished 11 of 14 for 128 yards. On defense he had intercepted two passes, one in each half. The final score was 56 to 7.

Morgan had played only defensive safety the second half for almost all the third quarter. He had a 31-yard interception return midway through the quarter. The Eagles had used 58 players in the game.

Coach Dills sat beside Coach Shaw on the trip back to Ridgeview. They got around to discussing the passing attack. The Salem assistant pointed out that, "Mentz would probably start at any other school in the state at quarterback."

Coach Shaw nodded in agreement. He did not doubt that for one moment. He told Dills that he wanted to use Mentz more at quarterback, but that Morgan was to be the starting quarterback the remainder of the year. He mentioned that next year with Winkler gone through graduation, he could take a look at moving Morgan to halfback and using Mentz at quarterback.

The young coach smiled as he asked, "Are you already looking at next year?"

Coach Shaw answered, "I always look ahead. With as much talent as we have on this team, our biggest problem is keeping our players happy with where they are playing, and how much they are playing."

It was around 5:30 p.m. Saturday afternoon when Morgan entered the snack bar in downtown Ridgeview. He ordered a grilled-cheese sandwich and a soft drink, then sat down at a table with Cobb and Mentz. They watched some of the college football game on the television above the counter. It was Doss State and Dent State in a Capital Conference battle.

Cobb said to no one in particular, "Boy, I sure would like to play for Dent state. They're my favorite team."

Mentz asked Cobb, "Have you gotten anything solid from any school yet?"

"Nah," answered Cobb, "just some questionnaires. Nothing from any major schools."

Cobb looked at Morgan, "How 'bout you, Kyle, any letters yet?"

Morgan answered back, "No, I haven't received anything from anyone."

Mentz retorted, "They won't go after you until your senior year in most cases. Bobby is talking with three-or-four schools and Hinsley is talking seriously with at least two schools."

"Morgan was curious," as he asked, "who is Bobby talking with?"

Cobb answered, "I think Clark State and Winston State are coming on the strongest."

Clark state was the number three ranked Division 1-A team in the major polls. Winston State had a great tradition with six consecutive bowl bids. Both teams had great seasons underway at this point of the season.

It was about 6:30 p.m. when Misty Porter and Jen Shaw walked into the store. They immediately made their way to the table and pulled up some chairs. Cindy Gray, Dora Purcell, Ann Mabry, and

Connie Hollis arrived shortly afterward and the next three hours were spent watching TV, dancing and just having a good time.

Sunday was church in the morning for the Morgan family. Kyle spent the afternoon watching professional football on the tube. Late in the afternoon, he walked over to Cobb's house. They spent about an hour shooting basketball in the front yard.

"If Coach Shaw hears about us even touching this basketball, he'll bench us Friday night," said Cobb.

"Really," replied Morgan, "are you serious?"

"You bet," answered Cobb, "he has made it clear to all of us basketball players he doesn't want us shooting a round ball until after football season."

Morgan could see that. He told Cobb, "Well, I guess we had better leave it alone. I'd sure hate to miss the football game Friday night." He grinned as he swished a set shot from the top of the circle.

Chapter Ten
The First Date

The month of October had blown in with miserable, cold weather. The October the seventh game against St. DaVinci and the Dawson Creek game on October the fourteenth were home games. A hard freeze had hit by Tuesday of the week and football practice outside was a miserable experience.

Most of the players would wear warm-ups beneath their regular practice gear. Morgan chose to wear a warm-up shirt beneath his shoulder pads, a sock cap under his helmet and two thick pairs of socks.

The temperature was in the low twenties on Wednesday when the team took the practice field. The ground was frozen. Coach Shaw chose not to have any contact drills on the day. Strong winds concerned the coach as he watched his troops run plays under the dark, wintry skies. He told Coach Powers, "We may have to play under these conditions Friday night, so lets work hard the next several days getting them accustomed to functioning in this type weather." Keeping the players moving to help keep them reasonably warm was a prime necessity.

After practice Morgan mentioned to Cobb that he had played a game in the snow the past year in Georgia. Cobb told him that last year their last three games were all played in the snow. Morgan shuddered as the thought hit home.

On Thursday night, there were probably 20 to 25 patrons in the Mentz snack shop. Mr. Mentz had already made plans to enlarge the area after the first of the year. He had just recently secured a loan to finance the building of an upstairs to the current teen center. James Mentz told his friends about it over a hot dog and soft drink that cold, windy night.

While Misty and Kyle were talking at a corner table, she mentioned the dance after the football game on Friday night. She rather sheepishly asked him if he was going.

He asked, "Misty, do you want to go to that dance?"

She was somewhat shocked as she in return asked him, "Would you go with me if I did?"

"I guess so!" Morgan answered.

Her look of surprise turned to a smile as she told him, "You silly, of course I want to go." She told him she would have to ask her parents permission, but she didn't think they would mind.

Morgan decided he had better run it by his parents, too.

That night Kyle talked with his parents at dinner about wanting to ask Misty to attend the dance with him. They smiled as they listened to him awkwardly explain what he wanted to do. "It won't really be a date or anything, because we'll just be in the gym right outside the locker room."

Mr. Morgan smiled as he said, " Son, you are at an age where you will start to notice the young ladies. We want you to experience the normal high school activities of any 16- year-old teen, including the dating experience. We only ask that you remember to respect the young lady and use sound judgment in all your actions."

Morgan knew exactly what they were talking about. He had no intention of any serious romances as this point of his life. His only concern was to finish high school and decide between college or professional sports.

As he started to leave the room to call Misty his father said, "Good luck tomorrow night in the game."

He returned a pleasant, "Thank you, Dad," as he left the room.

Misty had mentioned to a close friend that Morgan had asked her to attend the dance with him that Friday night. Word had spread quickly. Kyle got a lot of curious glances as he moved down the hallway at school. She didn't mention that she would meet him at the dance and that Cobb would drive them home after the dance. Morgan had his new car for almost a month, but he still rode to school with Cobb.

Cobb told Morgan he was one "weird duck." He had a new car parked in his driveway and didn't drive it.

Morgan simply smiled as he said, "quack, quack."

His father had noticed this, but was not interested in making an issue of it at this time. He knew his son was somewhat self-conscious about having the only new car among all his classmates. He had even given thought to buying him an older car and letting Lucille drive the thunderbird. He put it in the back of his mind, deciding to let Kyle come to him if the car was indeed a problem.

St. DaVinci High School was in McRae, which was about 75 miles from Ridgeview. Morgan was glad this was a home game. That would have been a long trip. He arrived at the gym at 5:00 p.m. After ankle wrapping and final coaching instructions, the team moved toward Memorial Field. The temperature was going to be around 12 degrees at kickoff.

The Eagles received the football and promptly moved 64 yards to the Lion 10 before Winkler took a pitchout, cut off his left tackle, and scored with over 8:00 minutes left in the quarter. The halftime score was only 14 - 0, Eagles. Penalties and fumbles stopped three drives after successful starts.

Coach Shaw was not in a good mood at halftime. Bobby Winkler went out briefly with a slightly-sprained ankle toward the end of the half, but it was not a problem as the second half stated.

In the middle of the third quarter, Morgan climaxed a nine-play, 71-yard drive with a 23-yard pass to Cobb for a 21 - 0 lead with 1:08 left in the quarter. With 9:02 left in the fourth quarter the Eagle star kicked a 37-yard field goal after a fumble and penalty had stalled a promising drive. With less than 3:00 minutes left in the game, Morgan rolled out to this left and behind a crushing block from Cobb raced 41 yards to the endzone. The final score was 31 - 0, Eagles.

Coach Shaw stood before his team and praised them for their performance in the very cold weather. By the end of the game it was four degrees and most of the fans had left at halftime. Even Coach Shaw huddled under a hooded coat during the game. The windy conditions made it difficult to throw the ball, so the entire second half was primarily play- action running plays.

Morgan threw the ball 16 times with 12 completions for 162 yards. He had carried the ball four times during the game for 72 yards.

Winkler had ran for 86 yards.

It was a tough game under the conditions it was played in.

A tired and cold-to-the-bone Morgan made his way into the gym where about 90 to 100 students danced to records, mostly of the slow rock or rhythm and blues variety.

Misty met Kyle as he walked in the door and they moved to a section where Butch Cobb and Cindy Gray were seated.

Cobb greeted Morgan, "good game, Kyle."

"Thanks, buddy," replied Morgan.

The dance was over at midnight. It was just a night of dancing and chatting for the two high school youngsters.

Most of their conversation was about school activities and basketball. Misty Porter loved to talk about basketball. She had started playing the game as a seventh grader. As an eighth-grade player she was five-foot-eleven-inches. This allowed her to easily shoot over the smaller girls she went up against.

After some degree of success as an eight grader, she had went out for the varsity the following year. She became a starter midway through the season and averaged around eight points per game.

As a sophomore she was, of course, the teams leading scorer and best player.

The busy young lady was involved in just about all the school extra-curricular activities including the Beta Club, Student Council, The S-Club for sports lettermen, Tri-Hi-Y, Science Club, the school newspaper, the annual staff and so on. She had even played clarinet in the band during her seventh and eighth grade years.

It was evident that the pretty girl sitting beside him was a very intelligent and somewhat fascinating work of art. One thing stood out that she told him. Her goal was to attend medical school and become a physician. Misty Porter was an intriguing as well as fascinating young lady. She had her mind set on becoming a surgeon. He never asked her why she wanted to become a doctor, but he could see her as being a success at anything she might choose to do.

On the dance floor she preferred slow dancing. Morgan was amazed that they danced so well together. Kyle had been taught to dance as an 11-year-old by his mother. He didn't think he had ever told anyone this, including his father. He was sure his mother had told the elder Morgan she was teaching him to dance. He was a good dancer with beautiful timing. While he enjoyed dancing to the faster beat songs, he acquiesced to letting Misty select the tunes she preferred to dance to.

It was a fun and enjoyable night for Kyle Morgan. He had really enjoyed the company of Misty Porter.

As Kyle and Misty made their way to his car after the dance, Cobb cautioned, "Be careful people, the parking lot may have some icy spots." Almost on cue, he stepped on a slight incline, lost his traction, slipped to the ground and slid down the hill on his back. As a concerned Morgan moved toward him, a small crowd that had witnessed the event began to clap and chatter as they gathered around. The good-natured Cobb just rose to his feet, smiled, waved at them and walked back toward his car.

After dropping off both girls at their homes, the two tired juniors drove toward their homes with very little to say.

Cobb did mention that he couldn't believe he was as open as he was on the pass play for the touchdown that night.

Morgan grinned as he said tongue-in-cheek, "I think the defensive back slipped down. You know how slippery it is out there."

Cobb said, "I think it was my perfectly ran route that got me so wide open."

Morgan laughed as he said, "I still think the defensive back slipped down."

Cobb just laughed along with him.

When he arrived home that night his parents had already turned in for the night. He took a seat in the den. He was lost in thought for several moments before deciding to turn in himself. He still quivered at the thought of the game. The ground was so hard it was like pavement. He felt the team was lucky to get through the night without some broken bones. He hoped next week would see a warmer week in practice and the game.

Chapter Eleven
A Sad Day!

A slight warming on Monday was a welcome sight for the football team as they made their way to the film review-room.

After watching the Dawson Creek Wildcats play against West Calvert and lose by a 35 - 14 score, there wasn't much concern about losing the next game. Coach Shaw could see this in the eyes and mannerisms of his players as he went about the job of preparing the team for the game. He suspected his major practice task for the week would be to keep complacency from descending on his Eagle squad.

Most of the week was spent working on defense with the normal pass emphasis on offense.

One new set was installed on Thursday while running through plays. Mentz was at quarterback with Winkler at one running back and Morgan at another. It was a split back set that drew great interest from the Eagle players as they saw it unveiled. They couldn't imagine the two speedsters in the same backfield. How could any defense hope to stop probably the two fastest backs in the state. Most of the blocking schemes were misdirection designed to get the defense going one way with the tremendous speed of the two backs going in the other direction. The team worked on the new set for about 15 minutes. The game was a home game with the temperature expected to be around the 25-degree mark.

Dawson Creek was not a very strong team as their 3 and 4 won-loss record indicated. They were primarily a running team that threw only as necessary to keep a drive alive.

Morgan was slated to play defense on third down for at least the first half.

Mentz was prepared to play quarterback the second half.

Coach Shaw was determined to show West Ridgeview at least two or three new plays to have to prepare for. He had no intentions of showing the two-back set with Morgan and Winkler at running back at the same time.

The game went pretty much as expected. By halftime ~ the Eagles had moved to a 24-0 lead on two touchdown passes from Morgan of 38 yards to Carter and 63 yards to Winkler. Fullback Van Greer scored on a three-yard burst off tackle and Morgan kicked a 39-yard field goal to account for all the first-half points.

The second half saw Mentz work at quarterback ~ while Morgan stayed under wraps beside Winkler and North on the sideline. Cobb, Hinsley and Mentz played most of third quarter on defense before sitting out the fourth quarter. Mentz threw two touchdown passes --- to Carter for 45 yards and to Shealey for 17 yards.

Sophomore halfback Jerry Phillips scored on a 22-yard run with less than three minutes left in the game to put the final 45 - 6 score on the board.

In the locker room Coach Shaw didn't spend a great deal of time talking about the game. He moved right into the next game and what it would mean as far as winning the region title. With only Murphy and East Ridgeview left on the regular-season schedule after the West Ridgeview game, it would put Salem in the drivers seat as far as the region was concerned. He told the team to start preparing mentally for the game, to expect a tough week of long practices. He said every moment of practice was of the utmost importance in preparing for the number two ranked Wolves.

While the Eagle players were dressing and preparing to leave for their homes, two coaches from Chesapeake Tech College were driving back to Chesapeake City. It had been their first look at the Eagles. They expressed disappointment at having seen so little of the Eagle starters. "I would like to see the quarterback play the whole game.

I'll guarantee you that tight end can play college ball." Coach Jerry Mealor said.

"I think you're right about the end, He really looks solid. I don't know enough about the quarterback to make a call after just tonight. We'll know more after next weeks game." Coach Tully West answered. Both coaches were slated to attend the West Ridgeview game.

Coach Shaw and the players weren't aware of it at this time, but 21 coaches from various colleges and universities around the country would be in attendance at the game. It was estimated that at least 10 players from both schools were Division 1-A caliber players.

After the weekend results were evaluated, the Eagles were rated the number three team in Class AAAA. West Ridgeview held the number two slot. A very good Sparrows Point team out of Hagerstown was rated number one.

It was Saturday morning around 9:00 a.m. when Mr. Morgan asked Kyle to step into the den. He needed too talk with him. After several moments of conversation, he got to the point. "Kyle, I have to be away for several weeks. I need you to step up and take care of your mother and the business while I'm gone." The elder Morgan continued, "There are issues in Vietnam concerning national security that I have to get involved in. This means going into the region and working with Army Intelligence to resolve these issues. It could mean being gone three-or-four weeks or possibly even longer."

Kyle Morgan wanted to ask his father why he bothered with a job like this. He made millions of dollars on his cafeteria business. He certainly didn't need the money ----- then, that uncanny ability to reason jumped out at him. His father needed the challenge.

Ken Morgan was not as unique as his son with absolute photographic memory capabilities, but his IQ level approached genius on many fronts. He needed the challenge of being one of the best at what he was doing just as much as Kyle needed the challenge of athletics.

As he hugged his father, he told him he would do what he had to do to protect the family interests.

Mr. Morgan told Kyle he would leave Tuesday. Another front that served his father would be the explanation used to explain his absence during this time. Morgan was a Colonel in the Air Force Reserves. The story would be that he had been called onto temporary active duty.

Kyle mentioned to him the prospect of staying out of school that Monday and Tuesday to be with him before he left. His father told him "that was not an option." Life had to go on as usual for him and his mother.

All day Sunday, Kyle and the family spent most of their time together. The prospect of not having his father at home for Christmas was very real. The thought of not having him sitting in the stands during his football games was even more sad.

Ken Morgan had always been the biggest supporter of his son when it came to athletics. He saw a need being filled. When Kyle was participating in sports he could be closer to normal than at any other time possible. Even with his immense talent, he was prone to get tackled, throw an incomplete pass or just make a bad judgment decision at times. In his normal world he was almost error free. He never missed making perfect scores on tests, speed-reading books in less than an hour and having his mind clogged with memories that would never leave him.

Many times, Morgan had wondered how his son had withstood the pressures of being a boy genius. One thing was for sure he decided as he drove toward the office that Tuesday morning. If he could make it back from this assignment, he would seriously consider leaving the agency for good.

Wednesday morning at the Pentagon, Colonel Morgan listened to Army Brigadier General Brian Hodges explain the problem in Vietnam.

Over the last six months four high-ranking officers had been "fragged" in the field in various commands. Two had died from their injuries and two more were seriously injured. All were over a 40-mile radius in Phong Lei Province. It was believed to be someone with freedom of movement among these locations that was committing the acts of violence.

"Fragging" was a term used when a fragmentation grenade was tossed into an officers tent, barracks or close proximity with intentions to kill or maim the officer ----- many times it was by a member of their own platoon.

It would be Colonel Morgan's job to find this serial killer and put a stop to the sideline horror that was plaguing the United States Military at the time.

It was 2:00 p.m. when Colonel Morgan climbed into the cockpit of a SPX-41 Spitfire fighter jet and revved up the engine to begin his flight to Vietnam. Ken Morgan had spent two years in advanced aviation and navigational training at the CIA Flight School in Brevard, California in 1958-59. He was considered one of the top CIA pilots in the service.

The takeoff went smoothly. Morgan turned his aircraft to the heading that would take him west across the Pacific Ocean, off the coast of Japan, over Taiwanese air space and into Ho-Chi-Mihn City. There would be briefings and refueling on two air-craft carriers as he made his way to his targeted destination.

To the left of his steering column he had taped a picture of his wife, Lucille. On the right he had taped a picture of his son in his Salem Eagle football uniform.

His thoughts drifted back to two-years earlier when an excited 14-year-old boy climbed into the rear cockpit of an SPX-35 fighter jet at the Langston Air Force Base Training Center.

It would be the first ride in a supersonic jet for the youngster. After the takeoff, the elder Morgan had carefully and in great detail explained all the various dials and compasses surrounding the cockpit. Less than 30 minutes after takeoff the teenager was literally flying the plane.

It was his fourth flight before young Morgan was at the throttle on the takeoff and during training maneuvers. He also brought the plane in for a landing on that day. At the age of 14, the teenage genius had conquered the art of flying a jet plane.

It had been about a year now since Ken Morgan had purchased a small plane and a company helicopter for his thriving restaurant business. Within a month after each purchase, Kyle Morgan had mastered the art of flying them.

Now the 14-year-old boy was 16-years-old. He was being entrusted to look after his mother's welfare and his father's business interests while the elder Morgan completed an assignment deemed as "in the best interest of national security."

All the logistics were in place. Now he simply had to complete the mission.

Chapter Twelve
Team by Team Perspective !

Misty Porter could tell immediately on Monday morning that all was not well with her friend. She asked him, "is there was anything I can do?"

He told her the "call-up story" although he was tempted to tell her the truth. He didn't feel good deceiving Misty on anything at this point. He asked her to give him a few days to let it settle in.

She said, "If there's anything that me, my family or the church can do, you just have to ask."

Morgan thanked her. He knew she was sincere and meant well. He turned and continued on down the hallway.

Monday afternoon at 3:30 p.m. ~ Coach Doug Martin of West Ridgeview stood before his number two-ranked football squad. The team had met on Sunday afternoon and reviewed the previous weeks game. They had viewed an Eagle game film. Martin had made it clear that beginning with the Monday evening practice session all focus was on the Salem Eagles. He turned on the projector and carefully reviewed the film of District-Heights and Salem High School.

He made no pretense that the keys to beating the Eagles was within that game. He didn't even bother to show their previous weeks game against Dawson Creek. He didn't feel it offered anything of value to the team.

He and his coaches had reviewed six different game films of the Eagles. They felt they knew the tendencies and strengths of the team as well as possible. The one thing that kept popping up in his comments was the speed of Winkler, Morgan, Carter, Mentz and even the big linebacker Hinsley. He continued to emphasize all during the film that much of their success was simply due to their blazing speed.

After the session he called his team together on the practice field. "Gentlemen, We are going to work hard this week on stopping the Salem passing attack. We can live with what they might do from a ground standpoint, but if they consistently move the ball through the air, it will present problems for us. We have to shut down the long ball and slow down their medium range success."

The West Ridgeview football program was considered the number-one program over the years in the state. The school had played football since 1942. Over this 21-year period of time they had won 15-region championships and six-state championships. Their last state titles were in 1958 and 1959. The Salem Eagles had not beaten the Wolves since 1953. In fact, most of the games were not even close.

West Ridgeview was a college football recruiters haven as 55 players over the last 10 years had received scholarships to play at Division 1-A schools.

There were at least 6 players on this years team that had good chances of receiving scholarships. Three seniors already had them in hand. Tailback Eddie Krees, quarterback John Sneed and linebacker Roland Merck were committed to college teams at this point with senior left end Ray Ogle and guard Carl Cross being considered by several schools. Junior linebacker Winfred Franklin and junior cornerback Gary Sneed, the younger brother of the Wolves quarterback, were high on some college lists.

The team ran a split back offense with two backs behind quarterback Sneed. These two backs were Kress, who had ran for over 985 yards in 7 games, and junior fullback Billy Nolan, who had ran for over 650 yards. The team was averaging over 33 points per game while surrendering only eight points per game.

At practice, Coach Martin lined up his offense in the Salem shotgun. He wanted to run a four-man front with Olman and Moulder at ends. Grisby and Stockstill would be at tackles, with Roland Merck,

Winfred Franklin and David Rogers at linebackers. In the secondary he wanted Cary Sneed and Wilson Sloan at cornerbacks. The strong side safety would be Steven Paschal.

Instead of their normal five-man front they would go with a free safety on every play. This would be the speedy All-State halfback Eddie Krees. Coach Martin assigned linebacker Merck, the fastest of his linebackers, the quarterback responsibility. "You have to stay with number 20 ~ Morgan," said the Coach. "Put him on the ground when you can. Blitz him at times in obvious passing situations, but be sure at least one of your teammate linebackers stays at home to cover the middle. The free safety will usually assist deep with number 22 ~ Winkler. Don't let him get behind you under any circumstances. If you see Winkler and Morgan at receivers with number 12 ~ Mentz in at quarterback, back off the blitz and cover deep first and the tight end second. On every play I want at least one blitz. It should come from a linebacker or corner. The ends are to go straight in and not directly at the quarterback. Don't let him or Winkler get wide. Push them back inside where we have some people to assist with the tackle."

The coach went over the various reverse potentials and the "flea-flicker" play he had seen against District-Heights.

He closed out the practice that evening by saying, "You have to be prepared for any situation with this team. They are so explosive. We feel we can score on their defense, but we have got to find a way to shut them down on offense."

He continued, "This week we will split the practice with offense working against the Salem defense and our defense working against the Salem offense. Their special teams are strong on punt and kickoff returns. We will need our kicker to put the ball in the endzone to prevent a runback. On punts we will kick away from Winkler when possible. If Morgan and Winkler are deep we will need to kick it out of bounds. We will call that from the sidelines as the situation dictates." With that comment the coach closed out the practice for the day.

Meanwhile, at Salem High School the afternoon film session consisted of a quick run through of the Dawson Creek game. This was followed by an extensive review of the West Ridgeview-Murphy film. Coach Shaw pointed out the explosiveness of the two Wolves running backs, Kress and Nolan.

He emphasized the passing ability of quarterback John Sneed and how he liked to throw to his two backs coming out of the backfield. These were two very good broken-field runners.

His primary points on defense were the exceptional speed of linebacker Roland Merck and the penchant the Wolves had to blitz. They seemed to blitz from somewhere on almost every play. With this in mind, Coach Shaw planned to emphasize audibles and play changing as needed to offset the West Ridgeview blitz package.

By the end of the practice session, the team was fairly familiar with what to expect from the Wolves on offense unless they were to slide in some new stuff. Coach Shaw would not rule out that possibility.

Last season the Wolves had beaten the Eagles 28 to 14. They had pretty much held the Eagle offense in check. Winkler had scored on a 56-yard punt return and a fumble recovery had allowed the Eagles to get a gift score late in the game.

The game was not as close as the score seemed to indicate. Coach Shaw had never beaten the Wolves. He had finished second to them in the region on two occasions with 9 - 1 records. The team was knocked out both times early in the playoffs.

With their win over District-Heights the Eagles controlled their own destiny. Win this game and the last two and they would be region champions. West Ridgeview still had District-Heights on their schedule the last game of the season. Coach Shaw hoped their battle would be for outright second place in the region after Friday night.

The crowd for the game at West Ridgeview Field was expected to be the largest in the history of Maryland for a high school game with the number two and three ranked teams in the states largest classification doing battle.

Wednesday night the Morgan family received a recorded phone massage from the Pentagon from Colonel Morgan. There would not be any direct calls to the family. All his calls would be to secure lines in the Pentagon with delivery to the family on tape from a liaison officer, usually about 12 to 24 hours after the original call. He said all was well, told them he loved them and would call at least weekly. The officer would then destroy the tape in front of the family. This was standard CIA protocol.

Misty Porter had been invited over for dinner after church the previous Sunday. Lucille Morgan told her the truth about where Kyle's dad was and how her son had felt bad about having to use the cover story with her. Misty told her she understood the reason for secrecy and appreciated her candidness. Mrs. Morgan felt her son needed a friend he could be comfortable with during his father's absence. She felt the vivacious young cheerleader and athlete was that individual.

Thursday night she arrived at the house with Kyle and they completed their studies and watched television until around 10:00 p.m.

As Morgan drove her home, she sensed the sadness he was experiencing as she spoke. "Kyle, it'll be okay. He'll be back soon, I'm sure of it."

On the way back home he turned on the car radio and listened as the Beach Boys and "Surfing USA" rang out from the speakers. He missed his dad, but he also had the utmost confidence in his ability to stay alive while accomplishing his difficult mission.

His mind jumped back to Misty. She was just the sweetest thing. He found himself thinking more of her everyday. He didn't want to think of ever having to tell her that he thought of her as the sister he never had. One thing he was sure of. He did enjoy being with her. She was the most fun person he had ever been around. She had a knack for saying the right thing to pick him up at the right time. He was also amazed at her ability to handle and shoot a basketball. He was really looking forward to watching her in action on the hardwood.

He sometimes wondered if there was something wrong with him for not constantly having girls and sex on his mind like most of the other boys. He would continue to let Misty be thought of as his girlfriend to keep from having to explain away his lack of a desire to get involved with girls at this time. He knew that there would come a time when he would have to tell her whether or not he wanted a steady romantic interest. Maybe it would be at the end of the school year - or even after high school graduation. He drove on toward his home. He found himself wondering what might lie in store for the Morgan-Porter relationship as time moved on.

Friday was fraught with anticipation all day. Just about everyone he passed in the hall coming or going to class would mention the game that night.

Plans were for the team to have a pep rally in the gym at 2:45 p.m. that afternoon. The game with West Ridgeview was only about four miles across town. The players would leave the gym at 4:00 p.m. for the pre-game meal, complete pre-game preparations by 6:30 p.m. and be on the field for warm-ups at 7:00 p.m. It was pretty much like a home game for the Eagles since it was so close.

The pep rally went well with the cheerleaders really raising the roof. A short skit had Misty Porter interviewing a boy with a baseball cap and whistle around his neck pretending to be Coach Shaw. She asked him, "Are the Eagles were going to win tonight."

He replied into her phony microphone, "We're going to run on 'em, and pass on 'em, and then we're going to grab them, twist them, beat them, and then rip 'em apart. Then we're going to come back to the gym and hug all the guys and kiss all the gals."

Everybody thought the skit was hilarious.

Butch Cobb just smiled as he said to Morgan, "I'll bet that's pretty close to what the coach is thinking."

As he walked to the bus, Misty came over and wished him luck. He smiled as she grasp his hand. He looked into her eyes as he told her softly, "We're going to win. I'll see you after the game."

She smiled and nodded her head in agreement.

At 7:55 p.m., the West Ridgeview Wolves won the coin-toss and elected to receive the football. Over 12,000 fans crammed into every nook and cranny screamed as Morgan boomed the kickoff eight-yards deep into the endzone.

On first down, the Wolves quarterback Sneed tried to hit his slanting end Steve Grutza, but linebacker North batted the ball down. On second down a swing pass to all-State halfback Kress went for 10 yards and a first down at the 30-yard line. For the third straight play, the Wolves quarterback threw the ball. This time it was a screen pass to Nolan the fullback for 18 yards to the Wolves 48. From a play-action set, a fourth consecutive pass was completed, again to Kress for another eight yards to the Eagle 44-yard line. The wily Wolves quarterback then ran an option, keeping the ball and gaining 12 yards before Winkler shoved him out on bounds on the Eagle 32. Another pass to their tight end Ratliff picked up seven yards to the 25. The Wolves were moving the ball.

Hinsley called time out.

"We stink!" he screamed as he walked toward the sideline.

He was an upset player as he stood with Coach Shaw and they talked about some needed defensive adjustments. The Wolves had decided to go with the passing game to confuse the Eagles. It was working to perfection early in the game.

A fullback dive netted four yards, then their greed jumped up and bit them. Norton threw a high bullet intended for Kress at the six-yard line. Morgan had seen the back start his route out of the backfield and picked him up at the 15-yard line. He stepped in front of the receiver and intercepted the pass. He was brought down at the Eagle 21-yard line.

The clock showed 8:06 left in the first quarter. On first down from the shot-gun, North plunged for four yards on a draw. A second-down pass intended for Carter on a sideline cut dropped incomplete. On third down, a pass was called in the huddle, but when Morgan saw the linebackers edging to the weak side of the field where Cobb was lined up, he called an audible for the draw to Winkler. The halfback moved from split back to the tailback slot, took the handoff and was dragged down by linebacker Roland Merck after five yards. On a fourth-and-one yard needed for the first down, Morgan punted the ball 51 yards to the Wolves 20-yard line. Kress called for the fair catch as the high and long punt was well covered by the Eagles outside contain players.

A tailback pitchout was diagnosed by Cobb and stopped for no gain. A quick pass to the flat fell incomplete on second down. On third down Sneed fired a pass to the sideline for 16 yards and a first down at the Wolves 36-yard line. Two running plays gained eight yards before the Wolves quarterback dropped back for a pass. Hinsley blitzed from the middle and Cobb crashed in from the left side. It was Cobb pulling the quarterback down for a nine-yard loss. The Wolves punted out of bounds at the Eagle 38-yard line with 5:41 left in the first quarter.

A pass intended for Carter was knocked down by the Wolves cornerback. A strong blitz from a linebacker that had moved up on the corner forced Morgan to throw just a split second before he was ready. On second down Morgan hit Winkler for 17 yards, but a holding penalty moved the ball back to the Eagle 23-yard line. On second down a draw to North picked up five yards to the 28. On third-and-20 for the first down, Morgan threw a slant to Carter for 14 yards to the Eagle 42 bringing up a fourth-and-six yards needed for the first down. Morgan went back to punt. As he took the snap he looked downfield and saw very little rush. He faked the punt, cut to the outside and was finally brought down after a 31-yard run to the Wolves 27-yard line.

It was Kress that was able to slow him down enough for his Wolves teammates to make the tackle. A handoff to Winkler gained six yards. On second down Morgan went play-action under the center intending to hit Cobb down the middle for 12 to 15 yards. As the quarterback made his drop and looked up he was hit by the blitzing Merck and the ball knocked free. It was recovered by the Wolves at their own 28-yard line with 2:16 left in the first quarter.

On first down a holding penalty on a toss-sweep moved the ball back half-the-distance to the 14-yard line. On first-and-24 yards for the first down, Sneed threw to Ratliff for 13 yards to the 27, bringing up a second-and-11 yards needed for the first down. A sweep by Kress picked up six of the needed yards. On third down Sneed threw the ball to Nolan on a screen for 12 yards and a first down at the Wolves 45-yard line. The first quarter ended without a score for either team.

On the first play of the second quarter Kress darted for 11 yards to the Eagle 44-yard line. A pass fell incomplete before Sneed threw to flanker Richard Gee for 27 yards down to the Eagle 17. Nolan picked up three yards. Kress gained six yards, but a motion penalty moved the ball back to the 19-yard line, making it second-and-12 yards for the first down. Kress ran for eight yards to the 11-yard line, bringing up a third-and-four yards needed for the first down. From play-action, Sneed dropped back to pass. Cobb literally threw two blockers out of his way and blindsided the quarterback at the 18-yard line. The ball came loose, but Nolan dove on the ball at the 21-yard line. West Ridgeview maintained possession. On a fourth down with the ball placed at the 28-yard line, one of the states best place-kickers, Mark

Ogle, kicked the 38-yard field goal to give the Wolves a 3-0 lead with 9:44 left in the first half.

The ensuing kickoff by Ogle was deep into the endzone. The Eagles started the drive from their own 20-yard line. Winkler ran for six yards on first down. On a crossing pattern with Winkler going long toward the right side corner and Carter going toward the left corner, Morgan hit the streaking Winkler at the Wolves 40-yard line. He ran 74 yards for the score with 8:15 left in the half. After Morgan kicked his fortieth consecutive extra point of the season it was Salem with the 7 - 3 lead. ~ 8:52 was left in the first half.

On the kickoff, a good runback by Kress to the Wolves 38-yard line was nullified by a holding penalty that placed the ball at the Wolves 22. A pass was complete for 13 yards to the 35-yard line. After two incomplete passes forced by strong rushes from a blitzing Hinsley, Sneed fired the ball between Mentz and Morgan to Grutza for 22 yards and a first down at the Eagle 43-yard line. Kress ran for 12 yards and Nolan cracked the middle for eight more and a first down at the 23-yard line. Kress and Nolan alternated on five carries before Nolan burst across the goal line from the two-yard line for the score. An Ogle PAT kick made it West Ridgeview 10 and Salem 7, with 5:22 left in the first half.

After the endzone kickoff, the Eagles once again started on their 20-yard line. On first down Morgan threw to Cobb for 16 yards to the 36-yard line. From the power-I formation, Winkler ran for seven yards. Morgan ran a sneak for four yards and a first down at the 47-yard line. Winkler broke for eight yards and then slashed off tackle for the first down at the Wolves 42. A quarterback rollout by Morgan started out with a lot of room on the outside before Merck dove and managed to trip up the quarterback at the 35-yard line. Van Greer ripped for five yards and a first down at the 30-yard line. The Wolves were bringing the mass on their blitz package. As Morgan gave the ball to Winkler on a delay, he was hit hard at the 33-yard line for a three-yard loss. A hurried and scrambling Morgan threw incomplete to Carter on the sideline just before he was crushed by three Wolves tacklers. On third-and-13 yards for the first down, Morgan called the "30-center-screen pass" to Winkler, but Wolves linebacker Winfred Franklin stayed at home and hit him as he caught the ball at the 35-yard line for another two-yard loss. With 1:56 left in the half, Morgan called time out.

As he walked toward the sideline, Coach Shaw had already called for the kicking tee ~ with Mentz as the holder ~ to go onto the field. Morgan glanced at Mentz as he walked by him and proceeded on toward Coach Shaw. The coach told Morgan to be on the alert for a blocked kick. He pointed out that he would be the safety if the ball was picked up by the blocking team. Coach Shaw shoved him toward the field as he said, "Kick the ball Morgan, no fakes, no delays, just kick the ball hard."

Morgan shook his head that he understood as he walked onto the field toward his huddled teammates.

The ball would be set down on the Wolves 42-yard line. If successful ~ it would be a 52-yard field goal. The longest in the state this year was 48 yards by three different kickers. The longest ever kicked in the state by a high school kicker was 52 yards. Morgan talked to his huddle, calling "field goal on one." Mentz placed the one-inch tee on the spot designated by Morgan on the 42-yard line. The lines were down and the ball was snapped to the holder. The ball was placed down and the junior place-kicker swung his powerful leg. The ball traveled in a high arch and cleared the bar with several feet to spare. The score was 10 - 10 with 1:46 left in the half.

Kyle Morgan had started kicking in the seventh grade on his seventh and eighth grade team. His coach noticed the strength and leaping ability he possessed in his legs and worked with him every day after practice on the kicking game. He preferred the soccer style of kicking over the traditional straight-on kicking style. His seventh grade year he had kicked a 25-yard field goal that had made state headlines in all the sports sections. His eighth grade year saw him kicking consistently good from 40 yards in practice. He managed to make a 38-yard field goal in a game. He would assume the kicking duties for his high-school team his freshman year. He had kicked 12 field goals as a freshman and 14 as a sophomore. His longest before this kick was 49 yards in the state quarterfinals the previous year.

The glad hands were extended to Morgan as he came to the sideline. He quickly refocused on the upcoming kickoff. It was long and deep in the endzone. The Wolves would start offense on their own 20-yard line.

Quarterback Sneed threw a quick pass to Kress in the flat for five yards, then tried to hit flanker Gee on a fly pattern down the left sideline. Tim Shealy tipped away the pass. On third down he fired the ball on a slant to Gee for 17 yards to the Wolves 42-yard line. A first down pass fell incomplete in front of Kress on the sideline. A draw to Nolan gained six-yards to the 48-yard line as time ran out in the first half. The score was West Ridgeview 10 and Salem High school 10.

Coach Shaw and the coaching staff moved from player to player giving individual instructions before the head coach moved to the front of the team. "We have one half left to get it done. He asked, "Can we get it done?" Loud screams of "Yea! We can do it!" and "We'll get "em," echoed from the locker room as he asked the team to bow their head for a short prayer. He ended the prayer with the words, "and Lord if it be Thy will, please protect Ken Morgan as he does his duty in Vietnam and return him safely to his family." There were tears in Kyle Morgan's eyes as he ran from the dressing room that night. It was as if he was suddenly dedicating the game to his father.

At the start of the second half, Morgan and Winkler were both back at the goal line to receive the kick. Ogle put a quick stop to that with a kick out of the endzone. From their 20-yard line, Morgan quick-pitched to Winkler on a 39-pitch for 13 yards. A quarterback rollout picked up 32 yards to the Wolves 35-yard line. North slammed for two yards. A quick-slant pass to Carter was incomplete. Winkler ran for 11 yards and a first down on the 22-yard line. Morgan ran a quarterback keep after a fake handoff to Winkler for 13 yards to the nine-yard line. Winkler ran for four yards to the five. On second down Morgan ran wide, drew the outside linebacker and corner toward him and fired a pass to Cobb for the touchdown. The PAT kick made it Salem 17, and the Wolves 10 with 7:58 left in the third quarter.

Another endzone kickoff put the ball in play at the 20 for the Wolves. Kress ran for 25 yards to the 45-yard line. Sneed kept for two yards. Kress ripped for another 12 yards. It gave them a first down on the Eagle 43-yard line. A Sneed pass was incomplete on the 25 as Mentz almost intercepted the ball. On second down Nolan ran a draw for eight yards to the 35-yard line. On third and two Sneed faked a handoff to Kress. The called pass route flooded the right side zone about 15 yards from the line of scrimmage. When Sneed threw into the coverage cornerback Shealey hit the receiver a fraction of a second early and pass interference was the call. It was a 15-yard penalty and placed the ball at the Eagle 20-yard line. With four-down territory as their aid the Wolves struck with reckless abandonment. Kress ripped for three yards, Nolan ripped for four yards and Kress again dashed for six yards to the seven-yard line. Nolan was held for no gain by Cobb and Boyd Massingale, the big tackle, but Kress then took over. He hit the right side for two yards and then barreled for four more yards to the one-yard line. With a fourth-and-one yard for the touchdown, the Wolves quarterback called time out with 2:44 left in the third quarter.

Hinsley, Cobb and Mentz talked defensive strategy including the possibility of a play-action pass. The coach sent Morgan in to act as a one side of the field safety. Winkler would cover the other side of the field. Mentz would have the middle. Eight men would be in tight on the goal-line defense designed to stop the short plunge. The quarterback for the Wolves went on a long count and the Eagles jumped offside moving the ball to the one-half yard line. On fourth down with all eyes on Kress, Nolan took a handoff and blasted into the endzone for the touchdown. An Ogle kick tied the score at 17 - 17 with 2:01 left in the third quarter. The Eagles had come out strong in the second half, but the Wolves had quickly answered.

From the 20-yard line the Eagles started their next series. Winkler was stopped after four yards. A second down pass intended for Winkler was batted down. On third down Morgan tried to sweep the right side, but Merck crashed through a Rudy Doyle block and knocked him down after a three-yard gain. With 0:22 left in the third quarter, Morgan punted 49 yards to Kress on the 24-yard line. He ran it out to the Wolves 36-yard line with 0.10 left in the quarter. A handoff to Nolan went for nine yards as the quarter came to a close.

The start of the fourth quarter saw Kress run for four yards and a first down on the Wolves 49-yard line, Sneed went long down the right sideline. Mentz stayed with the receiver all the way and batted the pass down. Kress broke loose on a quick-toss. Winkler caught him from behind at the Eagle 21-yard line. A 30-yard run. A slant pass to Ratliff was incomplete. On second down Hinsley was called for defensive holding on tight end Ratliff giving the Wolves a first down at the Eagle 10-yard line. Kress was hit hard by tackle Donald Walters and Cobb at the eight-yard line. He was slightly shaken and left the field. On second down from play-action, Sneed tried to hit fullback Nolan at the two-yard line, but Hinsley and Mentz put a punishing hit on him and knocked the ball loose. On third down, Kress returned to the lineup. On a play-action fake to Kress, Sneed went back to throw. Cobb crashed in from the left side and smothered the quarterback at the 11-yard line. On fourth-and-goal, Ogle came in and kicked a 27-yard field goal to put West Ridgeview up by 20 - 17 with 9:35 left in the game.

Ogle kicked the ball deep in the endzone where Winkler caught it and took a knee.

Morgan talked calmly to his huddle back on the 12-yard line. On first down, he threw to Carter for eight yards. On second down a quarterback sneak gained six yards to the 34-yard line. From the power-I formation, Winkler took a toss to the left, then tossed the ball back to Shealey on a reverse. The play started out with good potential, but linebacker Merck saw it all the way as he blitzed on the play. He slammed into Shealey and dislodged the ball at the 26. Only the speed of Morgan enabled the Eagles to keep possession of the ball as he recovered the fumble at the 25-yard line. In the huddle, Morgan asked Shealey if he had gotten the number of that run-a-way freight train. Shealey just shook his head. On second down a pass to Cobb was good for 12 yards to the 37-yard line. On third-and-seven yards for the first down, a blitzing Merck chased Morgan out of the pocket and forced a hurried throw that missed an open Carter at the mid-field strip. The Eagle quarterback dropped back to punt. The Wolves were not taking any chances of a fake as they played it as a normal series down without sending anyone deep. Morgan punted the ball to a stop on the Wolves 11-yard line. There was 7:21 left in the game. West Ridgeview still held on to a 20 - 17 lead.

Sneed brought his green-shirted Wolves to the line of scrimmage. He gave the ball to Kress for seven yards. Nolan gained two and then three yards for a first down at the 23-yard line. Sneed saw that the Eagles were in a seven-man front to stop the running attack. He called a quick-slant pass to Gee about 10 yards down the field. Mentz had watched the quarterbacks eyes all the way. He got a hand on the ball as it reached the streaking flanker. It was second down. Kress took a handoff and faked outside, cut back against the grain and rambled 17 yards before Hinsley and Devers ran him out of bounds at the Wolves 40-yard line. A draw play to Nolan gained six yards. A quick toss to Kress went for three yards and was about a foot short of the first down. On third down Kress ran behind his left tackle for three yards and a first down at the Eagle 47-yard line. Kress again got four yards on a misdirection play. Nolan was stopped after two yards on an off tackle slant. On third-and-four yards needed for the first down from the Eagles 41-yard line the Wolves called time out. There was no doubt that Kress would get the call on the third-down play. Morgan went in at sideback and Winkler moved close to the line. The power run by Kress was stopped after only two yards by the middle of the Eagle line. There was 3:27 left in the game when West Ridgeview called their last timeout. After a sideline discussion the Wolves dropped back to punt the ball. The Eagles played it straight. The possibility of a fake was always there with the Wolves. With no one back for the Eagles, Josh Herbert punted the ball dead at the Eagle nine-yard line. The clock showed 3:12 left in the game.

Morgan called the play. "Buttonhook to Cobb to get us out of the hole." It was complete for an 11-yard gain to the 20-yard line. Winkler ripped for six yards, then Morgan ran wide for eight more yards to the Eagle 34. A sideline pass to Shealey was complete for eight yards. Winkler cut inside for six yards and a first down at the 48-yard line. A Z-pattern to Carter was complete for 10 yards and a measured first down at the Wolves 42. Morgan emptied the backfield. Winkler split wide left. Carter wide right. A throw down the middle to Carter fell incomplete. Winkler was being doubled with a free safety and a cornerback. On second down Morgan took the snap and rolled right. He saw the cornerback following Carter on his middle-of-the-field route. Linebacker Merck was coming up on his left and defensive end Olman was coming directly at him. Morgan screeched to a stop, spun and reversed his field. He got a block from Shealey on the outside that left a small gap back toward the middle of the field. He quickly cut back into the gap. The big defensive tackle Stockstill tried to make the tackle, but the Eagle speedster simply ran past him. Corner back Gary Sneed, the quarterbacks brother, was leaving Winkler to come up and make the tackle. The galloping runner waited until he was within touching distance, then struck out with a wicked straight arm that drove the young sophomore onto the ground as he ran past him. Now, free safety Wilson Sloan was the only obstacle between Morgan and the goal. The speeding runner feinted inside and then stepped back outside, exploding by the overwhelmed Wolves defender. At the 25-yard line, there was suddenly nothing but the goal line in sight as the Eagle star turned on the speed. He raced into the endzone with 1:02 left in the game. The Eagles had the lead. The PAT kick by Morgan made it 24 to 20.

Needless to say the Salem supporters were overjoyed at what had just transpired on the field, while the very subdued home crowd hoped for a quick and positive response from their Wolves.

A Morgan kickoff went out of the endzone. From their 20-yard line Sneed went back to throw. He hit Kress in the flat and he ran for 17 yards to the 37-yard line. A furious rush from Cobb and Devers forced an out of bounds throw from Sneed just to prevent the sack. On second down, A screen pass to Kress was completed for another 12 yards with 0:37 seconds left in the game. From their own 49-yard line Sneed went back to pass. Winkler came off the left corner untouched and hit him for an 11-yard loss at the Wolves 40-yard line.

The clock was running, 26 seconds; 25 Seconds; Sneed took the snap and dropped back again. He tried to hit Kress on a swing pass, but the pressure from the Eagle line made him throw it early and it fell short of the speedy halfback. The clock showed 0:17 seconds as the Eagle fans cheered from the stands. The Wolves quarterback knew it would take a touchdown so he went for it all on third down with a pass down the sideline to Kress that was overthrown and out of bounds. There were 0:09 seconds on the clock as Sneed dropped back and fired long again to Kress, who was double teamed at the 10-yard line by Morgan and Mentz. The pass fell incomplete.

The clock showed 0:02 seconds when the officials put the ball in play. Mentz asked Morgan if he wanted him to take the knee to preserve his rushing average. He was smiling as he said it.

"This ones mine," Morgan said. He stepped behind the center and called the cadence. The ball was snapped and he dropped to his knee.

It was over. The Eagles had won the game 24 - 20 and were in the drivers seat for the region championship.

It was a mass of hysteria as Salem students, cheerleaders, fans, and parents converged on the players.

Morgan walked off the field with Misty Porter to meet his mother on the sideline.

She hugged him and said, "Your father will be so proud of you."

There were tears in his eyes as he said, "Mom, I miss him so much." He walked toward the locker room between his mother and Misty.

Coach Shaw met Morgan's mother at the door of the clubhouse and hugged her neck. After a few moments of conversation with his mom, he watched as she and Misty walked into the crowd of Salem supporters gathered around the clubhouse.

Coach Shaw asked the team to take a knee. He gave praise to the Lord for the victory, then calmly spoke to his squad. "I don't want to openly be dishonest with you. I have felt for sometime this team is something special. Now I see just how special you are. We still have to finish the job of winning the region before we think of winning the state. But I want to tell you that I will not be surprised if we do win the state. If you play as you are capable, you can play with any high school team not just in the state ---- but in the United States. Thank you for your efforts tonight." With that the coach turned to his assistant coaches and said, "I won't get any sleep tonight!"

When the Eagles arrived back at the school there were hundreds of students and parents waiting for the team. A hoard of media was waiting to get in an interview with the coach and some players if possible.

Another short speech was made by the coach as the team departed the bus and headed for the locker room. The coach agreed to meet with about 20 sportswriters for 10-to 15-minutes while the team was putting away their equipment. He made it clear he did not want any reporters talking with his players on this night.

Morgan walked out back of the school where his mother and Misty were waiting for him in his car. Mrs. Morgan moved over and the schoolboy climbed into the driver's seat. He would take Misty home first.

Afterward, as he drove toward his house, his mother and he talked about the many fun events he had been involved in while participating in high school athletics over the years. There was not much discussion about his father. That had already been said. Not many of his accomplishments were any better than the victory tonight.

It was after 1:00 a.m. when he finally turned in for the night.

Chapter Thirteen
Musings !

While Kyle Morgan was heading home, Coach Shaw and his assistant coaches were directing the media group back at the gym to a small classroom just off the gym floor. Here they would hold a brief press conference with them.

The first question they asked was where did Morgan go to school last year. The coach told them he would answer their questions about the game, but would not go into any specifics about any players past.

Coach Shaw told the media group that he had felt going into the game they would have to stop the multi-talented running back, Kress, and contain the passing game of Sneed to his experienced group of receivers to have any hope of winning the game. He had felt the team could put some points on the board, but wasn't sure how much ability they would have to shut down the high-powered West Ridgeview offense.

He was asked if Morgan was the best football player he had ever coached.

The Salem coach said he wouldn't answer that at this point. Maybe, later in the season.

One reporter asked him if Morgan was faster than Winkler and if he ran track. The coach replied, "I haven't timed Morgan in the 100-yard dash and, yes, he had said he ran some track."

For about 25 minutes the questions continued. Coach Shaw then proceeded to review the game statistics before adjourning the press conference.

The West Ridgeview team had 18 first downs to the Eagles 11. Total yards for the Eagles was 383 yards, with 406 yards for the Wolves. Morgan had thrown the ball 18 times with 11 completions for 157 yards. There were at least three dropped balls. He threw for one touchdown. Winkler had ran the ball 13 times for 87 yards. He had caught three passes for 89 yards, including the 74-yard touchdown pass. Cobb had caught four passes for 44 yards including his eight-yard touchdown reception. The time of possession was almost two to one with the Wolves controlling the ball for over 31 minutes with the Eagles having the ball for only 17 minutes. The Eagles big-play offense and their clutch defense had proved to be the difference.

For West Ridgeview, Sneed had throw the ball 29 times with 14 completions for 187 yards. The Wolves quarterback had been sacked on five occasions with Cobb having three of the sacks while Hinsley and Devers had one each. Kress had his usual all-star performance with 179 yards rushing on 24 carries and four catches for 57 yards. Nolan had ran for 60 yards in 17 carries. Everyone agreed it was an exciting and evenly matched game that could have gone either way.

After the group left, Coach Dills smiled at his head coach and asked, "Is Morgan faster than Winkler?"

Coach Shaw answered, "I guess you'll have to wait until track season to find out the answer to that question."

At 12:30 a.m., The coach walked out of the Salem High School gym. It had been a long night, but that elusive win over West Ridgeview had finally been achieved.

Around 10:15 p.m., Coach Douglas Martin stood before his West Ridgeview football team. He told them they had played a marvelous game, but things had just not broken their way. He reminded his team that with District-Heights still on the schedule, the opportunity to make the state playoffs was still there. He told his squad to get their heads up and move forward into the next game with the same intensity they had displayed on this night. "Make no mistake about it, you are an exceptional football team. We can play with Salem. If we can get to them again in the state playoffs, we will have a good chance to beat them."

With that he walked from the disconsolate dressing room and met with his assistant coaches outside the office. Assistant Coach Don McManus said, "You're right coach, they are a good football team. I can't believe the team speed they have."

Coach Martin answered, "We couldn't contain Morgan. He's the one that makes that team go. I don't believe I've ever seen anyone as fast on a football field. He's the best high school football player I've seen in 30 years of coaching."

It was almost 12:00 a.m. when the '63 Chevy pulled into the driveway of Coach Jerry Mealor of Chesepeake Tech College. He and Coach Tully West had just watched the game up in Ridgeview. On the way back to town they had discussed the performance of several players at length. Both were in agreement that probably the best back on the field that night had been Eddie Kress of West Ridgeview.

Winkler was outstanding, but it was felt he was already committed to Winston State.

Cobb, it was agreed would be the most sought after tight end in the state and maybe the country next year.

However; Mealor's mind kept going back to Morgan. He couldn't help but wonder just how good he could be if he were the central cog in the teams offense. If he carried the ball 20 times, how many times would he break it for a touchdown. He would love to know what his time was in the 100-yard dash and how strong he was in the weight room. Mealor was going to recommend to Head Coach Hugh Markham that they begin a recruiting process on both Cobb and Morgan the following week.

Letters would be sent to the players and the coach asking for interviews and presentations. He had seen numerous colleges and universities represented at the game earlier. He felt that the chase would probably begin next week to try and bring these two athletes into the fold.

Kress was already committed to Randall State, the number three rated team in the nation.

He was also impressed with James Mentz.

Coach Mealor was slated to attend another Salem game in two weeks and he would attend their playoff games. He wanted to get his foot in the door at Salem and with the parents of the two players as shortly down the road as possible.

Saturday afternoon another taped phone message arrived from Colonel Morgan. He told the family he was well and the case he was involved in was progressing well. There was still not a break that would allow him to come home.

The family made a recorded message to him that would be relayed through the proper channels.

Mrs. Morgan told him about the exciting game the previous night and that everything was going well in all the company stores.

Kyle told his dad he missed him and that all the team sent their best wishes to him. He also told him Misty said, "Hello."

Afterward, Kyle and his mother just sat and watched television without much comment. There seemed to be an understanding between mother and son that talking about the situation was not in their best interest, so they just let it go.

Sunday, after church Misty came over for dinner. She was excited that basketball practice was slated to start Monday afternoon for the November the twenty-second season opener at home against Murphy High School.

As Kyle and his mother sat on the steps watching the vivacious young lady tossing the ball toward the goal, Mrs. Morgan said, "She's really quite good, isn't she?"

"Yes Ma'am," Kyle replied, "she can play pretty well."

His mother said, "Can you help her with anything? You seem to play that game pretty well yourself as I recall."

Kyle smiled back at his mother and walked over to Misty. "Let me show you something. Bring your shooting arm in closer to your body. Fully extend your arm when you release the ball. You're short arming it on the outside shots. Let me show you what I mean." Morgan took the ball and shot it toward the basket. It parted the cords cleanly. He shot the ball with virtually no spin. It was almost like a knuckleball. After about 10 shots, with all but one finding the bottom of the basket, Misty gave it a try. She found that this shooting method did seem to improve her control of the ball and several even rolled around on the rim and then fell through. He spent the next half-hour working with her on a back-up dribble drop-step to enable her to get close to the basket for a quick-pivot one-hand shot. She was eager to listen and amazingly quick to learn. She and Kyle played basketball for over two hours. Mostly H-O-R-S-E and a loosely defensive one-on-one.

As they got ready to conclude their basketball session, she watched as Morgan walked up to the goal, jumped high in the air and slammed the ball down into the basket. She seemed awed as she said "I've never seen anything like that. How can you jump so high? I can't wait to see you play basketball."

Morgan quipped, "I hope you have to wait until after the state championship football game."

Chapter Fourteen
An Autograph for David Purcell

While there was great excitement around the school after the thrilling victory over West Ridgeview, it didn't seem to be as frenetic as the District-Heights aftermath.

Morgan reasoned that Salem fans and faculty were getting more accustomed to landmark victories with their latest climatic win.

At lunch, one of the cheerleaders, Dora Purcell walked over to where Morgan and several of the football team were having lunch. She wanted to introduce her younger brother to him. "He just worships the ground you walk on, Kyle," she said. There were smirks from Shealey, Bales and Massingale as the youngster handed him a sheet of paper and asked for his autograph. An embarrassed Morgan scribbled his name on the paper and handed it to the sixth grader. He extended his hand. Kyle shook it.

David Purcell walked away looking at the document like it was the autograph of some big-time professional athlete. Five years later, Purcell would become the most prolific passing quarterback in state history as he would lead the Eagles to two consecutive Class AAAA football titles. He would break many of the career records set by Kyle Morgan during his days at Salem High School.

William Edward Salem was a local industrialist. He had been the owner of four yarn factories in and around Ridgeview. In 1953, he had spearheaded a drive that raised funds to build a new school in downtown Ridgeview. The old Ridgeview-Central High School had been in existence since 1938. After construction of the new school, it had been named the William Edward Salem High School.

Salem had passed away in 1959 after serving as the   Board of Education Chairman for over 20 years at Central and at Salem High School.

The old high school was demolished in 1954 and a new shopping center was built where it had stood.

The football stadium and track complex were named Memorial Stadium in honor of Mr. Salem in 1960. It was said he never missed an Eagle football game in over 25 years.

It was 0:800 hours when Colonel Kenneth Morgan walked into 404 headquarters outside Ho Chi Mihn Delta. He had been informed the previous night of an attempted "fragging" incident in the barracks of First Lieutenant Larry Gardner, platoon leader of Bravo Squad, Unit 617.

He was met at the command tent by Lieutenant Colonel Whitt Weatherington. Fifteen minutes later, the Colonel looked over the scene where the young officer had been seriously injured when a grenade had been tossed into his sleeping quarters from somewhere outside the living quarters. The Lieutenant had just happened to be walking toward the doorway when the grenade entered the area. He immediate dove for cover behind the metal filing cabinet to the left of the doorway.

This quick-thinking act had saved his life. He had sustained serious shrapnel damage to his torso and extremities. He was, however, expected to recover fully.

Colonel Morgan carefully inspected the outside area and saw nothing that would provide an indication as to the perpetrator.

Back in the command tent, he spoke with the on-site commander. "Colonel Weatherington, I need a complete list of all your command by rank and serial number. I also need authorization to conduct appropriate background checks on all your personnel." Colonel Morgan asked, "Has there been any one coming and going from your station over the last two weeks?"

The commanding officer could not think of anyone specifically, but recommended that Colonel Morgan visit with his Chief Staff Officer, Second Lieutenant Frank Jarvis.

For the next several hours, Jarvis and Colonel Morgan went over all personnel that had been in and out of the camp over the last two weeks. Morgan had visited all the sites where the "fraggings" had occurred. He was now convinced that it was someone with some type of camp visitation privilege that was committing the criminal acts.

The usual clearances for site visits were for munitions/ordinance and commissary deliveries along with general supply and Red Cross visits. Eighteen individual names appeared that had spent time at the troop site during this time. Nine new squadron additions had come on board during this time.

At 1400 hours, Colonel Morgan climbed back into his jeep vehicle, driven by Corporal Andy Spindler and started his trip back to general command headquarters in Meng Lai.

There was something that was trying to jump out at him. He just couldn't quite put his finger on it. When he arrived back at headquarters he asked administrative clerk, Corporal Ted Mychelli, to get him the names of all the various supply unit members and Red Cross employees in the region. This would come to over 600 names. Colonel Morgan surmised that one of these names could be who he was looking for. It would take several days to accumulate this information and background checks would take several more days. He felt he was moving in the right direction.

Back at Salem High School at 3:30 p.m. the review of the West Ridgeview game started and was completed about 5:00 p.m. The coach repeatedly backed up the tape and reviewed all the positives and negatives individually. By 6:00 p.m. the Murphy game tape had been covered and a brief practice session concluded at around 7:00 p.m. Murphy was currently at 5 wins and 3 losses with sound defeats by both District-Heights, 43 - 7 and West Ridgeview, 38 - 0. They didn't seem to present a threat to the Eagles unless they were to receive a lot of gifts like fumbles, penalties, etc;.

Coach Shaw wanted to prevent this possibility at all cost. It would be an intense week of practice.

It was after 7:00 p.m. when Morgan climbed into the drivers seat of his car. It was his first day of driving it to school. He stopped by the Mentz Pharmacy and then proceeded on home. He picked up the phone and called Misty. "Hey Lady, How did practice go?" He asked.

Misty answered, "It went okay. We met for over an hour and just did some running. We didn't even touch a ball."

After finishing the conversation, he watched the evening news and started on his homework.

On Wednesday, Morgan had stopped as he walked out of the locker room when he saw a tall basketball player drive to the basket, go high above the rim and slam the ball into the basket. He watched several more minutes as the boy hit jumper after jumper from outside the circle.

He had seen the boy shooting in the gym during sixth period several times. He had spoken to him on occasions in the hallway and lunch room, but had never really spent a great deal of time talking with him about basketball. He looked like he knew what we was doing.

Upon his arrival home that evening, he found several letters addressed to him. They were from Winston State University, Chesapeake Tech and Dent University. They wanted to set up a home interview with him as soon as possible to discuss his playing football for their particular school. After discussing the letters with his mother, he decided to discuss the matter with Coach Shaw the next day. He told his mother, "If Dad were here he would know what I need to do next."

His mother replied, "Coach Shaw will give you good advice, you need to listen to him."

Misty had called Morgan Wednesday night and told him she was really shooting the ball well. "I'm using the method you showed me. I can't believe how well I'm hitting from outside."

Misty Porter was six-foot-two-inches in height. She was slender with good leaping ability and good quickness. As a sophomore she had averaged over 15 points per game, mostly on put backs and driving lay-ups. If she had a weakness, it was her outside shooting. She had worked on it all summer, but had not been totally satisfied with it until she started shooting like Morgan had suggested the previous weekend.

Now she was gaining more confidence in her outside jumper with every practice.

It was Thursday morning when Morgan met with Coach Shaw and they discussed the beginning of a recruiting process at length. The coach told him he would set up the recruiter meetings at the school during fifth and sixth periods if he wanted him to. He told him that was what Winkler had done and it had worked out well. He told Morgan that it might be better if he did not have the steady stream of coaches that he anticipated going after his services dropping by his home all hours of the night and on weekends.

Morgan agreed. He would meet with all recruiters and address all scholarship issues through the coaches office.

Most of the week was anti-climatic after the previous weeks game. Murphy was a road game with a travel time of about an hour to their stadium. The weather cooperated as far as no snow, but it was again cold and cloudy as the Eagles took the field.

The Eagles received to start the game and four plays later Morgan threw to Carter for a 31-yard score and a quick lead. By the end of the first half the score was 28 - 0 with touchdowns being scored by North on an eight-yard run, Winkler on a 44-yard run and Morgan on a 67-yard run.

Mentz played quarterback the second half. Winkler broke another touchdown run early in the third quarter for 73 yards.

There was 3:00 minutes left in the quarter when Coach Shaw looked over at Morgan and told him to go in at tailback. On second down from the 26-yard line, Morgan took a handoff, broke through the line, side-stepped a defensive side back into a missed tackle and ran 74 yards for the score.

The fourth quarter saw B-team personnel and third team players score one touchdown and surrender one to close out the 49 - 7 win.

Coach Shaw was not trying to run up the score. He just wanted to see the speedster carry the ball. He had seen enough. So had all the college scouts in the stands. By the end of the regular season there would be scholarship questionnaires to Morgan from over 40 colleges on just football alone.

Chapter Fifteen
Homecoming !

For the past six seasons the final home game of the regular season had been the Salem homecoming game. The Eagles had won them all. It was almost a certainty that Bobby Winkler would be Mr. Football and Connie Hollis would be the homecoming queen.

Misty had told Kyle that was definitely fact. She had heard it from some members on the selection committee.

Some of the Eagle players had began calling Winkler "Mr. Football" several weeks earlier. He would just smile and go on about his business.

Bobby Winkler was sort of a prodigy himself. He had found out early on that he was very fast. He was the only freshman to ever start a football game for Coach Shaw. He was virtually unstoppable in the open field and was a threat to break out of a broken field at any time. He was five-foot-eleven-inches in height and weighed 170 pounds. He was the epitome of the axiom, "tough as nails."

As a freshman he had rushed for over 1,500 yards and scored 13 touchdowns. As a sophomore he had ran for over 1,800 yards and scored 14 touchdowns. Last season as a junior, he had ran for over 2,300 yards and scored 23 touchdowns. This year was just as remarkable. The exception was that he had become so adept at catching the football with Morgan at quarterback, it had opened up new horizons as to his college potential.

Most recruiters felt he could excel at tailback, flanker or an defense. His potential for a professional football career someday had greatly increased this past season. He held all the Salem rushing records and now had taken over most of their pass-receiving records. He was an honor student that ranked in the top 10 in academic standing in his senior class. He had committed to attend Winston State University, the number two ranked football team in the nation. He was planning to also run track in college.

The week in practice was virtually all spent on passing offense. It was evident that Coach Shaw planned to open up the offense this week and throw about 70 percent of the time. The team now had twelve passing routes with five receivers. Coach Shaw was not concerned with Morgan remembering the routes with his amazing ability of total recall.

East Ridgeview won the toss and elected to take the ball. A quick three-and-out brought Morgan and the Salem offense onto the field.

On first down he threw low to Winkler, incomplete at the 40-yard line. A draw play to Winkler gained six yards to the 36. On third down Carter ran a Z-pattern, broke away from coverage at the Leopard 40-yard line, caught a bullet from Morgan and raced in for a touchdown.

The second Eagle offensive series saw Morgan fire a 69-yard touchdown pass to Winkler on first down.

After another three plays and out for the leopards he then took the Eagles on an eight-play drive completing four-of-five passes for 70 yards. It culminated with his throwing a 31-yard strike to Shealey for a 21 - 0 lead at the end of the first quarter. The second quarter saw touchdown passes of 73 yards to Carter and 19 yards to Cobb for a first-half score of 42 - 0, Eagles.

For the first half Morgan had threw only 11 passes, completing nine for 312 yards and five Touchdowns.

Five college scouts in the Salem stands were shaking their heads in amazement at what they were seeing.

Mentz played the entire second half at quarterback and threw for another score, while Winkler ran for 123 yards on only seven carries, including a 54-yard touchdown run.

The final score was Salem Eagles 56, East Ridgeview Leopards 14.

Morgan did not play at all the second half.

The Eagles had closed out the regular season with a perfect 10 - 0 season. Their first ever undefeated season. Winkler had rushed for over 1,800 yards and had scored 26 touchdowns. He had caught 54 passes for 1,263 yards.

Morgan had completed 72 percent of his passes for over 2,300 yards and had thrown for 23 touchdowns.

Cobb had made 109 individual tackles and had 18 quarterback sacks.

Mentz had led the team with 9 interceptions.

It was an all-star team with a final ranking of number one in the state polls. Salem was the heavy favorite to win the state title.

Coach Shaw stood before his team in the Eagle locker room. He spoke very evenly as he said, "Gentlemen, you have competed at a level we have never known here at Salem. I want to commend you for your efforts. Now, we have our greatest challenge ahead of us. We need to win four more games to become the first ever Salem state championship football team. You have the capability to accomplish this very difficult task. It won't be easy. We will see only the best teams from now on. They will be able to run with us, throw with us and play defense with us. Every week it will be a District-Heights up against us."

He paused slightly, then continued, "Tonight District-Heights defeated West Ridgeview 35 to 27 and finished second in our region. They will be going to the state, also. You can bet they want another chance at us. From what I know at this time, we will meet Chesapeake City at their place next Friday night in the first round of the state playoffs. We'll start preparing for them Monday afternoon. Again, I thank you for the amazing season you have presented to our school and our supporters this past season. See you Monday." With that said, he exited the locker room to cheers from his victorious Eagle team.

Coach Shaw looked up from the game stat sheet as Coach Dills walked in and took a seat across from him. Dills said, "You know it could have been 100 to 0 if you had left Morgan in, don't you?"

The coach smiled and elaborated, "It could have been bad. It's almost unfair to use Morgan against most teams. He's just so far above other players in his skill level. The coach of East Ridgeview came over to me after the game and told me that if we would just put him back there and let him throw the ball, we would score 75 points a game easy. I think he's right. I've never coached a player like him before. I find myself just watching him play at times and not doing very much coaching. He's like a coach on the field. Coach Dills, we have been blessed by having a young man like him come into our school and program. You can only wonder what his future holds for him. Will he become a professional in football, basketball, baseball? Will he go into politics and become the President of the United States some day? Just what will this boy be doing 10, 20, or 30 years from now?"

Coach Dills said, "Whatever he will be doing, I think he will be very successful at it, coach. I'll bet the mortgage on it."

A bemused Coach Shaw replied, "So would I, Coach, so would I."

Mihn Delta, Vietnam. Saturday, November the fourth, 1962. At 0:800 a.m. Colonel Ken Morgan looked over a list of 632 names that had on-going visitation privileges at all the camps that had been involved in the officer "fragging" incidences.

He was looking at troops from munitions, general supply, commissary and the American Red Cross. He felt that the answer was on that sheet of paper. He then proceeded to go through the profiles that been provided by the Pentagon of every individual listed on the ledger. He typed in prior military duty on all the Red Cross employees list and came up with six names. He then typed in discharge on the same list. All had honorable discharges. He then tried "brig time." He came up empty. From there he went to "prison time served." He had one of the six listed as having served time in a state-prison facility for drug usage. "I'm missing something," he thought. "What is it?"

There were 210 names on the Red Cross employee list that could have access to visit the various post compounds at any given time. Usually there were teams of 12 assigned to individual Red Cross groups that would travel to designated posts as scheduled by the Central Red Cross Director.

He decided to go over all the profiles in depth and try to see any obscure possibility of an answer that may jump out at him. Over 300 of the names on the ledger were no longer stationed on the war front within the 40-mile target distance from Ho Chi Minh City. None of the listed personnel had dishonorable discharges on their record. It would be a slow and tedious process, but he felt this was the right direction to proceed forward with at this time.

That night he sent home a message to his family that he felt he was getting close to an answer. Mainly, it was just for motivation and reassurance. He wasn't really sure just how close he was to solving what up to this time was a very difficult case.

Misty Porter and a couple of her basketball teammates came over after lunch that Saturday. Kyle and his mother watched them shoot baskets in his front yard while sitting on the steps to the driveway. Lucille Morgan spoke softly, "They are all quite good, aren't they, Kyle?"

Morgan smiled and answered, "They'll do all right, Mom. I'll think they'll have a good girls team this year."

Mrs. Morgan said, "Why don't you get out there and work with them on their shooting? That's what they say you do best on a basketball court, isn't it?"

Morgan laughed as he answered, "That's what you and Dad always told me, Mom, but I think you are both prejudiced." They laughed as Morgan arose and walked over to where the trio was shooting baskets.

For the next two hours he worked with the young ladies on shooting and passing.

Later that evening, Mr. and Mrs. Porter, Misty and Reverend Carl Darnell from their church joined them at the Morgan house for dinner.

The recorded message from Ken Morgan arrived as expected at 8:00 p.m. Afterward, there was prayer and the guests all went their separate ways. It was a solemn night at the Morgan house. It had been and would continue to be for as long as the man of the house was working in a distant land. Kyle was determined to be the man of the house his father expected him to be. He had went over the previous nights game in the recording that would be sent to his dad in Southeast Asia. He closed out by telling him to "get busy and close that thing out so you can make it home in time for the state championship game on December the first."

A pensive Kyle Morgan sat alone in the den late that night. He was in deep thought as to how to live up to the expectations of his father, his mother, his coaches and his teammates. There was a lot on the shoulders of a 16-year-old boy, even if he was a very mature 16-year-old boy.

Chapter Sixteen
The Choir Boy !

0:10:00 a.m. CIA headquarters. November seventh, 1962. For the past two weeks Colonel Ken Morgan had been studying the profiles of over 300 names that he had deemed as suspects in the "army fragging" incidences at three different outposts within a forty-mile radius of Ho Chi Mihn City in Southern Vietnam. Now he was ready to close out his information request as he met with Captain Reed Kelly of Army Intelligence at his Mei Deng headquarters located just outside the provincial Vietnam city.

"Captain, I need a complete listing of every Red Cross worker that has ever served in this sector of the military with full history disclosure. This must include any arrests at felony or misdemeanor levels. Find out if any of these people ever tried to get into the military and were refused admittance. Did they have family or friends that tried to gain entrance into the military that were denied entrance? Did any of the listed ever have altercations or violence associated with the military? Did any of the listed ever apply for commissions or assignments that were not granted? If so, I want all the details as to why they were not granted. And finally, I want all names of outside entry personnel coordinated with post entry on the same day of the crimes. Cross check the names that entered against any of the listed names and see if the entry times throw up a flag or may raise questions. Do this immediately."

"Yes Sir!" said the Captain. He then saluted his superior officer and left the office.

Colonel Morgan had eliminated through investigation and interviews all enlisted personnel. He was down to complete evaluations on all Red Cross personnel that served in the region. He was now beginning to feel it may not be a disgruntled soldier that was responsible for the irreprehensible acts of violence on the American Officers.

Monday saw an excited faculty and student body as they celebrated the region football championship with announcements over the school intercom system and with banners placed all over the halls by the cheerleaders.

The afternoon practice consisted of watching two films of the Chesapeake City Cardinals. The region 6 runner-up to Sparrows Point High School had lost to the number three rated Tigers 21 - 12 in an early season match-up. Coach Shaw felt there was much improvement for the Cardinals since that loss. He didn't see much difference between Chesapeake City and West Ridgeview from their own region. They were a strong defensive team with one of the top five quarterbacks in the state guiding their offense. They liked to run a multiple offense with a wide-open passing game that could put points on the board quickly.

The coach stressed that it was important for the Eagles to get out front early and force the Cardinals to throw into the strong Eagle secondary. He could see Mentz, Winkler, Shealey and Morgan having several interceptions against the Cardinal offense.

It was a windy, rainy Friday night when the home-standing Eagles took the field against the Cardinals. After a scoreless first quarter, the Eagles mounted a six-play drive that culminated with Winkler scoring from the nine-yard line with 10:32 left in the second quarter. The strong winds and slick-ball conditions were having an effect on the game. Two passes from Morgan to Carter and Bates slid through the receivers hands on the drive. As the rain picked up in intensity, the passing game was to be shelved for an old-fashioned ground game.

This proved to be a game killer for the pass-happy Cardinals as they consistently threw into the ground or short of their intended receiver.

Mentz finally picked off a Cardinal pass at the Eagle 40-yard line and returned it to the Cardinal 41-yard line with 8:07 left in the first half. From a power-I set with Winkler and North in the backfield, the Eagles methodically moved the ball toward the Cardinals Goal. Winkler ripped for eight yards, North for four yards, and Morgan kept for seven yards to the 23-yard line. Four plays later, North scored from the one-yard line to push the Eagles to a two-touchdown lead at the half.

In his halftime adjustment session, Coach Shaw established the two-back formation as their primary offense for the second half. He wanted to keep the ball on the ground. His primary emphasis was to hold onto the ball. No fumbles due to the elements.

The Eagles and Cardinals swapped touchdowns in the third period when Morgan ran a draw into the four hole, cut toward the middle of the field and ran 42 yards for a score with 2:23 left in the third quarter. With the score 21-7 the Eagles increased their lead to 28-7 when Winkler ran a punt back 63 yards for a score with 7:45 left in the game. A fumble by Chesapeake City at their own 33-yard line gave the Eagles the ball with 5:51 left on the game clock. A Morgan keeper carried the ball to the 11-yard line before he was bumped out of bounds. Two drives into the line by fullback Greer got the score with 2:47 left in the game. It was Eagles 35 and Chesapeake City 7. The game ended as the rain had increased to almost a downpour.

There was not too much of an uproar in the clubhouse as the Eagles showered and dressed before meeting with the coach for his post-game review.

Coach Shaw read off some statistics from the game. The Eagles had thrown the ball only six times with two completions for 21 yards. The running game had accumulated 296 yards with Winkler rushing for 126 yards and Morgan running for 93 more on only seven carries. He told the team, "We were able to adjust well to the adverse weather conditions. I don't believe many teams could work as hard as we have on our passing game all week, then switch to a ground game in the blink of an eye as you did tonight. Our opponent next week will be Jasper County. They won their game 7 - 0 tonight in a heavy downpour throughout the game like we saw late in our game. They will give us a battle defensively. As for the game tonight, don't let it lull you into thinking we have a cakewalk to the title. We just happen to have some good running backs that could adapt to the weather better than the Chesapeake passing attack. We did have a tremendous advantage in the weather conditions we encountered tonight. Maybe we need to change our name to the Mud-Hogs."

The coach closed out the brief meeting with instructions to his team to be careful on the way home as the storm outside continued to gain in intensity level.

Morgan's mother was waiting for him in the parking lot. The rain was pouring with loud thunder and lightning flashes literally lighting up the night sky. It was a slow trip to the Morgan house that night.

The following day, the sleek thunderbird pulled up in front of Coach Tom Shaw's house. Jen Shaw glanced out the window and saw her favorite football player walking toward the house. She met him at the top of the porch steps and hugged his neck. "Great game last night, Kyle!" Jen exclaimed excitedly.

"Thanks, Jen," said Morgan. "I need to see your dad if possible." She walked into the house with him and moved toward the den to tell her father he had a surprise visitor.

When Coach Shaw heard that Morgan was in the house and wanted to see him, he tried for several seconds to think of a reason his star player might have for wanting to see him. He could think of nothing in particular.

"Hello, Kyle," What can I do for you?" he asked as he motioned for Morgan to have a seat and then took one directly in front of him.

"Coach, I need to run something by you," said Morgan.

"Go ahead, son," replied the coach.

Morgan continued, "Coach, this past week I had meetings with seven different football recruiters during my fifth and sixth periods. I come home in the afternoon and there will be eight or ten letters asking to meet with me to start a recruiting process. It's really getting on my nerves, Sir. With my concern for the safety of my father, the school work I have to complete every day, and the work on the football team, I simply have too many irons in the fire at one time. What I want to do is ask you if you will let it be understood that I will not deal with any recruiters until the end of the basketball season my senior season."

An understanding Coach Shaw looked into the eyes of the high school super-star. He then spoke in a serious fatherly tone to Morgan. "Kyle, you know someone that has your athletic abilities will be sought by every school in the country. You can limit the face-to-face meetings, but they'll still bombard you with letters and possibly even phone calls."

Morgan replied, "I can go to an unlisted phone. I will personally send a letter to the head coach at all the schools that initially contact me asking them to wait until the designated time to start any recruitment process. Coach, I simply don't want to deal with it at this time."

Coach Shaw countered, "You can do as you have mentioned. The schools probably will honor your request. There will be a rogue recruiter pop up from time to time, but over-all you will be able to limit your contacts. Of, course, I'll help you in any way I can. I'll personally call some of the head coaches I know and ask them to refrain from recruiting you for the time being. By the way, Kyle, I've never asked you. Just what sport do you intend to play at the college level?"

Morgan looked at the coach, smiled and said, "Coach, I really don't know right now."

Coach Shaw said, "I understand you pole vault."

Morgan answered, "Yes Sir, I do vault."

The coach asked, "How high do you go?"

Morgan answered, "I have done better than 15 feet on several occasions."

Coach Shaw said, "We have never had a pole vault athlete that could do over 10 feet. How did you develop that particular skill?"

Morgan answered, "I just started fooling around with it when I was in the sixth grade. I found out I could vault over 10 feet by the time I was in the eighth grade. My freshman year I cleared thirteen feet. Last year I was able to win the state with a vault of 15 feet, 3 inches."

Coach Shaw asked, "You use fiberglass, I suppose?"

Morgan answered, "Yes Sir, I use a 14-foot sky-jump pole with a 200-pound strength level. I depend on speed, form and the catapult factor to get me over the bar."

The vaulting pole that Salem had was a 12-foot steel pole.

Coach Shaw said, "Kyle, I'll order two new poles for you next week. This will give you time to check them out and be sure they're what you need. I'll also get you a couple of pairs of spikes and flat soled shoes for rubberized tracks or for use when you're not on the track. I'll have them in over the next few weeks. I'll notify you when to come in and look them over."

Kyle Morgan nodded his head and arose from the chair.

As he headed toward the door he stopped and said, "Coach I appreciate what you have done for me. I know you have pretty much tailored the football team offense around what I can do. I really appreciate it."

Coach Shaw replied, "Kyle, You could be successful in any kind of offense I put on the field. I'll take care of your recruiting request. See you Monday."

As Morgan approached the door ---- Jen Shaw walked over to him and said, "When are you going to ask me out, Kyle?" I'm not going to wait around on you forever." She jokingly exclaimed, "If Misty Porter don't like it, I'll beat her up!"

Kyle Morgan liked Jen Shaw. She was a sophomore football cheerleader that would start at point guard for the Lady Eagles basketball team during the upcoming season. They both laughed as he went out the door.

When Kyle started attending Westside Baptist Church, he had gravitated toward the choir and quickly became their lead soloist. He had sang in front of the assembly on several occasions, usually at the behest of Misty or his mother. He didn't think too much of it when Youth Minister David Bartleson asked him if he would sing with the choir at a church charity benefit the following Saturday night in Woodbury. He told him he would be happy to participate.

On the way home, his mother asked him, "What will you solo on next weekend, Kyle?"

He replied, "Whatever Reverend Bartleson wants me to sing."

She said, "You're always fooling around with writing new songs, why don't you write a special one for this occasion?"

He laughed as he answered, "Mom, I just do that for fun, I really don't know much about song writing."

She smiled as she told him, "Kyle, just let your common sense and inner feelings tell you if your song is something you feel good about. Then if you do feel good about it, you'll have the right words in the song."

Morgan replied, "Since I won't have any recruiters bothering me during fifth and sixth period, I might be able to find time to do that. Thanks, Mom."

Chapter Seventeen
A New Beginning

Monday saw a dreary day as heavy rain continued and the temperature hovered around the freezing mark. Weather predictions for the week were not very optimistic as to a clearing by Friday nights game.

Coach Shaw did not dwell on the weather as he reviewed the previous game with Chesapeake City. Afterward, the team went through warm-up and passing drills on the concrete parking lot in front of the school. The practice field was saturated. By Wednesday it was apparent that the weather was worsening. Ice greeted the arrival of the morning with a weather forecast of icy rain and snow through Sunday evening.

The Wednesday practice consisted of about an hour of defense against the Jasper County offense. Their primary threat was a senior halfback that had scored over 25 touchdowns during the past season. He had scored their only touchdown from the eight- yard line in their 7 - 0 win in the previous weeks game. Coach Shaw called him a good "mudder" and warned that he would enable the Jasper County team to hold onto the ball if the Eagles couldn't stop his quick off tackle bursts.

After practice, Morgan sat beside the court and watched the boys basketball team go through their shooting drills. He was really impressed with Jack Ellerson. That was the tall boy that had caught his attention on several occasions as he left the gym after dressing from football practice. He ran the floor like a small guard and literally played above the rim on offense.

After about 10 minutes Misty had dressed and came over to him. She told Morgan, "I'm ready when you are, Kyle." Misty had asked for a ride home so her mother would not have to get out in the weather to pick her up. On the way home, she said, "It's going to be messy this weekend."

Morgan just nodded his head.

She asked, "Can I help? You look like you are so down."

He answered, "No, not really. I just miss my Dad. I wish he could be at the game Friday night."

During the week, Morgan had spent all of his sixth period study hall writing a special song for the Saturday night Choir Concert with his church choir. He had finished it the previous day and was looking it over and getting the tune and music clear in his mind. Morgan was an excellent guitarist and had played the piano since he was seven. He could pick up an instrument and after a few notes he could figure out in his mind just what it took to play it. Another trait of a 16-year-old genius.

His song was entitled, "If it be Thy Will." It was a sad, but spiritually uplifting song about how things may not always start out as you intend them, but will eventually work themselves out if it is the Will of God. Morgan liked what he had written --- so would a lot of other people.

The game that night was down at Jasper County, about 45 miles south of Salem High School. Snow was falling at a fairly heavy rate as he boarded the bus for the trip over to the Morgan Cafeteria for the pre-game meal. A large contingent of fans were going to have the meal with them on this day.

Morgan sat by Cobb on the bus afterward as they made the trip down to Jasper County. His friend and teammate chatted about just about everything until they approached the stadium.

The Salem coaches could easily see the blasé mood of the team as it departed the bus for the locker room. They immediately began to work to uplift the spirits of the team as they dressed and prepared to do battle with the Stars.

Jasper County had won the Region 2-AAAA title. They were a sound defensive team with an adequate passing attack to supplement their excellent running game.

Bobby Winkler and Randal Hinsley led the team onto the field. The conditions were terrible for a football game. Snow and ice covered the entire field. The Eagles had all decided to go with one-inch cleats instead of their standard one-half-inch cleats to help them get better footing. The temperature was around 10 degrees. Any moisture on the ball would immediately freeze, making an accurate throw extremely difficult.

Salem won the toss and elected to receive the football. It didn't take long to see that footing was going to be a major problem. After North trudged for three yards, Winkler tried to cut into the six hole, but slipped down for a four-yard loss. A quick pass to Cobb gained eight yards but was short of the first down. Morgan punted to the Stars 36-yard line.

Jasper County tried to establish a running game with Young carrying for a first down on three carries. Three more rushes netted seven yards, resulting in a punt that Winkler watched roll dead on the Eagle 29-yard line.

With 9:02 left in the second quarter both teams had completed two series of three plays and out.

Salem started a drive on their 31-yard line that produced a first down at their 43. On first down, Winkler ran a draw that saw some daylight as he crossed the mid-field stripe. A Stars defensive player took a wild swipe at the wet football and knocked it from the Eagle tailbacks grasp. The Stars recovered at the Eagle 48-yard line.

The drive stalled at the Eagle 23-yard line with a fourth-and-six yards for the first down. On fourth down, Young drove off tackle and picked up a first down at the Eagle nine-yard line. On fourth down from the one-yard line, the elusive and powerful tailback crashed into the endzone for the touchdown. The PAT kick was wide with 3:45 left in the half. The Eagles were able to pick up a first down and entered intermission on the short end of the 6 - 0 score.

At halftime, Coach Shaw worked on closing the off tackle play that seemed to be the yardage maker for the Stars and their tailback, Young. He made it clear that the game was still the Eagles' to win.

To start the second half, the Stars put on what was to be their most productive drive of the night. Starting at their own 30-yard line, Young carried five consecutive times gaining seven, 16, 13, 11, and nine yards to the Eagle 15-yard line. Two crashes into the line netted four yards to the 11. Coach Shaw turned to Morgan and said, "They're going to throw, get in there at free safety."

Morgan ran onto the field. He watched the play develop and never took his eyes off the quarterbacks eyes. He noticed a receiver cut toward the sideline under the gaze of the Stars quarterback. He turned on the speed as the quarterback cocked his arm for the throw. It was headed in the direction Morgan had guessed. He had a good jump on the ball as he dove for the low throw at the five-yard line. He caught the ball and rolled over on his back while cradling it in his arms. It was the biggest interception of his life.

The Eagles managed to start their own drive behind the running and throwing of Winkler and Morgan. After a 23-yard run by Winkler to the Stars 44-yard line, Morgan dropped back and threw a pass that Carter caught behind the Stars safety. He completed the 44-yard touchdown play untouched. Morgan had seen the flag go down as he released the ball. Tackle Boyd Massingale had been called for holding on the play. Instead of a game-tying touchdown, it was a 15-yard penalty back to the Eagle 39-yard line. Two plays later after a recovery of his fumble of the wet, elusive pigskin, he punted the ball to the Stars 38-yard line with 8:54 left in the game.

A three and out gave the ball to the Eagles on their 29-yard line after a 39-yard punt by the Stars punter.

Three carries by Winkler and Greer got a first down on the Eagle 41-yard line. Morgan decided to cross up the Stars defense with a slant pass to Winkler. He threw the ball to the speedy tailback at the Stars 45-yard line. Winkler was hit hard by a Stars linebacker and cornerback at the 43. Morgan prepared to call the play when he saw Bobby Winkler walking to the sideline holding his right arm. He called a "42 dive" with Greer ripping off five yards to the Stars 38-yard line. On second down he went back to pass, scrambled to his right and slipped at the Eagle 47. ---- A 15-yard loss. A pass to Cobb picked up 12 yards to the Stars 41-yard line. It was fourth-and-13 yards needed for the first down with 5:28 left in the game. The Eagles called time out.

A somber Coach Shaw approached Morgan as he walked to the sideline. Bobby Winkler was being looked at by Dr. Long, the team physician that always attended all the Eagle games. Coach Shaw said, "It doesn't look good. The doctor thinks he has a broken bone in his right wrist. We're going to have to do this without him." The coach purposely did not call the play. He just told Morgan, "get that first down, we're running out of time."

Morgan gave instuctions in the huddle back at the mid-field stripe. He told them, "We don't have Bobby. We have to get it done without him. Cobb, take out that left end. Carter, you and Shealey go after that cornerback. Get me some room on the outside. Lets go with an "18 rollout on one."

The Eagle quarterback took the snap and rolled out to his right. He raised the ball as though he intended to pass the ball to freeze any defensive player he could and then tucked the ball in the crook of his arm. He watched as Cobb took out the end and a linebacker that got too close to him while closing for the tackle. Shealey and Carter were moving toward the cornerback. North was throwing his body in front of an oncoming linebacker. Suddenly, Morgan saw an open field in front of him. It was clear sailing after he crossed the Stars 30-yard line. He ran in untouched for the tying touchdown. The PAT kick was usually automatic with Morgan. He had kicked 63 consecutive up to this point. The state record was 78 consecutive established in 1958. No one had ever kicked as many consecutively in one season as Morgan. James Mentz went in to hold for the kick. With 3:03 left in the game, Morgan's kick split the uprights and Salem led by a 7 - 6 score.

With the snow coming down so hard you could hardly see the goalposts, the Stars took the kickoff at their own 18 and ran it out to the 34-yard line. Two passes were batted down by the charging Cobb. A screen pass to Young went for nine yards to the 43-yard line. On fourth down Young went over the top for the first down at the 45-yard line with 2:01 left in the game. On first down, Stars quarterback, Jamey Gilbright, went back to pass. Cobb came in from the blindside and hit him high, knocking the ball loose. Salem recovered the loose ball at the Stars 33-yard line.

The Stars had one timeout left as North took the handoff and was tackled for no gain. Jasper County called their last timeout.

Morgan told his huddled team, "I'll take it from here. All keepers from this point on. He told center Hinsley, "Don't snap it until I say "Now!" We want to run the clock down as much as we can before the snap." Morgan took the snap and moved a few steps to his right, then fell to the ground carefully covering the ball. 1:28 left. He watched the referee bring his hand down ~ signifying the start of the 25-second clock. He counted silently to himself ~ 1,001, 1,002, 1,003. At 1,020 he gave the "Now" call to his center, took the snap and fell to the ground. On fourth down he took the snap and ran wide, broke a tackle at the 30 and was knocked down on the 18-yard line ~ a key first down. All eyes were on the tall quarterback as he stood in front of them awaiting the end of the game. It was all over. The Eagles had won the game, 7 - 6.

All concern now turned to the condition of their captain Winkler as they made their way to the locker room.

Inside the locker room, Coach Shaw did not sugarcoat the Winkler situation. "I don't know what they have found out as of yet. The doctor felt his arm was broken when he took him to the emergency room at the hospital for x-rays. We'll know the story by the time we get back to the gym."

On the bus back to Salem High School, there was not a great deal of celebrating or conversation. Losing Bobby Winkler was the last thing anyone could have imagined happening during this magical season. Cobb and Morgan sat together. They didn't have anything much to talk about on the way back home.

While the team dressed, Bobby Winkler and his father arrived at the coaches office. It was confirmed that Winkler did have a broken arm and was through for the year.

As he walked through the locker room, Winkler had tears in his eyes. He had been an integral part of the Salem football program since he was in the sixth grade. He had never had any injury of any kind that threatened his playing status. Now, he was done for the year. When he arrived at the locker of Morgan, he shook his hand and said, "You're going to take this team all the way, Kyle. There is not any doubt in my mind you'll find a way to win these last two games. I'll be right beside you and pulling for you with everything I've got."

Morgan replied, "Thanks, Bobby. You're a great football player and a great friend. I'm sorry I called that pass play. You wouldn't have been hurt if I hadn't."

Winkler said, "You've called it all year. There was no reason to stop now. Besides, I probably would have broken my arm on my next running play. It was just my destiny, I guess." Bobby Winkler walked away from Morgan. He meant what he had said. He had never seen anyone like Kyle Morgan. He just refused to lose. There was tremendous mutual respect between these two high school athletes.

Coach Shaw addressed the team shortly thereafter. "I don't need to tell you how proud I am of you for your accomplishment tonight. We could have mailed it in after we lost Bobby, but you sucked it up and went after the win. Morgan, you made a good run on that touchdown, but I think you will see in the film Monday that there was some extraordinary blocking on that play. Make no mistake about it, this was a team win. Now we have two games left to bring home the title. Winkler is still one of our three captains on this team and will represent us on the coin-toss every game we have left. He will also serve as a student coach for the remainder of the season." There was applause from the team as the coach concluded his comments.

As he walked out of the gym that night, Morgan agreed with his coach about the blocking on that touchdown run. He knew that with his speed and that kind of blocking, there was not any way he could not have scored that touchdown.

Kyle's mother waited for him in the parking lot with the parents of Misty Porter. She had went to the game with them. As his mother moved into his car, Kyle chatted with Misty and her parents about the loss of Winkler for the season.

Mr. Porter said, "We'll miss him, son, but you boys are still the best I've seen. You'll be fine."

Morgan smiled as he said, "I see where Misty gets her tremendous optimism."

On the way home, Mrs. Morgan saw the look of disappointment in the eyes of her son. He enjoyed football, but it was fairly evident he had no real intentions of pursuing the sport after high school graduation.

Bobby Winkler was committed to the sport as something that he wanted to provide him an education and play professionally. It was tremendously important to him. She could almost read in his eyes the unfairness Kyle felt was being unduly thrust upon Winkler. Only two games to go, and not getting to play anymore. It just did not seem fair.

Saturday morning, Morgan sat at the piano and sang his new song for his mother. She listened intently as he completed it. She had always said that anything he might do would never surprise her. She had never heard anything more beautiful than his voice and the words that were in that song. There were tears in her eyes after she heard it for that first time. He sang several songs that he wanted to do that night. There was a strong realization to Lucille Morgan that her son had abilities and talent that far transcended his athletic skills. For the first time, she realized that he very well could do anything he wanted to do.

The trip to the Woodbury Chapel would be by bus. Kyle, his mother and the Porter's boarded one of the three chartered buses' for the trip to the concert. The choir members would sing as they went down the highway. Misty asked Kyle to sing a solo just before the arrival at the church. He sang a couple of their gospel favorites. Everyone had a wonderful time on the trip.

The Woodbury Chapel was the largest Baptist denomination church in the nation with over 3,000 members. There would be twelve choirs from around the state that would appear at the Christian Unity Society Function. All donations would go to local charities. The church was full.

The second choir to perform was the Westside Church group. After several group songs, Kyle stepped forward and sang as lead soloist on two songs. He then announced that he had written a song he wanted to sing. After Morgan completed his rendition of "If it be Thy Will" the applause was deafening.

After the program was completed, a man walked up to Morgan and asked if he could talk with him. He introduced his mother and they listened as he spoke.

Ben Curruth was a producer with Revele Record Company out of Baltimore. He had scoured the countryside for 20 years looking for potential recording talent for the company. Now, it seemed that a potential had just fell into his lap while he was attending his regular church service. He was impressed with the voice of Morgan and the beauty of his newly-written song. He wanted to offer an opportunity for him to make a sample recording at the studio at his convenience sometime over the next several weeks.

It could be an existing top-forty song, a country song or he could write one of his own if he desired.

Lucille Morgan listened quietly to the proposal being laid out to her son.

Kyle Morgan agreed to do a demonstration record with the producer the following Saturday at 2:00 p.m. at the Revele Recording Studios. He said he preferred to write his own song.

Later that night after Morgan's arrival back home, Mrs. Morgan told Kyle, "Well, you've done it now."

Morgan asked, "What have I done?"

Mrs. Morgan answered, "You've gone into show business."

Both laughed as they took a seat in front of the television in the living room to watch the late news.

Chapter Eighteen
The Break-out Of Kyle Morgan

Monday morning broke with a clearing around the Ridgeview area. The ice and snow was melting as the temperature was expected to rise into the upper forties. There was much conversation about the game the past Friday night. The loss of Bobby Winkler was now becoming a reality.

Coach Shaw had met with his coaching crew most of Sunday afternoon as they tried to formulate a plan to maximize their remaining talent as they moved into the state semi-finals. Their opponent would be Sparrows Point. The Region 3-AAAA champions. They were unbeaten and ranked number two in the state. Coach Shaw also noted that District-Heights had also won this past Friday night and could very well be on a path to meet the Eagles again if they could find a way to beat Sparrows Point.

It was decided that with the loss of Winkler, the running game had a serious setback, and would need a complete renovation. Coach Shaw had decided to move Mentz in as the starting quarterback and move Morgan to tailback. Plans were to use them interchangeably in the backfield at quarterback and flanker with Morgan the featured running back. This would mean that at times Morgan would be at quarterback with Mentz at flanker and at other times, Mentz would be at quarterback with Morgan at either flanker or at tailback. All the coaches agreed the possibilities with this direction were without end. Morgan would return punts and kickoffs at times with Shealey and Carter as a backup. On defense, Mentz would stay at safety with Morgan at the sideback slot.

015:00 p.m.   Meng Deng Province, Vietnam.   November twenty-one, 1962. There it was. After scrutinizing over 600 names and histories, one name jumped out at Colonel Ken Morgan. Carl Ridzik. He was stationed with the American Red Cross at Kwi Zant Supplemental Headquarters just outside Ho Chi Mihn City. He had been in the area for five months. His history was that of a former Army volunteer that had left the service in 1958. He had never served in Vietnam. He had been assigned to motor pool and vehicle repair after completion of his on-the-job training at Fort Gray, Alabama. He had completed his service obligation at Fort Brady, California with an honorable discharge. After his release from the service he had gained employment with the Red Cross out of Carlton, Alabama. He was the son of a former U.S. Army Officer that had served 30 years in the military. The finding that stood out in the profile was that Ridzik had applied for Officers Training School early on in his enlistment, but had been rejected for reasons deemed as not compatible with military tradition. He had opinions that clashed with established military protocol.

As Colonel Morgan continued to read the text on him, it was becoming clear that he was someone that had opportunity and motive to make him a prime suspect in the officer "fragging" investigation he was heading up at this time. His next step was to set up an interview with Ridzik.

That Monday afternoon at Salem High School the new system implementation started. There was not any running it by Morgan or asking if he would be happy with the change. Coach Shaw knew the young man would do whatever it took to win a football game. He would play tackle if asked to do so, if it would help the team win. Mentz threw the ball well. Morgan was a blur at tailback. He hit the hole so fast he was in the secondary before the defense could react. Once he saw a gap in the defense, it was dodge and dart until time to turn on that blazing speed.

Winkler worked with him on drop steps and hesitation counts as the week progressed.

Tuesday was a day of great anticipation. The Salem basketball teams were to open play that night at home against Murphy High School. Jen Shaw, Connie Hollis, Ann Mabry, and Misty Porter were understandably excited all day and were eagerly awaiting their season opening tip-off.

Morgan was also interested in watching the big man he had seen around the practice floor in action. He and his mother arrived at the gym around 6:45 p.m. They took seats next to Mr. and Mrs. Porter.

Butch Cobb's girlfriend was not on the basketball team, but served as the basketball cheerleader captain. He came over and sat down beside Morgan. The Lady Eagles, under Coach Molly Donaldson, played exceptionally well for a season opener as Porter hit a variety of jump shots and driving lay-ups to score 36 points in a 63 to 56 win.

When the Eagle boys took the floor, all eyes were on the 6-foot-nine Ellerson. He quickly demonstrated that he was a highly skilled basketball player as he poured in 39 points in a 78-49 Eagle win. Point guard Walter Hogan had scored 16 points.

Misty Porter sat between Kyle and Butch, and screamed the entire game.

Cobb and Morgan, along with Mentz, who had joined them late in the girls game, spent their evening laughing at the screaming Lady Eagle star.

Lucille Morgan laughed as her and Kyle were going home when she said, "When she sees you play Kyle, they'll hear her screaming all over the county. She really gets excited."

The Thanksgiving Holiday was a quiet day for the Morgan family. Mrs. Morgan had prepared a turkey. Her and Kyle had a quiet, uneventful Thanksgiving dinner together.

She told Kyle, "I'm going to fix you, your father and myself a plate, put them in the freezer and save them until Ken gets back. Then, we'll all have our Thanksgiving dinner together."

Young Morgan smiled as he said, "Only you would think of something like that, Mom."

Mrs. Morgan responded with, "Do you think you and your father have all the brains in this family?"

Morgan cheerfully answered, "Mom, You are not only smart. You're mighty good-looking, too!"

As the Thursday practice closed out, the team felt good about the upcoming battle with Sparrows Point. The shock of not having Winkler had subsided somewhat. The team anticipated a victory over the highly rated Beavers.

November twenty-four, Red Cross headquarters. Vietnam. Carl Ridzik was a 29- year-old father of two. He was divorced and made his home in Reeceville, Alabama. He had volunteered for a one-year Vietnam service tour with an option to renew his commitment for another year at his discretion. He stood over six-feet tall and weighed around 180- pounds. He looked normal in every respect as he sat before Colonel Morgan and answered a series of questions that brought out a strong emotional tie to his failure to become a career officer in the United States Military. After the session, Colonel Morgan was convinced that Ridzik was the individual he was seeking.

A search of his quarters had turned up a U.S. Military Glock Z-38 automatic weapon. A serial-number check showed it was assigned to Corporal Randal Ballinger of the 323rd Infantry Division stationed in outpost 31 just outside Lang Quin province. The assignee had been killed in action four months earlier in a sniper attack while on a routine patrol with his unit. He was assisted by the Red Cross unit with Ridzik in its membership. Colonel Morgan theorized that the weapon was taken at that time.

A further search of his belongings turned up four grenades and a C-4, six-inch land mine. These articles were hidden in a duffle bag on the upper shelf of a storage room where Ridzik frequented and had easy access to. His fingerprints found on the items confirmed he had handled them at one time or another. When confronted with all the overwhelming evidence that was piling up around him, the suspect wanted to deal with the army to assure the death penalty was not on the table when his final sentence was levied.

Colonel Morgan, after consultation with the Attorney General, agreed that with a full disclosure, the death penalty would not be sought. A life sentence without parole would likely be the alternative. Ridzik opened up. He told how he had taken the munitions articles from wounded or deceased soldiers as the Red Cross unit worked on medical missions at the various bases in their assigned vicinity. His hatred for the military stemmed from his failure to be allowed to attend Officer Training School.

He had been a military brat as his officer father had moved around from base to base early in his childhood. He had it entrenched in him at an early age that he would follow in his footsteps and become an Army Officer. When that failed to happen, he turned to the Red Cross with the intention of someday exacting revenge for his being refused entrance into the Officer Training Program. When the opportunity to volunteer for overseas duty came up, he had seen this as a venue to carry out his retribution plan against the Army. Two deaths, and three major injuries were the results of his vendetta. Colonel Ken Morgan stood outside the office where the interrogation of Ridzik had occurred. He looked at the man sitting beside the wooden table, smoking a cigarette and sipping on coffee. He had not seen any remorse in the eyes of Carl Ridzik. He believed he would have killed every officer he came in contact with if he had the opportunity.

When Morgan had left his home in Ridgeview, Maryland, he had given serious thoughts to getting out of the agency. He didn't need the money. His restaurant franchise business and the units he owned made him independently wealthy. But as he walked out of the building that evening, he knew he was not ready to call it quits just yet. He still had that urge to give something back to the country that had been so good to him and his family. There were still some loose ends and a lot of reports to complete, but It looked like Ken Morgan would get to see his son play football again this season.

Friday night came on cold but clear. The game-time temperature was at the 30- degree mark. Coach Shaw gave his usual pre-game pep talk and ushered the team onto Memorial Field. It was the last home game. The state championship game would be at the Winston State University Stadium in Baltimore if they were fortunate enough to make it.

Winkler, North and Hinsley walked to the mid-field stripe for the coin-toss. Sparrows Point won the toss and elected to receive the ball.

Morgan kicked the ball out of the endzone to give them a 20-yard line start. On first down, quarterback Jerry Pledger threw to tight end Mike Holloway on the left hash mark for 13 yards to the 33-yard line. Tailback Mickey Kinsey ran for six yards to the 39. Butch Cobb let his presence be known quickly as he crashed in on Holloway as he backed up to pass, tackling him for a nine-yard loss. A pass to Wilkes was almost intercepted by Mentz. A third-down draw play netted only five yards so Kinsey punted to Morgan on the 31-yard line. The Eagle tailback took the ball on the dead run and bowled over a tackler before he was run out of bounds on the Eagle 43.

Mentz talked to his typewriter huddle at the Eagle 35-yard line. On first down he gave to fullback North for four yards. On second down, Morgan took a pitchout at the 40- yard line and cut it inside before being tripped up at the Beaver 39-yard line. On the next play, Morgan went off tackle, cut to the side line and ran for the touchdown. With 8:31 left in the quarter, a Morgan PAT kick made it 7 - 0, Eagles.

The Beavers failed to move the ball after the kickoff, so Kinsey punted to the Eagle 37.

On first down Morgan zipped for 12 to the Eagle 49. On the next play he took a swing pass in the flat and ran by two defenders completing a 51-yard touchdown play. His PAT kick made it Eagles 14, Beavers 0, with 6:48 left in the first quarter.

Another endzone kickoff gave the ball to the Beavers at their 20-yard line. With Kinsey running and Pledger throwing short dump passes, the Beavers picked up three first downs and moved to the Eagle 38-yard line. On a fourth-down play, Kinsey was stopped a yard short of a first down and the Eagles took over the ball.

Greer ran for six yards. Mentz hit Cobb for 16 yards to the mid-field stripe. On first down Morgan sliced off tackle and raced for 24 yards before being tripped up at the Beaver 26-yard line. A holding penalty moved the ball back to the Eagle 35. Two Mentz passes to Cobb and Carter got back all but five of the yards. From the Beaver 45-yard line Mentz threw long to Carter. It was intercepted at the Beaver 19-yard line by safety Phillips. The Sparrows Point offense could not get anything going with the furious rush of Cobb and the backside blitz of Hinsley completely disrupting their offense. After two first downs, Kinsey punted to Morgan at the Eagle 12-yard line.

Morgan pulled in the ball and started to his left. He did a pivot to his right and turned on the speed. 88 yards later, he crossed the goal line for a short lived 20-0 lead. A block-to-the-back penalty erased the punt return touchdown and moved the ball back to the Eagle nine-yard line. When Mentz saw a nine-man front for the Beavers he sent Morgan in motion. The audible put the speedster in a fly pattern down the left sideline. The speed burner flew by the astonished cornerback at the 25-yard line and caught the Mentz floater at his 35. He raced 91 yards for the score. Then he saw it. Another yellow flag lying at the five-yard line. The Eagles had been offside. Guard Johnny Meyers had jumped the gun. The long touchdown play was nullified by the infraction.

The Eagles had a first-and-15 on the four-yard line. In two plays Morgan had gained 179 yards and scored two touchdowns, but neither one had counted. Coach Shaw was shell-shocked as Morgan ran off the field. He told him, "Hang in there, we'll get you one that counts sometime tonight." The Eagles ran Greer for two yards and four yards before Mentz was blitzed by the Beaver linebacker and sacked at the three-yard line.

Morgan came in to punt the ball. Standing one yard from the back of the endzone line, he took the snap and kicked the ball. It was unbelievable as the ball rose into the cold night sky. It went over the head of the surprised Beaver punt return man and rolled to the 16-yard line. It was an 81-yard punt with the roll from the line of scrimmage. It had covered 68 yards in the air. Take the distance Morgan was standing in the endzone and add it to the kick --- it was 94 yards with 80 yards in the air. There was at first a deafening roar from the home team, followed by a stunned silence as the fans suddenly realized what they had just witnessed.

The Beavers managed two first downs before punting away from Morgan and out of bound on the Eagle 34-yard line.

Morgan moved under the center. His first pass intended for Carter was overthrown. A draw play to North gained seven yards. On third down, Mentz back under center, tossed the ball over the head of Morgan on an option play and the Beavers recovered at the Eagles 31-yard line.

It took three plays for the Beavers to score with Kinsey running the final 18 yards for the score with 2:17 left in the half. The score was 14 - 7, Eagles.

The ensuing kickoff was a squib kick to Greer at the 25-yard line. He was brought down at the Eagles 32. After Morgan and Mentz ran on the field, Morgan talked to his typewriter huddle on the 15-yard line. He had told the team the play was "Banana two" with Carter and him going long. Everybody else stay in and block to give Mentz time to get the pass off.

Mentz took the snap and dropped back. He spotted Morgan breaking away from his defender at the Beaver 45-yard line. He heaved the ball as far as he could throw it toward the middle of the field. Morgan saw the angle of the ball and went after it. There was not anyone close as he caught the ball cleanly in his hands at the Beaver 20-yard line and trotted in for the 68-yard score. Mentz had thrown the ball over 60 yards in the air. A Morgan PAT kick made it 21 - 7, Eagles, with 1:23 left in the first half.

Starting at their own 20-yard line, the Beavers managed a first down on a screen pass to Tannan to the 36-yard line. Two draws to Kinsey netted 14 more yards as the first half came to a close with the Eagles leading, 21 - 7.

Coach Shaw's halftime communication was primarily directed to elimination of penalties and continued defensive pressure.

As the team walked out the door, Coach Will Powers walked over to Coach Shaw and said, "You know, of course, they can't stop Morgan."

The wily Eagle coach replied, "I know that, and they know it, too. We need to put them away quickly."

The second-half kickoff went short to Shealey at the 25-yard line. They had no intention of kicking the ball to Morgan. Mentz came out throwing. Cobb caught a slant for 11 yards. Carter pulled in a sideline toss for 14 yards. Two passes fell incomplete before Mentz threw a screen pass to Morgan for 26 yards to the Beaver 24-yard line. A pitch-out to Morgan was stopped after six yards. North got three to the 15-yard line. On third-and- one, Mentz pitched the ball back to Morgan. As the tailback raced to his right, he suddenly fired the ball to an open Carter all alone in the back of the endzone. A PAT kick made it 28 - 7, Eagles.

Will Bolton Kicked off for the Eagles to give Morgan a brief rest. The Beavers started play on their own 33-yard line. On first down Kinsey ran for seven yards. A draw play to the fullback lost one yard.

On third-and-four for the first down, Cobb sacked Holloway as he attempted to hit Kinsey on a fly route. Kinsey punted a low kick that bounced out of bounds on the Eagle 29-yard line.

Morgan, Mentz and the Eagles turned up the pressure at this point. Morgan ran for seven, then 11 yards. Greer ran for six yards, before Mentz kept the ball for six more yards and a first down at the Beaver 41-yard line. On first down Greer broke through the line, but fumbled the ball at the Beaver 36-yard line. The Beavers had held off the Eagles ---at least for the time being.

A fired-up Beaver team moved the ball methodically down the field with strong inside running by Kinsey and quick, pinpoint passing by Holloway. Kinsey rushed for 34 yards on the drive that carried the ball to the six-yard line. With a first and goal, Kinsey completed a 13-play drive for a touchdown with 1:06 left in the third quarter. The successful PAT kick made the score 28 - 14, Eagles.

The Beaver kicker completed the short kick to Shealey again, who turned and tossed the ball back to Morgan. He was again off to the races. Another penalty, this time on Bates for a clip, brought back a third touchdown by Morgan. The 82-yard touchdown return was erased.

The Eagles started play on the 12-yard line. Morgan raced for 16 yards, North ran for six yards and then for seven more. A motion penalty set the Eagles back to the 27-yard line. On first down Mentz threw to Cobb for eight yards. Morgan ripped for 17 yards, but a holding penalty moved the ball back to the Eagle 18-yard line. A screen pass to North fell incomplete on second down. On third down Mentz pitched back to Morgan, who quick-kicked the ball dead on the Beaver 22-yard line. A 62-yard kick.

The Beavers tried to move the ball but tremendous pressure from Cobb, Hinsley and Devers forced wild throws that were far short of their intended receivers. After one ground out first down the Beavers punted to Shealy at the Eagle 27. He was dragged down at the 32-yard line. Greer ran for two yards, Mentz hit Cobb for eight yards and a measured first down at the Eagle 42-yard line. Mentz missed Carter on a sideline pattern on first down. On second down, Morgan took a handoff into the four hole and broke through the line. He ran through two tackles and broke free at the Beaver 40. This time there was not a penalty flag on the 58-yard touchdown run. A Morgan PAT kick made it Salem Eagles 35, Sparrows Point 14, with 4:17 left on the game clock.

Bolton kicked off for the Eagles. It was returned to the 38-yard line. A series of penalties and a fumble by quarterback Holloway moved the ball back to the 23 with a fourth-and-25 yards for a first down. The Beavers coach decided to go for it on fourth down with less than 3:00 minutes left on the clock. A pass down the middle was batted down by Mentz.

The Eagles had the ball with 2:17 left in the game. Mentz moved in a quarterback. Sparrows Point had one timeout left, but wasn't anxious to stop the clock. Mentz let the clock run down as far as he could before snapping the ball and quickly took a knee on three successive plays. The officials weren't in a hurry to get the play clock started. They let as much time run off as possible while spotting the ball. The clock ran down to 0.00 with the scoreboard reading Eagles 35 and Beavers 14.

The Salem Eagles would play in the Maryland State Championship game the following Saturday night at Winston State University Stadium in Baltimore.

The stat sheet on Morgan was somewhat amazing. He had rushed for 163 yards on 10 carries, passed for 15 yards on one completion out of two throws, returned a punt 12 yards, and caught three passes for 152 yards. The most amazing statistic was penalties wiping out an 82-yard kickoff return; an 88-yard punt return; and a 91-yard pass reception. All had went for touchdowns. He also had 24 and 17-yard gains on rushes brought back for penalties. This was 302 yards in lost yardage due to penalties. His total yardage in the game could have been 644 yards instead of the 342 official yards.

The game was a coming out party for the amazing skills of Kyle Morgan. The state sports reporters now knew about the amazing athletic prodigy that made his home in upstate Maryland.

The District-Heights scouts had left the game shaking their heads and wondering if there was any way to slow down the Salem speedball.

James Mentz had performed admirably in his first start at quarterback. This game had shown what the Eagles would look like in the senior season of Morgan, Mentz, Shealey, Greer and company. They could very well be an offensive juggernaut.

Coach Shaw moved in front of his team. He looked them over quietly then spoke, "Well, I've just heard the news. District-Heights will be our opponent next week in the championship game. They beat Hardwick Academy by a 35 to 7 score tonight. They have openly campaigned on getting a second chance at us. Now they have that opportunity. We'll start to prepare for them on Monday."

He looked around the locker room, then said, "I just want to say that I'm proud of you for coming out and playing so well after losing our leading rusher last week. We'll work on fine tuning this week, eliminating mistakes and try to work towards what will give us the best chance to win the game. I speak for every Salem faculty member, every parent and all of our coaching staff when I say we are proud of you regardless of whatever happens against District-Heights next weekend. Thank you for the effort." With that he left the locker room.

Bobby Winkler walked in the coaches office where coaches Shaw, Powers and Dills were sitting and said to no one in particular, "They didn't have a chance of stopping him. Nobody can stop him. We're going to win it all!"

Coach Shaw walked over to Winkler, put his arm around his shoulders and said, "You were a big part of all this, son. We couldn't have done it without you."

Winkler smiled and said, "I don't know Coach, maybe I held that guy back. Morgan might have scored eight touchdowns a game if he had been at tailback all season."

After Winkler left, Coach Dills said, "You know he's right, we are going to win it all. There is not a player in high school that can stop a boy that size with that much speed. He can literally do anything he wants to do on the field."

Coach Powers chimed in, "Did you see him on that kickoff return? He wasn't even touched. He would have had seven touchdowns tonight without the penalties. I can't wait until next week."

Coach Shaw answered, "We have to play the game. District-Heights will not just give it to us. We have to cut down on the errors to beat them. They'll score some touchdowns against us."

Misty Porter sat across from Kyle as he pulled into her front yard. She would often find herself staring at him for no apparent reason. She wasn't in love with Kyle Morgan. At least she didn't think so. She felt that both of them were too young to make solid commitments to each other, but she knew she thought more of him than anyone she had ever known. He was just the sweetest and best all-around person she had ever seen. He was kind and considerate and had the biggest heart of anyone she had ever met. If anyone was ever worthy of having a big-head, it was Kyle Morgan. She knew that would never happen. He was far above that kind of attitude. It was if he were some kind of young God. She knew that this exciting young man was certainly not in love with her, but she felt that he also thought a lot of her. Her thoughts seemed to always jump ahead years down the road. If there could be continued communication and friendship, there might be a serious relationship somewhere in the future. It was like he was an adult and she was an adoring child. She wanted to remain friends with Kyle Morgan and would not intentionally jeopardize that friendship in any way. She liked being looked upon as his girlfriend, even thought she knew it was not really that kind of relationship at the moment. She wondered to herself how could things so simple sometimes be so complicated. It would take a mind like Kyle Morgan to figure them out. If even he could.

Saturday started with Kyle practicing his new song in the living room. He had worked on two songs for several days the past week and completed the last one at home on Thursday night. He stroked gently on his guitar as he sang his new slow rendition called "Only the Heart Can Know."

His second song was an upbeat dance song he entitled, "The Dance Song." His mother heard him singing and sat at the top of the stairs as he put the music with both songs.

He saw her and asked, "Well, how do they sound?"

She looked down at him and answered, "They're good, Kyle. I knew you would write a great song. You have always been able to express yourself in written words. That's one of your strong points." She added, "We'll leave at around 12:30 for your 2:00 p.m. appointment."

He nodded as she left the room.

The next day it was just past 2:00 p.m. when Ben Curruth welcomed the teenager into the sound studio where he would cut his demonstration record.

Two hours later he walked out of the room with his recordings complete. He had completed 12 takes of the slow song and almost as many of his dance tune. He had adjusted his voice flex and tones as he went along and felt that the last several takes were the best of the lot.

Curruth told him they would start prepping the record for possible release on Monday. He said he would let him know by the next week if there was any interest in Revele Records discussing a recording contract with him.

On the way home, Mrs. Morgan looked at Kyle and asked, "Are you sure you want to move forward with this?"

He answered, "I don't have a problem with it, Mom. I don't think I want to be a singer as a career, but I wouldn't mind the pursuit at this time."

She smiled as she said, "Your father is going to want an explanation of how I let you become a rock and roll singer while he was away. What am I going to tell him?"

Kyle answered jokingly, "Just tell him I finally found my calling."

Saturday night the call from Ken Morgan was presented to the family at around 7:00 p.m. He told the family that he was finishing up the assignment and expected to be home in time for the game Friday night.

It was a happy Lucille and Kyle Morgan as they recorded their message to be delivered to Colonel Morgan. The crux of their message was that they loved him and would be glad to see him.

Da Nang Province, November twenty-eight, 1962. 0:800 a.m. Colonel Ken Morgan was closing out the bizarre "Officer fragging" case that he had been working on for the past six weeks. He had made plans to leave Vietnam on the following Friday and arrive back in the Virginia Headquarters by Monday evening or Tuesday morning. Tentative plans were for a debriefing and documentation period throughout the week at the Virginia CIA Headquarters. His assignment release date was expected to be on Friday morning. He had plans on attending his son's state-final football game that Saturday night in Baltimore.

Mrs. Morgan and Kyle went over to the gym where the Eagle basketball teams were entertaining the Chesapeake City Cardinals. The Lady Eagles blasted the Lady Cardinals by a 65-39 score. Porter scored 38 points and had 16 rebounds --- 26 points in the first half. The Eagle boys had a close game with the Cardinals before pulling out a 66-61 win. Ellerson scored 34 points.

After the game, Morgan walked down to the court and shook his hand. "Great game, Jack," he said.

Ellerson answered, "Hurry up and get that football over with, Kyle, we need you."

The basketball program was published and available for all the Eagle home games. It mentioned under Morgan's name that he had averaged over 30 points per game the previous year.

The following Tuesday night the Eagles would travel to meet the defending AAA state champion Galveston Hawks. Their winning streak had now reached 65 games.

Morgan was looking forward to seeing the Hawks in action.

Sunday evening all the football team met at the gym. They viewed the previous game film and looked at four District-Heights' films of games this past season. The Eagles earlier 42-41 win over the Cougars was a good tool to help formulate an offensive game plan.

Morgan felt that relatively close wins over several other schools presented more of a capsule as to their capabilities. He couldn't take his eyes off their All-State running back Thurmond on every play. This guy could run, block, throw the halfback pass, catch the ball and he played defense like a man possessed. He was really a great high school player.

The Eagle star left with the feeling that if any team in the state could play with the Eagles it was District-Heights.

Chapter Nineteen
Happy Days Are Here Again

The week started off with a bang as the quarterly report cards were passed out.

Misty Porter ran down Morgan at the morning break and asked him to let her see his report card.

He laughingly told her his report card "is none of your business."

She said, "ashamed of it, huh! Not very good is it!" ----- "You're just another dumb jock --- Kyle Morgan."

Kyle asked her to let him see her card first. They swapped cards. He looked at the string of straight A's on her report card. Her grade point average was 98.7, which put her in the top three in the junior and senior class.

Porter looked at the 100.0 grade-point average of her friend and smiled. She shook her head slowly from side to side as she said, "You are some kind of Martian, aren't you?"

Morgan quickly answered, "No! ---- I'm from Jupiter."

They both laughed as they walked toward their next class.

With a big basketball game coming up with Galveston Tuesday night, another game with cross-town rival East Ridgeview slated for Friday and the state championship football game coming up Saturday, it was a huge sports week around Salem High School. You could feel the excitement in the air as the team gathered for football practice that Monday afternoon.

The Winston State Stadium would hold 65,000 fans. It was anticipated there would be 35,000 to 40,000 football fans in attendance at the game. Over 200 college coaches from around the country and virtually every high school coach in the state would attend the state championship game in the states largest classification.

There would be at least 10 seniors in the game that would attend Division 1-A schools on football scholarships and 6 to 10 juniors that would be widely sought after the following year.

Most newspapers around the state were proclaiming this game as potentially the most interesting game ever played in the state.

There had been an interesting article in the Sunday edition of the Baltimore High School weekly as it featured the high school football powers. It had pointed out that the loss of Winkler had put the Eagle team at a strong disadvantage going into the game. It suggested that District-Heights would put all their efforts into stopping Morgan and would probably win the battle of the state football powers. Coach Shaw read the article with interest, laid the paper aside and turned on the local news.

Monday and Tuesday were spent on defense with every possibility explored as to what the Cougars might do offensively. Hinsley would shadow Thurmond on every play. North would cover the middle with emphasis on fullback Hal Damons. Cobb was to blitz on virtually every play from the weak side. Devers would hesitate at the line unless specifically designated to blitz. He would cover the flat and look for the screen pass. If Thurmond flanked wide, Morgan would go with him. All other pass defense was to be zone with Mentz to be the free safety if Morgan was on Thurmond. If Thurmond was not flanked on a probable passing situation, Morgan would be at free safety with Greer moving into the game as a corner back to provide a five-man pass defense. The possibility of misdirection and counter plays were covered at length. Every gadget, or trick play imaginable had been covered as the Tuesday afternoon practice came to a close.

After practice, Cobb, Mentz, Hinsley and Morgan dressed quickly and started the drive to Galveston to watch the Salem basketball teams play.

The girls game was just underway as they moved to their seats.

Cobb noticed her first.

There was Mrs. Morgan.

Beside her sat Mr. Morgan.

Cobb nudged Kyle and pointed toward them. Tears came to the eyes of young Morgan as he moved toward his father. It had been a well-planned surprise. Kyle hugged his father and sat down beside him.

Down on the court ~ Porter looked up into the stands. There were tears in her eyes as she purveyed the reunion of father and son that night in Galveston.

Principle Collins and Superintendent Gray came over and joined the welcoming back festivities.

Meanwhile, the Lady Eagles battled hard with the Lady Hawks. After trailing throughout the game, Porter led a charge in the fourth quarter that enabled the Lady Eagles to escape with a thrilling 47 - 41 win. She had scored 28 points with Jen Shaw scoring 11. Connie Hollis pulled 14 rebounds.

Coach Tom Shaw sat and watched his daughter play. Afterward, he walked over to shake the hand of Ken Morgan. He told him, "It's good to have you back."

Mr. Morgan replied, "I'm glad to be back, Coach. Ya'll go get 'em Saturday."

The Galveston Hawks story was well known around the state of Maryland. The 1960 season had seen the Hawks make it to the state finals with four freshmen and a senior. Their leading scorer was a freshman point guard --- Vince Stevens. They had lost that final game 69 - 63 in overtime.

The next season they had ran roughshod over every team on their schedule. They won the state AAA title and All-Classification Tournament with a 31 - 0 record in 1961.

Their best player was six-foot-three-inch junior shooting-guard Vince Stevens. He was rated as one of the top five guards in the country. He had averaged over 25 points per game over the last two seasons. Their center was six-foot-five-inch Ron Eddy. At forwards they had six-foot-four-inch Mike Rison and six-foot-three-inch Jimmy Watts. A sophomore point guard rounded out their starting five, six-foot tall Ricky wade. As a team they averaged almost 90 points per game. Either of their Junior stars could score 30 points in a game on a given night. They played a tight 1-3-1 zone defense that forced opponents into a 2-1-2 offense and virtually closed down scoring in the paint. Their defensive strategy was to make teams try and beat them from outside.

Morgan watched closely as Stevens moved from side to side on the court, popping jumpers or feeding inside to one of his tremendous inside scorers, Hall or Rison. Hall would fire from outside at will. The young point guard --- Wade --- didn't shoot much, but with the other four players on the court, he didn't have to.

By halftime the Hawks had ran out to a 49 - 26 lead. Stevens had 23 points by halftime. The Hawks had played their zone defense to perfection with a double team on Ellerson any time he got the ball within ten feet of the basket. He was able to hit a few outside jumpers to run up his 28 points for the night. Hogan had also dropped in some outside shots for his 16 points. The Eagles just did not have any inside play and not enough outside shooting as the streaking Hawks ran off with a 94 - 61 win. Win number 66 in succession.

Kyle rode back home with his mother and father that night. They talked about events over the last few weeks since Mr. Morgan had been away. It was a happy moment for the Morgan family as they arrived back in Ridgeview shortly before midnight.

The Wednesday and Thursday afternoon practice sessions were devoted to offense with emphasis on first-and-third down. The goal was to use Morgan on first down as much as possible to get them into short-yardage situations for a first down. Second down could be a primary throwing down, with third down to be Morgan again or a quick-slant pass. All the various gadget plays were reviewed. Friday would be a short practice in shorts or sweats with emphasis on special teams and changing the play at the line of scrimmage.

The trip across town to the East Ridgeview gym only took about 15 minutes. Morgan went by his house and picked up his mother and father.

On the way to the game, the discussion was more on basketball than football. Kyle told his father, "Watch number 33, (Ellerson) Dad, he can really play. He might be the best I have ever seen in high school from an individual standpoint. When the football players get on the court and take some of the scoring pressure off him, he could really be dominating."

One thing was for sure, the irrepressible junior Misty Porter had become dominating on the court. She hit from every conceivable position on the court as the Lady Eagles remained undefeated with a 66 - 39 win over the Lady Trojans. Her work for the night netted 41 points.

Mr. Morgan smiled at Kyle and asked, "Does she do that every night?" He exclaimed, "God, she can play!"

Kyle Morgan just nodded his head. He was proud of Misty Porter. She was not only a very wonderful person, she had become an outstanding basketball player.

She would join the Porter and Morgan family midway through the first quarter of the boys game and start her standard screaming and cheering session.

Mr. Morgan thought to himself, "She is a very sweet and pretty young lady. He could easily see why his son thought so much of her."

Jack Ellerson piled up the points against the smaller East Ridgeview team. He scored on tap-ins, put-backs, jump shots, foul shots and even threw in a sky-hook or two as he completed the night with 47 points. He hit the boards for 20 rebounds. The Eagles won the game 79 to 64. The 47 points were a new Salem scoring record. The old record had been 44 points.

On the way back home, Mr. Morgan said, "You're right about Ellerson. He is good."

Kyle answered, "I think we're going to have some kind of strong basketball team."

Saturday morning broke with a temperature of 40 degrees. The game time temperature was expected to be around the freezing mark. There was not a lot of jabbering and talking as the team prepared for the game that night.

Morgan sat on a table in the locker room.

Coach Will Powers went over the plays that had been prepared as the most likely to have success against the Cougars defense. One thing about Morgan, he thought as he read them off ----- he's not going to forget them.

At 7:55 p.m., eleven seniors followed Winkler, North and Hinsley to the center of the field for the coin-toss.

The Cougars won the toss and elected to receive.

The game was now underway for all the marbles.

Morgan kicked the ball deep into the endzone.

On first down, quarterback Raymond handed the ball to Thurmond for six yards. Damons cracked for two more yards before Thurmond pounded out to the 25-yard line for a first down. A sweep by Thurmond was played well by Devers and he was stopped for a two-yard gain. Hinsley called the defense.

Morgan looked at Cobb and said, "He's going to pass. Go after him hard."

On second down, Raymond took two quick steps back to throw as Hinsley crashed from the front and threw him for a five-yard loss. On third down a pass intended for wide receiver Cronin was batted down by Shealey. Thurmond punted out of bounds on the Eagle 49-yard line.

Morgan reached behind him for the pitch on first down from Mentz and was hit behind the line by one of the two All-State linebackers for the Cougars, Richard Clinton. The result of the play was a two-yard loss. In the huddle, Mentz said, "My fault, Kyle, it won't happen again." He called a 34 screen. The screen was well set up, but Clinton was with Morgan all the way and batted the ball away just as it reached the tailback. After only a few plays it was evident that Clinton had Morgan as his containment assignment. A third down-draw to Morgan picked up 11 yards, but was short of the first down. Morgan punted into the endzone.

Two smashes into the line netted five yards for the Cougars. On third down, Raymond threw a bullet intended for Danny Whitman that Greer broke up with a hard hit on the intended receiver. Thurmond punted long and high to Morgan. Morgan fair caught the ball at the Eagle 38-yard line.

On first down Morgan burst off tackle for four yards. It was again Clinton that made the tackle. On second down Mentz went back to pass, was hit hard by the other District-Heights All-State linebacker Marcus Fitzpatrick and lost 11 yards on the sack. A third-down pass intended for Morgan was batted down by Whitman at the Cougar 45-yard line. Morgan again punted into the endzone.

Damons hit the line for six yards on first down. A draw to Damons brought up a measured third-down-and-inches. Quarterback Raymond dropped back from play-action and threw long downfield. The ball was intended for wide receiver Terry Culver. Mentz was with him all the way and intercepted the ball at the Eagle 34.

Morgan moved in at quarterback. On first down he rolled right and hit Carter on a slant pattern for 10 yards to the 44-yard line. A dive play to Greer gained two yards. On second down he threw a quick buttonhook to Cobb for nine yards to the Cougar 45-yard line. A Morgan keeper gained six more yards to the 39. On second down, Morgan dropped back to throw, was pressured by Clinton, and threw incomplete to Shealey. Guard Rudy Dolye was flagged for holding on the play. The 15-yard penalty moved the ball back to the Eagle 45. Replaying second down resulted in a rollout by Morgan getting four yards to the Eagle 48-yard line. On third down a fierce rush by Clinton and Fitzpatrick forced the quarterback to scramble from the pocket and overthrow Carter at the Cougar 40-yard line. He punted into the endzone. He did not want Thurmond having the opportunity to run back the punt.

On first down from the 20-yard line, Thurmond broke a tackle and picked up 23 yards before Morgan brought him down on the Cougar 43-yard line. Damons rushed for four yards. Lewis got two yards up the middle to the Cougar 49. The first quarter came to a close without a score.

The first play of he second quarter saw Thurmond ran off tackle for five yards and a first down at the Eagle 46-yard line. Raymond threw a quick slant to Westbrook for eight yards to the 38. Thurmond ripped for seven yards and a first down at the Eagle 31. The District-Heights coach had noticed that weak side cornerback Shealey was cheating toward the strong side. He called a flanker reverse with a pitchout to Thurmond moving toward the strong side, who in turn would reverse toss the ball to the flanker, Whitman, coming back toward the weak side. It worked beautifully with the flying flanker swinging wide to the Eagle nine-yard line before Mentz could run him out of bounds. A first down plunge by Damons netted only a yard to the eight-yard line.

On second down the Eagles jumped into a nine-man goal-line front at the last second before the snap. Hinsley crashed into Thurmond behind the line for a two-yard loss back to the 10-yard line. A third down pass from Raymond was tipped by a charging Cobb and fell short of its intended receiver. In the regular season game, Cougar place-kicker Kelly Keino had his PAT kick blocked after the Cougars third touchdown. It had eventually been the decisive point lost in the 42-41 Eagle victory. Now he was being called on to kick a 27-yard field goal to give his team a lead. The kick was good and the Eagles trailed 3 - 0 with 6:49 left in the first half of play.

The kickoff was short to Greer at the 24-yard line. He was brought down on the Eagle 31-yard line. Mentz gave to Morgan for three yards.

Morgan asked Mentz if he could say something in the huddle.

Mentz said, "Of course you can, speak up!"

Morgan told him, "Go to the shot-gun, empty the backfield, use a man in motion and go quick passes to open up the run. They're killing us with that eight-man line."

Mentz called "speed pass series five." This would send five receivers on short routes to allow the quarterback to get the throw off. On first down he threw incomplete to Cobb on a buttonhook, second down connected with Carter for eight yards to the Eagle 39-yard line. A third down pass to Shealey on the sideline picked up six yards and a first down at the Eagle 45-yard line. A quick pass to Morgan on a slant was good for 12 yards to the Cougar 33. Mentz went back on first down to throw, was rushed from the pocket and threw incomplete at the 35-yard line. A holding penalty moved the ball back to the Cougar 48 . On first and 25 yards, Mentz threw a screen pass to Greer for 18 yards to the Cougar 26-yard line. Back under the center, Mentz gave to his tailback for eight yards and a first down at the Cougar 18. A quick pitch again to Morgan went for eight more yards to the Cougar 10-yard line. A second down run by the Salem workhorse gained one yard before a third-down dive by the same back went for two more yards and a first down at the Cougar seven-yard line. On first down, Mentz ran play action to Morgan, kept the ball and hit a wide open Cobb in the endzone for the touchdown. The PAT kick by Morgan made it Eagles 7, District-Heights 3 with 2:23 left in the first half.

Morgan boomed the ball out of the endzone on the ensuing kickoff. The Cougars came up at their own 20-yard line with 2:08 left in the half. Thurmond took a quick pass down the middle at the 35-yard line. A beautiful block was thrown on safety Mentz by the wide receiver Whitman that effectively took him out of the play. Suddenly, the state 220-yard dash champion was free at his own 40-yard line. Morgan had a receiver in his zone that he left after seeing the ball in the air. He was far behind the speedy Cougar receiver when he caught the ball at the 35-yard line. Morgan had a slight angle that would enable him to catch up to the fast moving cougar at the Eagle eight-yard line. There was a loud roar from the Salem fans and a stunned silence from the Cougar faithful. They had never seen anyone catch the swift back when he got past the defensive coverage. There was a realization from everyone in the stadium that Morgan was not just any football player, but something super special on the field. Two plays later with 0:47 left in the half, Thurmond crashed into the line, broke a tackle at the four-yard line and dove into the endzone for the touchdown. The PAT kick made it Cougars 10, Eagles 7, with 0:38 left in the half.

The kickoff was short to Shealey. He quickly turned and tossed the ball to Morgan at the 21-yard line. The Eagle speed merchant broke for the sideline and was finally pulled down by Thurmond at the Cougar 41-yard line. On first down. Mentz threw to Morgan for 21 yards to the 20 with 0:06 left on the clock. After a timeout by the Eagles, Morgan kicked the field goal from the 37-yard line to make the halftime score, Cougars 10 and Eagles 10.

It was a tired group of Eagle players that sat before Coach Shaw in the locker room. Coach Shaw told the team, "We are 30 minutes from achieving the ultimate in high school football in the state of Maryland. The State AAAA title is within our reach. Lets take it."

The second-half kickoff was a squib kick with reserve center Howard Seeley falling on the ball at the Eagle 29-yard line. Morgan took a quick pitch for seven yards then rambled for eight more yards to the 44. A motion penalty moved the ball back to the 39. On the first-and-15 yards needed for a first-down play, Mentz threw to Carter for eight yards on a sideline route. Morgan ran for four yards making it third down and three yards to go for the first down. A crushing Cougar defense hit the Salem tailback just as he took the handoff at the mid-field stripe and brought him down for a three-yard loss. Morgan punted high and long ----- again into the endzone.

The Cougars came out growling. Thurmond carried three straight times for six, three and eight yards to the 37-yard line. Damons ripped for 11 to the 48-yard line. A motion penalty moved the ball back to the 43 before a Raymond pass was intercepted by Devers after a tip by Cobb at the Eagle 47-yard line.

Two attempts wide by Morgan netted only six yards to the Cougar 47-yard line. A quick pass to Carter was thrown low and bounced incomplete. Morgan took the snap and faked the punt. He pulled the ball down and broke off of his left side. He was forced back into the middle of the field and brought down on the Cougar 36-yard line after a 17-yard run and a first down. Greer ran for three yards on a play-action dive. Mentz threw to Cobb for seven yards, who attempted to pitch the ball back to Shealey. The pitch went wide and District-Heights recovered the ball at their own 38-yard line.

Thurmond ran for four yards, Damons got three yards on a quick hitter. On third down Thurmond ripped for eight yards and a first down at the Eagle 47-yard line. On a play-action, quarterback Raymond faked to Thurmond, pulled the ball from the pocket and dropped back to throw. James Mentz had tripped on a Whitman fake and the Cougar receiver was open on the Eagle 30-yard line. Raymond threw a perfect strike to him for an easy touchdown and a 16-10 lead. The PAT kick made it 17 - 10 with 2:28 left in the third quarter.

Another squib kick was recovered by the Eagles at their 31-yard line. Morgan moved to quarterback. On first down he threw to Mentz for nine yards, then scrambled for eight more yards to the Eagle 47-yard line. On first down, Morgan rolled right making it look like a run all the way. He then threw off a dead run to a streaking Carter at the Cougar 20-yard line. The Eagle receiver made the catch and jogged in with an easy touchdown. The score was Cougars 17 and the Eagles 16 with 0:52 left in the third quarter. It was at this point the impossible happened. James Mentz kneeled for the PAT snap. The ball was high and wide from center Hinsley. Morgan reached out with one hand and managed to control the ball. He was hit before he could start any forward movement. The PAT was missed. It was the first PAT the team had failed to convert all year.

Morgan kicked the ball six-yards deep in the endzone with 0:29 seconds left in the third quarter.

On first down, Raymond threw incomplete from the 20-yard line. Thurmond ran for nine yards to the 29.

The third quarter ended with the score, 17 - 16, Cougars.

The first play of the fourth quarter saw Damons stopped for no gain. On fourth down-and-six-inches for the first down, Thurmond crashed for four yards and a first down at the 33-yard line. A pass interference call on Carter resulted in a 15-yard penalty and an automatic first down out to the Cougar 48. Thurmond ran for two yards to the mid-field stripe. A quick pass to Whitfield was complete for nine yards to the Eagle 41-yard line. Another pass to Whitfield was good for 16 yards to the Eagle 25. A delay handoff to Damons gained nine yards to the Eagle 16-yard line. Thurmond ran for three yards, then for seven yards and a measured first down at the Eagle six-yard line. Damons was stopped for no gain on first down. A pass in the flat to Whitfield was incomplete. On third down, Thurmond took a swing pass from Raymond out of the backfield and ran into the corner of the endzone for a 23 - 16 lead. The PAT kick made it 24 - 16 with 7:21 left in the game.

Another squib kick kept the ball out of the hands of Morgan, but it was recovered at the Eagle 39-yard line by end Joey Bales. On first down Mentz threw to Cobb for eight yards to the 47. Morgan was stopped after a one-yard gain by Clinton. Another attempt to spring Morgan gained only three yards to the Eagle 48-yard line. On third down, Mentz flipped a short swing pass to Morgan for 10 yards and a first down at the Cougar 42-yard line. Morgan bolted through the four hole and picked up 23 yards before he was hit by Whitman and Thurmond at the Cougar 19. Mentz lost three on a pass attempt with Fitzpatrick getting the sack. A motion penalty on left tackle Donald Walters moved the ball back to the 27-yard line. On second down Mentz threw down the middle to Cobb on a rare tight end fly pattern. Coach Shaw had called this play from the sideline. It was good for 23 yards to the Cougar four-yard line. On first down, Morgan took a pitchout and dove into the corner of the endzone for the score. The PAT kick by Morgan made it Cougars 24, Eagles 23 with 3:01 left in the game.

An attempted onside kick was recovered by the Cougars at their own 43-yard line. The Eagles had two timeouts remaining as the Cougars came to the line. A nine-man front faced the Cougars as they ran Thurmond into the line. He was held to two yards by the swarming Eagle defense. On second down, a wide sweep by Thurmond was diagnosed by side back Morgan, who came up and hit the speedy tailback for a two-yard loss. On third down quarterback Raymond went back to pass and was sacked by an all-out blitz by the Eagle ends and linebackers. On a fourth and 17 from the Cougar 36-yard line, Thurmond went back to punt the ball away with 1:04 left in the game.

Salem called time out.

Coach Shaw looked into the eyes of his junior running back. He was amazed at the seemingly lack of emotion as the player told him, "It's okay, Coach, we've got plenty of time. I want to go gun all the way with Mentz wide left and Carter wide right with an empty backfield the rest of the game."

The veteran coach said simply, "Call your plays, the games in your hands now."

Morgan smiled and nodded as he ran back onto the field.

Thurmond kicked the ball out of bounds on the Eagle 37-yard line with 1:01 left on the game clock.

When Morgan, who came up in the shot-gun, saw the defensive alignment of the cougars he quickly decided what his plan of action was. They had two defensive backs about 20-yards downfield. The linebackers were also back about five yards deeper than normal. Morgan stood back in the shot-gun with the empty backfield to accent his charade on planning to throw the ball. He had other intentions. On first down he took the snap and fired the ball intentionally high over the head of Carter on a down-and-out pattern. This was to stop the clock and conserve what precious time that remained on the clock. He carefully noted in his mind where every defensive player was on the play. He would call the same play drawing the same coverage on second down. He had no intentions of throwing the ball. He now knew where there might be some running room. Now he was ready to go to Plan A. He took the snap, dropped one step to freeze the defense and then darted to his right. He turned the corner and was not brought down until he had crossed the mid-field stripe. He was forced out of bounds on the Cougar 47-yard line. It was a 16-yard run. On first down, from the same set, he again called the same play. Again he kept the ball, ran over two tacklers and was finally gang tackled at the Cougar 38-yard line. With his eye on the clock, Morgan called time out and walked to the sideline.

The clock showed 0:09 left in the game. Coach Shaw looked into the eyes of his quarterback, smiled and asked, "What do you think?"

Morgan wiped his hands on a towel. He then reached down and wiped off the inside of his right shoe. He looked at the coach and gave him a closed-mouth grin. Again he replied, "I think we're okay, Coach."

Coach Shaw nodded. He knew what Morgan had in mind from the on-set of the series. He only wanted to get the ball somewhere in his field goal range. With the wind behind him, a kick from the 45-yard line, or a 55-yard field goal was certainly a possibility. He had seen him do it many times in practice. All of the team had seen it. They also knew what the Salem super-star had in mind.

Morgan ran on the field and handed the kicking tee to Mentz, who took it without any display of emotion. Morgan talked to his huddled team at the Eagle 45-yard line. The Cougar team suddenly realized what was happening and quickly called time out.

Morgan didn't go toward the bench. He recalled the huddle and told his team, "No penalties! We can't afford even a five-yard penalty right now. Just block them long enough for me to get the kick off." Not one word was said as the team moved forward to the line of scrimmage.

Not one fan was seated as the center Hinsley, prepared to snap the ball. Mentz called the cadence. The ball was snapped. He caught it cleanly and placed it on the tee.

Morgan kicked the ball in a low trajectory that seemed to rise as it moved toward the goalposts. It seemed as if the ball was in the air for an eternity.

The referee's under the goalposts threw their hands up as the ball passed over the crossbar with several feet to spare.

Morgan had split the middle. The kick was good!

The William Edward Salem Golden Eagles were the State Class AAAA football champions of 1962. The final score was posted, Eagles 26 and Cougars 24.

There had been instances of chaos and pandemonium after several big Eagle wins over the season, but none that matched this one. It took almost 30 minutes for most of the Eagle players to get off the field.

Morgan was patted on the back by every Eagle fan that could get close enough to pat him, kissed by every girl that could fight her way up to him, and just touched by every kid old enough to know what had just occurred. He didn't see his parents or Misty Porter on the field. There would be time for their congratulations later. He knew they wanted this to be his moment.

The previous year Morgan had been a part of a state championship team in Georgia. It was a Class AA school. He never imagined the thrill winning a big school championship could bring. It was definitely one of the greatest thrills he could imagine.

In the locker room, Coach Shaw asked the team to kneel in a word of prayer. Afterward, he spoke quietly to his AAAA state champions. "I don't know exactly what to say to you at this time. You dream of winning the big one as a coach, but it doesn't happen very often. Not in a football crazy state like Maryland. You gave everyone in the Eagle Nation the greatest thrill we can ever experience. We may win it again next year, but nothing will ever top this first one."

Looking around the locker room he said, "Bobby Winkler, come up here, son." He proceeded to hand him a shirt that had the Eagle logo and the words, "1962 State AAAA Champions" on it. He told equipment manager Riley Gates to pass out the shirts to all the players so they can wear them as they leave the stadium tonight and to school on Monday.

Boyd Massingale and Randal Hinsley walked over to Morgan and extended their hand. "Thanks man," said Hinsley.

Morgan just grinned at them as he said, "You are both going to be some kind of players in college. Good luck to both of you."

The warm shower felt good after the cold night on the gridiron. He was just about the last one to finish dressing.

Morgan walked toward the group gathered in the parking lot. Most just didn't want to go home. They wanted to savor this moment for as long as they could. It had been a long time coming for the proud Eagle program. Morgan felt good for Coach Shaw. He was a good man and a good coach. He finally saw his family and the Porter family standing together off to one side of the crowd. He walked through them and hugged his mother, father and the young lady that it seemed was becoming more of a soul mate every day ~ Misty Porter.

Everyone that attended his church must have been at the game. He received congratulations and pats on the back from just about everyone there. Three months earlier he had been just a guy trying out for the football team and looking for a place to worship. Now he was a member of a state championship team and an integral part of the Christian environment that made up Westside Baptist Church. As the bible said, "The Lord did work in mysterious ways."

Chapter Twenty
A New Ball Game

Monday morning at Salem High School was just one big party after another. All the faculty had brought cookies, cakes and soft drinks for their classes. You couldn't walk 10 feet without a sign proclaiming the Eagles the greatest team in Maryland history. The school management had declared that if the team won the state title the week would be dedicated to the football team. There would be essays on the past season and class work dedicated to classroom discussions on the season.

All the players wore their pullover shirts that had been passed out the past Saturday night.

Many of the discussions of that week were about Kyle Morgan and how he was able to accomplish the miracles he brought about on the football field.

A sports writer had asked Coach Shaw if Morgan was the best player he had ever seen.

Shaw didn't hesitate with his answer. "He probably is, but I haven't seen many players outside of North Maryland. We haven't went far enough into the playoffs for me to even see the best players all over the state. I would find it hard to believe that anyone could compete with a higher level of skill sets than this young man. He can do everything imaginable on a football field. I would imagine you will be asking that same question after you see him play basketball, run track and play baseball. I understand he is outstanding in those sports, also."

All the team would meet with their coach at 3:30 p.m. to review the championship game film and close out the season.

Honors would abound for the Grid-Eagles.

Coach Shaw would be named the Region, District and State Coach of the Year in AAAA. The Eagles would be rated the number one team in America by the Indianapolis High School Sporting News.

Kyle Morgan was not named as the first-team quarterback on the Maryland All-State team. That honor went to the Senior Raymond of District-Heights. Morgan was, however; named as the AAAA Back of the Year and was selected as captain of the All-State squad. He was called the best all-around back ever to play in Maryland. He was cited in superlatives as being the best passer, punter, running back and placement kicker in the state.

Cobb, Mentz, North, and Hinsley were named first-team All-State on defense. Cobb and Morgan were named to all the high school All-America teams. Winkler was a first team All-State selection at running back, and second team All-America. Carter was at second team wide receiver on offense. Named to the honorable mention list were Doyle, Greer, Massingale, and Shealey. It was an impressive list of honors for a very impressive football team.

The basketball players were excused from the final football team meeting. Coach Breyer wanted to start getting them ready to play the following night when Mitchell County would visit the Eagles Nest.

The young Eagle head coach had eagerly anticipated the arrival of his three big guys since the season started. Now it was show time. Could Morgan possibly be anywhere as good on the court as he was on the gridiron? Was Mentz and Cobb the answer to freeing up Ellerson for better shots with their inside presence?

At 3:30 p.m., Butch Cobb, James Mentz and Kyle Morgan walked onto the gym floor for their first day of basketball practice.

Coach David Breyer and Assistant Coach Will Powers watched the three youngsters as they shook hands with all the players and casually shot the ball toward the basket.

After about 15 minutes the coach called his team together. He welcomed the football players to the squad and started the practice with a figure eight lay-up drill. All went smoothly as he moved into rebounding and fast break drills.

It was about 30 minutes into the practice session that he went to what he called the "survival" drill. This particular drill would have five defensive players in a typical 2-1-2 or 1-3-1 zone defending the goal with two players trying to score against the five. He put Morgan and Mentz on offense against his starting five on defense. Morgan took the ball out front, dribbled once and left the floor for a jump shot. It parted the cords. On the next possession he sped around the defensive guards and passed the ball to Mentz, who gave it back to him for another jump shot 15 feet from the basket. He simply jumped above the defense for an easy shot. In 10 shots at the basket, the two new players scored on eight of the attempts. Morgan on seven of them. Coach Breyer had seen enough. He called for offensive and defensive lineups on the floor. The current starting lineup went through several offensive series against the defensive team consisting of the three new players and a couple of Eagle reserves.

The only player who was able to even get a decent shot at the goal was the six-foot-nine Ellerson. On several occasions he stepped out to the free-throw line and popped turn-around jumpers. With the football additions on offense, the head coach watched as Morgan drained three shots from outside and continuously penetrated the lane. He would finish the play with a dish to Cobb for a lay-up or kick the ball back outside to Mentz for a 15-foot jump shot. After about 15 minutes the coach moved Cobb to pivot, Morgan to the three guard and Mentz to a wing. With these three players were Ellerson and Hogan.

The amazed coach watched the team score virtually every time they ran the offense.

Coach Powers said, "I've never seen anything close to this team as far as height. There may not be a college team in the country as tall as we are."

Coach Breyer answered, "We have about 30 minutes left of practice to get them ready to play tomorrow night."

The rest of the practice session was spent working with the new starting team on defense and offensive sets.

When the team practice concluded, the players were told to finish up their practice with individual foul-shot practice. The coach watched as Morgan stepped to the line. After watching his new guard hit 25 consecutive free throws he walked over to him and asked, "Do you ever miss a foul shot?"

Morgan answered, "every now and then!"

The next day at school Morgan was having lunch with Porter when she asked, "How did practice go yesterday?"

He told her, "It went well, we really have some good players on the team. We should be able to play with just about anyone if we play well."

That night the Salem girls, behind Porters 29 points, downed the Mitchell County team 54 - 42 for their fifth straight win.

There was a buzz when the Eagles took the floor. All eyes were on them as they went through their shooting drills.

The game started with Ellerson jumping center and tapping the ball to Morgan. The ball flowed around the top of the circle until Morgan exploded toward the basket. He went high into the air for what appeared to be a jump shot. Suddenly at the apex of his leap, he dropped the ball off to a breaking Ellerson for a slam dunk. The Salem High School Wonder Five was now a reality. With Morgan dropping long jump shots off his 60-inch vertical leap, and the tremendous size advantage inside, the Eagles pulled away for an easy 103 - 64 win. Ellerson had 33 points, Morgan 28, and Mentz 14 to pace the win. The starting team was pulled from the game with a 92-53 lead with just over 3:00 minutes left on the game clock. That would become the standard as the season progressed toward the state tournament. The team record was now 4 - 1 with the lone loss to Galveston.

The Salem basketball program had always been pretty much a joke among their region 8-AAAA peers. The last and only state appearance for the boys team was in 1948. They had lost in the first round. The last winning season for the Eagle boys was in 1951 when they compiled a season record of 16 wins and 8 losses. Over the last 10 years the boys had won only 83 games with 164 losses.

The girls had fared somewhat better with 147 wins and 96 losses. They had won 16 and 14 games the last two seasons. The Lady Eagles had made one lone trip to the state tournament in 1956, losing in the first game.

Around Salem, the support for the basketball teams were primarily just some die-hard student loyalists and the players parents. Now Coach Breyer, who had been the Eagles coach for the past three years, looked at his starting lineup and could not believe the amount of talent he had on the team.

At the point was six-foot-two-inch sophomore Walter Hogan. He had led the Eagle B-team in scoring the past season with over 21 points per game.

Holding down the other guard slot was the prep superstar, six-foot-five-inch junior Kyle Morgan. He was a Georgia All-State selection the previous season as he led his state championship team with a 31.6 scoring average.

In the middle at center was the lone returning starter for the Eagles, six-foot-eight-inch junior Butch Cobb. He had averaged 10.2 points per game the previous year.

Manning one forward was the six-foot-seven-inch junior jumping-jack James Mentz. He had averaged 21.3 for his Virginia high-school team.

At the other forward was the nations highest ranked sophomore from the previous year, six-foot-nine-inch junior Jack Ellerson. He had averaged 28.4 in leading his team to the state AAA Pennsylvania state championship.

About the only question Coach Breyer had was whether there would be enough basketballs to satisfy this type of firepower.

In analyzing their abilities it was easy to see that Morgan was a scoring machine that could probably score 100 points in a game if he chose to do so. He shot the ball so well. He was incredibly quick and fast for a player his size. He could totally dominate and take over a game.

Cobb was an animal inside. When he went up for a rebound, it was an almost certainty he would come down with it. He was a good jumper and could score if the team needed him to fill that role..

Mentz was an exceptional leaper. He was tremendously strong on defense. He was an excellent shooter with good rebounding skills.

Hogan was a talented point guard. He was willing to pass the ball, play good defense and set up the team scorers with good penetration. He could be a solid scoring threat if he looked to shoot the ball.

And last, but certainly not least, was the amazing Jack Ellerson. It was almost a crime to have him and Morgan on the same team. Throw in Mentz and Cobb and it was demoralizing to play the Eagles. Ellerson literally played above the rim. He was extremely quick for a player his size and could jump out of the gym. He and Morgan would become expert on the ally-oop pass where the guard would toss the ball up around the rim and Ellerson would go up and slam it into the basket. He would have eight dunks in one game late in the season.

Coach Breyer asked himself, "How would I defend a team like this if I were coaching against them?" He had no answer.

Word quickly spread around school about the talented Eagle basketball team. West Ridgeview would be their next opponent. The Eagles had lost 14 straight games to the Wolves. The Lady Eagles had beaten them once the past season and lost to them by one point in another game. The games would be in West Ridgeview Friday night.

On the way to the game, Morgan sat down beside Porter and they chatted about various subjects. One thing he still never discussed was his plans for the future. Misty continued to wonder, "Could I be somewhere in those plans?" The future was still a long way off for her and Kyle Morgan.

The Salem girls lost their first game by a 43 - 39 score. Porter had scored 26 points for her team, but didn't get much help from her teammates in the scoring column. Ann Mabry had chipped in with nine points.

The Eagles jumped out in front of the Wolves 31 - 9 at the end of the first quarter and poured it on until halftime for a 59 - 23 lead. Morgan led all scorers with 24 points at the intermission. He would finish with 36, Ellerson chipped in with 22 and Mentz threw in 21 points. Morgan had hit 14 of 15 field goal attempts and eight of eight from the foul line. It was an awesome display of shooting. The final score was 106 - 67, Eagles.

On the bus back to Ridgeview, Porter was somewhat disconsolate after the disheartening loss to their cross-town rival.

Morgan told her to "just put it aside and get them next time."

She smiled as she said, "You can bet on it, big guy."

The bus pulled out of the Salem High School parking lot at 5:15 p.m. the next night headed over to District-Heights. Only one week earlier the football team had played the Cougars for the state football championship. Now they were headed over to play their basketball team,

Porter took out her frustrations from the previous game loss at the expense of the Lady Cougars. She poured in 46 points as the Lady Eagles won easily 63 - 29.

When the Eagles took the floor, shouts of "revenge" came from the Cougar stands. Not on this night! Morgan put on a shooting clinic, finishing with 36 points. Ellerson had 24, and Mentz chipped in with 18. The Salem starters went to the bench with five minutes left in the game. The final score was 103 - 58. The most exciting play of the game was a pass to the rim by Hogan that Morgan had went about a foot above the basket, caught the ball with one hand and slammed it down through the basket. The play had brought the house down. Ellerson had two dunks and Mentz got his first of the season early in the third period.

On the way back to Ridgeview, Porter turned to Morgan, sitting beside her and asked him, "You think you could teach me to dunk the ball?"

They both laughed!

Chapter Twenty-One
A Big Decision

After basketball practice on Monday most of the team went by the Mentz Pharmacy snack shop. Morgan had come to the conclusion that James Mentz was a nice guy. He was an above-average student that was a four sport participant. He played on the football team, basketball team, track team and baseball team. As he and Morgan sat and talked, he gave off an impression that his goal was college basketball with a degree in pharmacy. He planned on carrying on the family tradition. Morgan thought that made good sense. The family pharmacy would probably be left to him someday. It was a good business.

When he heard other people talk about their plans for the future, it brought out a feeling of envy in the mind of Morgan. He had plans to go one of two directions after his senior year. He would go on to college to play basketball and participate in track or, if drafted by a professional baseball team, turn pro immediately. He really didn't know at the time just which direction he would go. He was still batting it about in his mind.

One thing was for sure with him. He would not go with the Central Intelligence Agency. He had watched his dad hang in there over the years and have to do things that he totally abhorred. But one thing was certain about his father's situation. He admired his dedication and loyalty to the agency. He was currently set to gain ownership of twelve

Morgan Restaurant's upon his twenty-first birthday. The trust was already completed. It was estimated his income off these stores would be over $10 million per year. He was not in any danger of needing to pursue a career that was not to his liking. He would have the ability to choose exactly what he wanted to do. Not many people were blessed with that opportunity.

When he arrived at home that night, his mother told him that Ben Curruth of Revele Records had called earlier. He would call back around 8:00 p.m. He said he needed to talk with him.

It was just after that time when Morgan picked up the phone. "Hello, Kyle, Ben Curruth. Do you have a few moments?" Curruth asked..

Morgan answered, "Yes Sir!" "What can I do for you?"

Curruth told him, "Our company has made a decision to release your record. You need to come in next Saturday, if possible, and we'll finalize the deal. You can bring your attorney if desired."

Morgan replied, "I'll bring my Dad, he'll help me with all the decision making process."

Curruth asked, "Is 11:00 a.m. a good time for you?"

Morgan told him he felt that time would be acceptable. If there was a problem he would get back with him the next day.

After hanging up the phone, he ran it by his father. Ken Morgan had no problem going with his son and working out the details of a record release with the recording company. One thing he did want Kyle to do was let him hear the songs he was supposed to be making a decision on.

Morgan complied with his request as he walked over to the piano.

Afterward, Mr. Morgan told his son, "I knew you were good on gospel songs, but I had no idea you could sing like that. We'll back you all the way if you want to take a shot at the singing profession." He then asked Kyle, "Will this get in the way of your high school sports priorities?"

Kyle answered, "No Dad, I'll quit the music stuff if it does. You know I have to participate in sports."

His father nodded as he smiled at Kyle's mother and said, "Well, it looks like we'll have a rock and roll singer in the house."

Later that night, Dawson Creek came into the Salem gym and played the Lady Eagles a close game before succumbing 44 - 36. They had double-teamed Porter most of the night and held her to 28 points.

As Morgan jogged onto the floor, he told her, "Ya'll just Win!, Win!, Win!"

She yelled back at him, "We're the best basketball team in this school!"

Morgan laughed as he began the pre-game lay-up drill.

The Wildcats were not much competition for the much taller Eagles. By halftime, Ellerson had 22 points, while Morgan had 16. The Eagles ran out to a 53 - 21 lead. They would end their night midway through the fourth period with 29 and 26 points respectively. Mentz threw in 11 and Cobb had 10 in the 104 - 59 win. Mentz had blocked eight shots in an awesome defensive display.

Another easy win came against East Ridgeview Friday night as Morgan exploded for 42 points, while Ellerson had 24. Mentz chipped in 15 points. The Lady Eagles had demolished the Lady Trojans by a 65 - 38 score. Porter had played only three quarters and scored 35 points. Connie Hollis had her best night with 18 points. The Lady Eagles were currently ranked at number 10 in the state while the Eagle boys came in at number five.

Kyle and Ken Morgan pulled into the Revele Records parking lot at 10:45 a.m. on Saturday morning.

Ben Curruth was already in the office when they arrived.

He said the demonstration record had been a big success with the in-the-know company people and they wanted to make him a contract offer. The offer was $100,000 on a three-year deal that would pay him 40 percent of all record sales. Revele Records would get 40 percent with the other 20 percent going into recording cost, advertising and administrative cost. It called for a minimum of three recordings each year of songs written by Morgan. There would be a minimum of three personal appearances specified in the contract to be established by Morgan each contract year. After one year, a possible album would be negotiated if any of his records had achieved one-million in sales.

Ken Morgan looked over the contract and had no problem with it. He wanted a clause in it that specified that Kyle could void the contract with a $100,000 buyout if he decided he wanted to leave the recording business.

Curruth agreed. There was also a provision on movie rights that stated that Revele Records would not be involved in any negotiations involving motion-picture rights nor have any claim to revenue derived from any motion-picture rights. Both parties signed the agreement and the Morgan's started their trip back home.

He had been assured his record would be released within the next 30 days. He smiled at his father and said, "I don't think it'll do very well, Dad."

His father replied, "You never know until you give it a try. Now, what are you going to do with a $100,000?"

Morgan laughed as he said, "It's getting close to Christmas, Maybe I'll buy Mom and Misty a set of ear rings?" They both laughed as they continued on their way.

The Salem High School basketball squads would close out their before Christmas schedule with easy wins over Rock-Hill. The girls won 59 - 43 with Porter netting 31 points. The boys rolled over Rock-Hill by a 104 - 59 score. Morgan led the team with 28 points, while Ellerson threw in 24. Both the boys and girls had 11 - 1 records as they prepared for the Christmas Holiday break. The Eagle boys were ranked number 3 in the state with the girls in at number 6.

It was on a Monday, December nineteenth, that young Morgan and his mom went shopping for Christmas Gifts for family and friends. Kyle had decided to give Misty a gold-plated charm bracelet with 31 charms on it along with a 10-carat diamond pendent. The bracelet had a charm for every point she was averaging on the basketball team. It had cost over $700. His gift to his mother was a diamond necklace with a price tag of over $900. He purchased his father a set of diamond cuff links and a diamond studded tie clasp with a price tag of over $450.

His mother asked, "What's going on with this diamond buying spree?"

Kyle answered back, "It's just something I want to do."

The church was having a Christmas Dinner on the Sunday before Christmas. The Porter and Morgan families attended the event together.

It was a time of good food, developing friendships and the singing of Christmas Carols.

On the way back to his home, Morgan thought back to past Christmas seasons. He had always loved the season with all the color and cheerfulness.

He had received several Christmas Cards from friends back in Georgia. He had not thought much about his time back there with all the happenings going on in his new home-place. He thought about visiting the local mall and getting some Christmas Cards off to all those that had sent him one. Several more old friends popped into his mind that he also wanted to send cards.

Basketball practice would be every day at 2:00 p.m. for the girls and 4:00 p.m. for the boys. The only days they would not practice would be Christmas Eve and Christmas Day.

It was after supper on Christmas Eve when Kyle walked up to the front door of the Porter house. He had placed the charm bracelet under the Porter family tree the previous Saturday night. Misty had spent several moments trying to guess what it was. Morgan just let her ramble on without an indication of what it might be.

She was again throwing out guesses as to what the gift was when her father said, "Misty, you'll find out what it is tomorrow, sweetheart. Now let it go!"

She replied, "All I know is it had better be something nice after what I got him, or I'll give him a good whopping!"

Morgan smiled as he said, "You'll have to catch me first, Lady, and I run fairly fast."

Christmas morning, Porter opened the gift and quickly put the bracelet on her arm. A note with it explained the 31 charms as one for every point she was averaging on the basketball team. Also, there was a small basketball charm with the initials KM-20 along with a small charm bible with the initials MP on it. Misty Porter was happy with her Christmas gift from Morgan. She cheerfully told her mother and father, "I guess Kyle saved himself from a bad whopping."

Her Mother and father smiled as they continued to open presents.

Meanwhile ~ over at the Morgan residence, Kyle Morgan picked up the present from Misty and opened it. There was a note attached to the first item in the box that read, "It's hard to give something to somebody that has everything. Love you ~ Misty."

In the box was a football jersey with his name and number 20 on the back, ten comic books, four 45-rpm records and a small box that Kyle slowly opened. The box contained a small medal that read "Basketball Most Valuable ~ 1961-62 ~ Misty Porter." It was her "Most Valuable Player" medal award from last basketball season. Morgan would later try to get her to take it back. He realized this was something she probably cherished very much. When she told him she wanted him to have it, he bought a chain and wore it around his neck for the remainder of his junior year.

It was an enjoyable year for the Morgan clan. They welcomed in the New Year the following week with a luncheon for all their friends at the Eastside Cafeteria.

Afterward, all the men and Morgan classmates would watch the football bowl games on a new color television just above the main dining room. For many in attendance it was their first viewing of a colored set. Most of the women and young ladies would just sit around and chat about anything that came to mind. Misty Porter took delight in showing off her bracelet to all that wanted to see it.

At one point, Morgan walked by and asked Connie Hollis if she wanted to look at the Batman comic book Misty had given him for Christmas.

Porter shrieked back at Morgan, "I'll get you for that." Again, it was obvious that it was a joke among two teens that probably got along together as well as any two individuals possibly could.

Coach Shaw, Coach Breyer and all their staffs and families along with all the school administrators and their families attended the luncheon.

It consisted of a buffet style setting of chicken, steak, vegetables, deserts, and just about everything else a person could want. Some would stay on a while. Others would leave. All agreed that the Morgan family was indeed unique. They were about the most amazing family that had ever graced the city of Ridgeview. Most by now felt strongly that the town was indeed blessed with their presence.

Chapter Twenty-Two
A New Elvis ?

It was the first week of January, 1963. Mrs. Morgan was entering the living room when the phone rang. It was an excited Misty Porter who exclaimed, "My God!" Mrs. Morgan, I just heard Kyle on the radio. I can't believe it! He's a rock and roll singer! Is he at home? Can I speak with him?"

Mrs. Morgan explained that he and his father had left to visit one of the family restaurants. He would not be back until later. She said, "You can call the Eastside store and get him there. I think that's where they were going."

When Porter called the store, she was placed on hold as the younger Morgan was being sought.

"Hello," said Morgan as he answered the phone, "this is Kyle Morgan."

Porter said with a shriek, "You devil, why didn't you tell me you had made a record? I just heard it on the radio."

Morgan replied, "I wanted it to be a surprise to you."

She replied, "Well, it was that all right, I can't believe it."

Morgan told her, "I'll explain the recording situation to you when I get back home. I'll give you a call."

It was an excited Misty Porter that rejoined the group at the Mentz Pharmacy.

Her first knowledge of the Morgan record had indeed been a surprise. She and several of her friends were eating burgers and talking when Mrs. Mentz came over and told them, "They're playing a Kyle Morgan recording on the radio." As she and her friends listened to the song there were shrieks from the girls and cheering from the guys.

James Mentz chimed in, "Hey, he's pretty good!"

It was the second day of the record release. Morgan had not given it much thought up to this point. He told his dad as they made the return trip home what Misty had told him.

His father gazed at him and said, "You haven't told Misty you made a recording? I would have thought she would have been one of the first to know."

He answered back, "No Dad, I wanted to wait and let it be a surprise to her. I really haven't said anything about it to anyone."

Porter and her snack shop friends weren't the only people to hear the new record. Just about everyone in town was talking about the record release of Kyle Morgan.

All the teachers and students at Salem would smile and wave at him as he moved about in the hall and classroom. Kyle Morgan - the football hero - was suddenly a folk hero. There simply was not an end to the potentials and capabilities of young Mr. Morgan.

When Morgan was about 10-years-old he had become a serious rock 'n roll fan. He had stood in front of a mirror and emulated many of the top singers of the time. It was easy for him to remember the lyrics of all the various Top-10 hits as he heard them. He had not really developed a particular singing style, but knew that he liked a lot of movement as he performed a song. He felt he would need to work hard over the next few weeks to develop that certain style that defined him as a singer.

Plans were made by his record producer for him to be on two nationally syndicated television shows doing a song over the following two months.

One show spot was to be recorded on a Saturday morning at the recording station. The other was to be a live presentation on a Saturday night in New York on the American Good Time Hour show on CBS television.

Misty Porter went with the Morgan's on the New York trip. They would leave Ridgeview about 8:00 a.m. and make the 140-mile trip with an arrival in the Big Apple around 3:00 p.m. The show was at 8:00 p.m. that Saturday night.

Everyone in Ridgeview was tuned into that show.

When he was introduced to the live audience, he was somewhat surprised at the enthusiasm exhibited from the screaming mass. He went into his song and all agreed it was a good presentation. Morgan had performed on stage much like he did on the high school athletic field. With style and grace.

He had a little dance step he performed while singing that really brought emotion and sound from the teenage audience. Later, as he viewed a replay of the performance, he would see little things he could do to step up the excitement to even greater heights.

Young Morgan roomed with his father that night while Porter and his mother stayed in an adjacent room. They would head back home early the next day.

Lucille Morgan looked at the very pretty young brunette as she read from a magazine that was provided in the room by the hotel. She then spoke to her in the kind, motherly tone of voice that came to her so easily. "Misty, I just want you to know that Ken and I are very proud that you and Kyle have become such good friends. He has never been able to have anyone other than his father and me he could talk with and relate to. You and he get along so fabulously."

Porter replied, "Mrs. Morgan, your son is the most extraordinary person I have ever seen. He just defies the imagination. I'm just proud to be a small part of his life."

Mrs. Morgan answered her, "Misty, I think you are far more than just a small part of his life. I think you play a great part in the life of our son. Far more then you can imagine at the moment."

Misty Porter hugged Mrs. Morgan and said, "Thank you, Ma'am, I appreciate your telling me this."

Meanwhile, Morgan and his father sat in their room and talked for some time about the show. Mr. Morgan said, "You need a clothing style, unique to you. Something that sets you aside from all the other singers. You still want to keep the short hair, even with all the other singers having long hair?"

He answered, "Yes, I do, Dad. I don't want to be a copy of anyone or any style. I'll present the image of a high school student that participants in athletics. My main interest is still high school athletics at this time. Singing is the sideline activity for me."

Mr. Morgan replied, "I understand what you're saying and I agree. You do need to have your own personality and mannerisms."

As they made their way back to Ridgeview on that Sunday morning, Morgan was working on a new song. He would write a few lines and then sing it to Porter. There were a lot of laughs as she critiqued it as they moved along the freeway.

They stopped at a Morgan Cafeteria for lunch just inside the Maryland state line. Kyle dined on shrimp and seafood while his dad enjoyed a steak. Mrs. Morgan and Misty had vegetables and pasta.

It had been six years earlier when Ken Morgan had come up with the Morgan Cafeteria concept. He was in and out of town all the time with his government job. He decided to put together a venture that would provide a profession for the family. He came up with a restaurant after eating at a small diner in upstate Virginia that he really liked. He would model his establishment after that restaurant. From there everything just fell into place.

The Morgan Cafeterias were all built in much the same style. They were large buildings with huge dining halls, meeting and private rooms with all tools and materials needed to conduct training seminars and classes. All were neatly landscaped and had a distinct frontal style that set them aside from any other at the time.

The cuisine was mostly of southern origin with a combination of Louisiana Cajan, South Georgia and Florida deliquesces. Spicy foods with the New Orleans taste, beef and pork cooked in a southern bar-b-que style or thick, luscious steaks from six-ounces to forty-eight ounces with all the trimmings. There was also seafood brought in from the shores of Florida. The Morgan Restaurant was one of the first in the nation to feature a salad bar with virtually every vegetable known to man. It was a family style eating experience that literally took off. Four months after opening his first restaurant he opened three more. The business began to grow in leaps and bounds. While now all the Morgan Franchises were in the south and on the east coast, there was still the desire to grow. Now almost seven years and 46 stores later he was looking at carrying the chain national.

Ken Morgan was not recognized by anyone at the restaurant. The manager was not in on the Sunday shift, so no one there knew the owner was a customer in the store. All went well. The waitresses were all friendly and provided the necessary service to them during the lunch experience. The dining room was elegant and provided a good dining experience. Afterward, Ken Morgan tipped the young waitress a five-dollar bill.

She put it in her pocket and thanked him.

He smiled and said, "I appreciate your hospitality. You people have been very nice."

It was two weeks later that the waitress saw a picture of Mr. Morgan in a company newsletter and recognized him as the man that had been in the restaurant that day. She still remembered that five-dollar tip. She quickly told her manager, who called the corporate office in Ridgeview and asked to speak with Mr. Morgan.

When the Morgan Restaurant owner moved to Ridgeview, he had leased office space at a downtown location. He brought in a franchise general manager, a secretary, an accounting staff and purchasing manager.

There were now about 30 employees that worked out of that corporate office. He would visit the office on occasion and hold regular meetings with the general manager. His secretary was updated daily on ways to contact the company president in emergency situations or in times of need.

The call from Hollis was transferred to Mr. Morgan's home.

"Hello Michael," said Morgan as he picked up the phone, "it's good to hear from you." Michael Hollis was the restaurant manager of the Camden Plaza Restaurant where the Morgan's and Misty Porter had dined that day.

After several moments, in which Morgan explained he was just passing through the area, the conversation ended. Hollis seemed relieved his restaurant visit was not an audit or specific problem solving mission.

Ken Morgan did visit his restaurants on a fairly consistent basis. He had quarterly meetings with all his store managers to review performance. He kept all profitability statements before him and always knew how well a store was doing from a performance standpoint. He firmly believed in training for all his managers and their staff. It was mandatory that all his directs and middle management would attend various seminars and training classes. He paid his employees well and treated them well in the area of benefits and work environment. He had his hand in virtually every decision that was made in the huge Morgan Cafeteria corporate structure.

Over the last several months, the elder Morgan had been training his son on all the specifics of running a restaurant business. He was capable of handling just about any situation that might arise during the daily operation of the business.

Mr. Morgan had plans to take the business national over the next two years. International expansion was considered a strong possibility sometime in the future.

Now Kyle Morgan had added record recording and quest appearances to his already full schedule of high school athletic participation, learning the family business and just being a growing and maturing teenager.

Ken Morgan often thought to himself, "How long can he go on like this?" He suddenly remembered that his son was not your everyday teenager. The local newspaper had called him a high school super-star. To Ken Morgan he was just a super-star son.

Chapter Twenty-Three
New Year ~ Same Results

When school resumed after the Christmas and New Year Holidays, the Eagle boys and girls teams continued to pile up the victories. The boys romped past West Calvert 97 - 44 with Ellerson erupting for 36 points. They blew by Mitchell County 106 - 63 with Morgan scoring 33 points. They popped West Ridgeview 99 - 68 with Morgan again the high point man with 31 points. Finally on January 10, they destroyed Murphy 106 - 63. James Mentz had a season high with 28 points, while Ellerson had 26. Eight of his baskets were dunks.

The girls won all four games easily with Porter scoring over 30 points in all games. She was now averaging over 32 points per game for the season. The Eagle boys were the number one ranked Class AAAA team in the State with the girls ranked second.

Now the states number one ranked AAA team and the number one ranked team in the nation was coming to town. On Friday night, January 13, the Eagles and Galveston would meet for the second time this season. The last time they played the Eagles were without, Morgan, Mentz and Cobb, who were playing football. Galveston had won that game easily. Their winning streak had reached 82 games. A Maryland record. A record crowd was expected including as many as 25 college head coaches. The game was at the Eagles Nest and a new all-time attendance record was expected. Temporary bleachers were installed everywhere possible in the gym to accommodate an overflow crowd.

The Salem head coach stood back and watched his team practice on the day before the crucial game. There wasn't a lot he could tell them. They knew the stakes. To defeat Galveston would seal their standing as the best team in the state and maybe the best team in the nation, but a loss would not throw out the possibility of a AAAA state title. Coach Breyer wanted his team to look at it as a crucial game, but still stay focused on winning that state title in their classification.

Coaches Breyer and Powers shouted instructions as the team worked on the fast break with a zone press after every score. The Salem coaches never failed to be amazed at what they were seeing on the court.

Morgan was a work of art on the basketball court. He handled the ball like it was a part of him. His peripheral vision enabled him to instantly spot teammates anywhere on the court. His quick-thinking mind would tell him the best pass or option to allow an open shot to the basket. On many occasions a behind-the-back pass or deceptive shovel or bounce pass would find an open teammate for an easy lay-up. When he went up to shoot he would be far above the outstretched arms of the defender. He used either hand as needed to allow him the best opportunity to put the ball into the basket. He was so quick off his first step and had such tremendous quickness and straight-up speed he usually left his defender far behind as he went about his business of either scoring or setting up a teammate for a score.

Morgan had started playing basketball in the youth leagues at the age of six. He seemed to always be able to score at will. He had a great ability to bank the ball off the backboard at this early age. By the time he was in the sixth grade he could stand under the backboard, jump up, and touch the rim. By grade eight, as a six-footer, he could stand flat-footed underneath the basket, jump straight up and dunk the ball with either or both hands.

He also could hit from anywhere on the court shooting left-handed or right-handed. He started at guard as a freshman for his 23 - 6 region-champion team averaging over 34 points per game. As a sophomore he had averaged 32 points per game on a 29 - 3 state- champion team. Two of the three losses were to the Georgia Class AAAAA State Champion.

One of those losses was an 89 - 86 loss where he had scored 61 points to establish a new state Class AA scoring record. At one point during the season he had hit 83 consecutive foul shots, missed one, then hit another 41 in a row. He was a 98-percent shooter from the foul line up to the moment. Almost as consistent as he was at kicking extra points on the gridiron. He had also hit 29-consecutive field goals over a two-game stretch (17 in one game) that had been featured in a nationally syndicated sports magazine.

He was not expected to average 30 points per game with the unusually talented Eagle team that featured three of the finest scorers in the state. Not many people doubted that he could if he took the shots, but there was just so much talent on the team it was highly unlikely. Already this season, he had hit 123 foul shots in a row at a recent practice session. He was as close to perfection from the foul line as anyone at any level of the sport at the time.

Morgan considered basketball as his favorite sport. He honestly felt that if you could excel on the basketball court you could be an asset in any team sport. He had a personal rule about dunking the ball. He would dunk only if it increased the percentage of making the shot. It could never be just to play to the crowd. If wide open he would just lay the ball in the basket, or kiss it gently off the back board. He had never missed an uncontested lay-up. He was not into showboating or in any way embarrassing the opposition. Every move he made on the court was employed to help his team win.

Eagle Coach David Breyer did not spend a great deal of time working with his starting team on fundamentals. He saw the talent level that had been handed to him by fate and just primarily let it take its own course. He managed the game and situations in the games as they came up. He tried to impress upon his young players that what they were seeing from Morgan, Ellerson, Mentz and Cobb were God given talents that had been honed with hard work and dedication. He stressed the importance of that hard work ideology. He seldom mentioned Morgan when referencing ways to accomplish positive results on the court to his kids. What Morgan could do was unique. He didn't want to create frustration in his younger players by having them try to emulate plays that only the super quick and high flying high school super-star could accomplish.

Coach Powers would work with Morgan and Hogan on various passing drills. Morgan continuously did the impossible on the court. He could make unbelievable assists to his teammates. He could thread the needle on a precision pass to a teammate breaking for the basket or rifle the ball the length of the court to set up an easy lay-up. He made blind passes that were unbelievable to say the least.

His ability to hang in the air was a breathless experience for those that witnessed it. He would leave the floor at the foul line, and be so high he could look all around the floor for the open player. After several double clutches, he would flip the ball gently off the backboard directly into the basket, or make the easy outlet assist pass. The Salem fans were constantly amazed at the skills being demonstrated by not only Morgan, but by the play of Mentz and Ellerson. The boundless skills of these high school basketball players simply boggled the mind.

Now it was time to cut bait. Was Vince Stevens or Kyle Morgan the best guard in the state? Head Basketball Coach Jerry Farris of Winston State University already thought he knew the answer to that question. He had seen Morgan play in the Georgia State AA tourney the previous year while looking at another player that was high on the Leopards recruiting list. He had seen him score 36 points in a semi-final game. He had written his name down as a player to watch in the future. Now he was in the stands to watch Stevens of Galveston, but he was interested in seeing how much progress the former Georgia high school sensation had made in the past year.

There was a tradition unlike any you had ever seen at the Eagles home game warm-ups. Fans would throw dimes onto the floor as a ball went through the basket. Six elementary school kids each game were assigned to have the responsibility to pick up the coins as they came out of the stands. The dimes were theirs to keep. Someone made the comment that Morgan, Mentz and Ellerson were costing the Eagle fans a lot of money that season. Ball after ball swished through the nets from the three Salem shooters.

As the National Anthem was played by the Eagle band, Morgan looked into the stands. He had never seen so many people packed into a gym. It brought back memories of the state-title football game with District-Heights earlier in the school year. He hoped it would feature the same winning results.

Chapter Twenty-Four
Hack that Hawk !

In the girls game, it was the usual story. The Galveston Lady Hawks double-teamed Porter the entire game. She hit time-and-time again from the top of the key to score 36 points and dominated the defensive backboards as her team won 61 to 48. Connie Hollis had scored 11 and Jen Shaw had played a good game at the point. She scored nine points with eight assists.

As Morgan and his teammates walked toward the locker room to get dressed, well-wishers lined the hallway. You could see the excitement in the eyes of the Salem supporters. There was this tremendous hope that this team could realize the impossible dream and beat the greatest team ever to play on Maryland soil.

Mr. Morgan had told Kyle before he left the house to "just play your game, go with the flow early and take over the game late if the game is still close." That was a good strategy. Morgan was literally capable of taking over a game.

The pre-game environment was similar to just about all the previous games of the season. No one seemed uptight or to be pressing. It was obvious that all the team was focused. Morgan thought to himself as he trotted onto the floor for pre-game warm-ups that if Galveston did beat them, they would simply be the best team. He had never seen a team so ready to play.

The dimes rained down on the team from the stands as they took pre-game warm-ups. He looked in the stands and saw Porter toss a dime his way and yell, "This is one for good luck, super-star." He just smiled at her and went on about his pre-game preparations.

As the teams lined up for the jump at mid-court the gym was so loud that all the players looked into the stands at the tremendously festive atmosphere. It was a happening. All the players knew this.

Mentz jumped at center and tapped the ball to Hogan, who brought it across the time line. The ball floated around the top of the key for about 25 seconds before Morgan let the ball fly toward the hoop on an 18-foot jumper. It swished the net. The action was officially underway.

Vince Stevens was an awesome basketball player. He was probably the best opponent Morgan had ever went up against on a basketball court. He was cat quick with great leaping ability. He penetrated so quickly that even Morgan was amazed at how well he handled the ball and controlled the flow of the game.

The first quarter was primarily a swapping of baskets with Stevens draining several long jumpers and scoring on two driving lay-ups. He had 11 points the first quarter, while Ellerson had eight and Morgan six for the Eagles. The first quarter score saw the Hawks with a 21 - 20 lead.

The second quarter was much of the same. The quick Hawk players were amazing shooters. They hit constantly from around the circle and every time they penetrated it seemed like there was a whistle for a foul. Midway through the second quarter, James Mentz picked up his third foul trying to guard Stevens one-on-one.

Coach Breyer called a time-out. "Go to a 2-1-2 zone. Mentz in the middle. If they get the ball in there, let them have the basket and then get it back on the other end. Don't foul," instructed the coach.

With 0:17 seconds left in the first half, Stevens hit a fast break lay-up to put his team up by 46 - 45. It gave him 22 points for the game.

Morgan brought the ball down and drove toward the basket with 0:06 seconds left. He jumped high in the air and kissed the ball off the backboard, points 16 and 17 of the game.

Salem led at intermission by a score of 47 - 46.

Jack Ellerson had scored 16 points for the Eagles.

Coach Breyer wanted more penetration the second half. The Hawks 1-3-1 zone was suffocating the Eagles inside game. Cobb was virtually left out of the offense, with Mentz being denied the ball on most trips down the court. Morgan was being double teamed almost every time he touched the ball. Ellerson was being doubled anytime he was within 10 to 12-feet of the basket.

The Eagle coach gave his instructions, "Morgan, bring the ball down every chance you get. Take the shot or look for something inside. Try and get to the foul line. We're going to need points."

Morgan nodded that he understood the directions and moved toward the door of the locker room.

The third quarter saw Morgan take control of the game for the first six minutes. He started looking for the outside jumper and it was obvious the Hawks had no one that could jump high enough to prevent his jump shot. He scored 11 points in the first six minutes of the quarter as Salem built a 68-61 lead.

Stevens brought the Hawks back quickly with two long jumpers and a driving lay-up that drew a foul from Hogan. After converting his foul shot he had 36 points with just over a minute left in the third quarter.

An Ellerson foul shot and Mentz basket kept the Eagles out front by a 78 - 75 score as the third quarter came to an end.

The Eagles turned up the heat early in the fourth as Morgan, on four-consecutive trips down the court, converted four foul shots and made two baskets. The Hawks were forced into three turnovers in the next three minutes that saw three baskets scored by Morgan and one by Ellerson.

The shot that brought the house down occurred with 2:28 left in the game and Salem out front by an 91 - 83 score. Morgan stole the ball from the Galveston point guard at mid-court. He took the ball to the basket, went high for a slam dunk, and was fouled in the act. The foul shot by Morgan with 1:26 left made it Eagles 94 and Hawks 83.

Stevens would not give up as he took the ball to the hoop and drew a shooting foul. His two foul shots with 1:18 left made it 94 - 85 Eagles.

For the remainder of the game, Morgan would control the ball for the Eagles. He took the inbounds pass and was immediately fouled.

He made the two foul shots for his forty-first and forty-second points of the game, giving Salem a 96 - 89 lead.

A miss by Stevens on the other end of the court saw Cobb get the rebound and quickly get it over to Morgan. He was immediately fouled. He again went to the foul line with 0:29 seconds left in the game and made two more foul shots to spread the lead to 98 - 89.

The inbounds pass was intercepted by Morgan with 0:23 seconds left and he was again fouled. Two more foul shots made it 100 - 89.

The game ended with a miss by the Hawks and another Cobb rebound. The outlet pass went to Morgan, who dribbled out the last 0:11 seconds of the game.

Morgan had scored 46 points, Ellerson gave strong support with 28 points, and Mentz had added 11 points.

Stevens had scored 44 points in a valiant effort to keep his Hawk team undefeated. On this night the Salem Eagles were the better team.

It was pandemonium as the hometown fans rushed onto the court. The Eagles had established themselves as the team to beat in the All-State Tournament to be held later in the season. Most sports writers were conceding the AAAA state title to the Eagles after this game. One thing was for sure. The two best teams in the state and maybe the nation had battled it out and the odds were good they would meet for a third time later on in the season.

Morgan had been 14 for 14 from the foul line. He now had hit 94 consecutive foul shots and had missed only two foul shots for the season. He was also 16 of 18 from the field in the game. It was quite an exhibition of basketball prowess that left the college basketball coaches almost speechless as to the potential of the Salem guard.

In the Salem Locker room, Coach Breyer told his team, "We have five regular season games left and then the region tournament. We can't afford a letdown."

Afterwards, as the Salem coaches sat in the gym office, they chatted about playing more youngsters during the remainder of the season to get them some experience. There was not a team left on the Eagle schedule that could come within 40 points of them if they were allowed to play all out.

The Salem girls were to meet the only team that had beaten them the next night at home against West Ridgeview. It was a nip n' tuck game that saw it tied at 38 - 38 at the end of regulation. West Ridgeview had played a slow-down game that kept the ball out of Porter's hands as much as possible. She still had accounted for 26 of the 38 points during regulation. The overtime saw it come down to the wire.

With 0:12 seconds left in the game and Salem with the ball, Jen Shaw took the inbounds pass from Connie Hollis. She drove the left side of the court, tossed the ball back to Porter at the top of the key for the 16-foot jump shot. It split the cords with 0:02 seconds left. Time expired with the Lady Eagles winners by a 46 - 44 score. Porter had scored 34 points.

The boys blew past West Ridgeview 97 - 64.

The wins kept coming as the boys closed out their season with wins over Rock-Hill, Dawson Creek, Chesapeake City and District-Heights. None were close. The Eagles scored 121 points against Rock-Hill. Their final season record was 21 wins and one loss.

The W.E. Salem Eagles were the number one ranked boys team in class AAAA and in the overall rankings for the state of Maryland.

The Lady Eagles rolled over the same opponents easily with only a 59 - 48 win over Chesapeake City being reasonably close. Misty Porter had scored 49 points against Rock-Hill to establish a new Salem scoring record. The Lady Eagles were the number one rated AAAA team in the state and were the number three team in all state rankings with an identical record to the boys. 21 wins and one loss.

The boys region tournament started on Tuesday night , January 31 with a first round match-up with Murphy. The Eagles won easily with Ellerson scoring 33 points in a 104 - 67 game. Lopsided wins over District-Heights and East Ridgeview followed as the Eagles easily won the region title.

The Lady Eagles had two easy wins over Dawson Creek and Murphy, followed by a reasonably close 61 - 55 win over cross-town rival East Ridgeview. It was the first time the Salem boys and girls had ever won the region in the same year.

In their last and only trip to the state tourney in 1948, the Eagles had been beaten 81 - 49 in the first game by Aldridge High School.

All agreed it was unlikely this same scenario would be played out on this trip.

The Lady Eagles last trip to the state was in 1956. They had also lost in the first round to a good East Lansing team by a 61 - 53 score. For the season Misty Porter had averaged 32.50. She was the leading scorer in the state regardless of classification. Jen Shaw had averaged over eight assists per game. It was a solid team that was expected to give a good account of itself in the state tournament.

Chapter Twenty-Five
On To The State

The state tournament for both boys and girls would be in Baltimore at the Civic Arena.

Both teams would leave Ridgeview on Tuesday evening at 4:00 p.m. for the Perimeter Center Hotel. They would stay there as long as they remained in the tournament.

As Morgan entered the bus, he was munching on some grapes. Porter sat beside him as they spent most of the trip to Baltimore talking about his new song "My Dream." He had recorded it the past Saturday. Morgan felt it was the best song he had ever written.

Porter agreed it was his best ever. She felt it would be a chart buster.

Virtually all the players parents and town dignitaries would attend the state tournament. It was their first since the 1956 girls had made the tourney. The boys had been to only one prior tournament. That was in 1948. Neither Eagle basketball team had ever won a state-tournament game before.

The girls would open with the Miller County Pelicans on Wednesday at 7:00 p.m. followed by the boys game at 8:30 p.m.

Porter put on a show in that first game. She scored 52 points on 19 of 26 from the field and 14 of 15 from the foul line. The Lady Eagles won easily 72 - 56.

The Eagles met the Denton Rockets and blew by them by a 102 - 67 score. Mentz scored 33 points, Ellerson 24. Morgan had taken only three shots the second half and scored 18 for the game. He constantly set up open shots for Mentz and Ellerson and finished with 21 assists.

On Thursday evening at 4:00 p.m. the Lady Eagles beat Wilkes County 59 - 44 behind 28 points by Porter. Connie Hollis had 18. Jen Shaw had 11 assists.

In the 8:30 p.m. game, the East Marshville Terrapins were outclassed by the taller Eagles by a 96 - 77 score as Morgan again turned offensive and poured in 32 points to pace the Eagle attack.

On Friday evening at 4:00 p.m. the Lady Eagles faced the Richland Lady Leopards. They were the state runner-up the previous season and were rated number two just behind the Lady Eagles in the final state rankings. It was a physical contest with the bulkier and more aggressive Richland team literally beating Porter to death. She was pounded every time she went to the basket and hammered on the defensive boards. The depth of the Lady Leopards wore down the smaller Lady Eagles and saw Richland win a 72 - 61 game. Porter had scored 44 points, with 16 of them coming from the foul line.

As the Eagles ran on the floor for their game with Case Academy, Morgan stopped and hugged Porter briefly. He whispered in her ear, "It'll be all right, you were great. Ya'll have nothing to be ashamed of. Keep your head up. I'll see you after the game." The tears continued to flow as she walked away toward her mother and father.

Case Academy was one of the smallest teams in the tournament. It was evident early on they could not match up with the taller Eagles. James Mentz had 29 points and Ellerson added 23 as the Eagles blasted them by a 106 - 68 score. Morgan had 16 assists to go with his 16 points. He took only 7 shots.

That night Porter, Morgan, Cobb and Cindy Gray sat in the stands and watched as the Kanapolis Knights beat Mt. Evans 83 - 79 to advance to the finals against the Eagles.

Coaches Breyer and Powers came over and pointed out the speed of the Knight point guard as he consistently beat the Mt. Evans defender down the floor and set up easy scores for his teammates. Chip Meade was the highest ranked point guard in Maryland. He was headed for Southwest Virginia on a scholarship.

Back at the hotel, Ken Morgan knocked on his sons door.

Walter Hogan, Morgan's roommate answered the door. "Good to see you Walter, you played a good game tonight," said the elder Morgan.

"Thank you, Mr. Morgan," said Hogan as he exited the room.

"Hi, Dad," greeted Morgan.

"Hello. Son. Good game tonight," said Mr. Morgan.

"Thanks, Dad," replied young Morgan. For the next hour they talked about various subjects before Mr. Morgan left the room.

Kyle Morgan sat down on the foot of his bed. His thoughts drifted back to the look of disappointment he had seen in the eyes of Misty Porter after the loss that afternoon. He tried to realize how she felt after such a disheartening loss. He found himself wishing he was with her to console her. He suddenly had come to the realization that he really did think a great deal of Misty Porter. She had been very quiet during the game they watched together that night. He knew she was hurting. She was a competitor much like him. The girls had won 26 games with only 2 losses. It was a good season, but it had not turned out the way she wanted it to. She did not like to lose. He briefly wondered what he might feel like should his team lose in the championship game the following night. He concluded that he had to do whatever it took to prevent such an occurrence. His final thoughts before turning in for the night was that he might call her, then he decided against it. It was about 11:30 p.m. before Morgan turned in for the night.

The state championship game the next night was really never close. Morgan put on a shooting clinic with 52 points for the game. He was 21 of 24 from the field and 10 of 10 from the foul line. With four minutes left in the game the Eagles led 98 - 65. Coach Breyer pulled his starting five from the game and put Tate Manning in at the point. He put seniors Gene Downing, Richard Howell, and Dan Richmond in to play the rest of the game. Larry Phillips, Rip Steel, John Winters and Harvey Meadows would also get some playing time.

The final score was 107 - 76. The William Edward Salem Golden Eagles were the 1962-63 Class AAAA State Champions.

In the locker room, Coach Breyer gazed over his team and said, "I want you to know, I expected this since early in the season. I also expected us to meet Galveston again in the State All-Classification

Tournament. I just learned that Galveston has won their second consecutive Class AAA tournament. We'll get to see them again next week at College Park."

A loud roar went up from the Eagles. They didn't have a problem meeting Galveston again. Another win over the Hawks would solidify their standing as the best high school team in America. Kyle Morgan had known since seeing the Hawks for the first time that the State All-Classification Title would run through Galveston.

On Sunday, a motorcade left Baltimore heading back to Ridgeview. They would stop off at the Ridgeview First Baptist Church where there would be a brief prayer meeting at 11:00 p.m. before the regular service. Everyone in that motorcade stopped at the church and stayed through the prayer service.

At school on Monday morning there was an assembly in the gym to honor the basketball teams --- boys and girls , for their exceptional seasons.

All the coaches and school administrators had their say. All spoke highly of the respect earned for the school by their highly skilled basketball squads.

Morgan was asked to speak to the student body. He walked to the microphone and said, "On behalf of our boys team I want to thank you for your support this past season. We could not have asked for more support and enthusiasm than you people provided for us all season." He then paused and said, "I'm disappointed we were not able to bring home a girls state title this season, but I feel confident that Misty Porter, Jen Shaw and the Lady Eagles will join us next year in celebrating state titles at the conclusion of the state tournaments." The Gym went bonkers.

Misty Porter was invited up by Principle Collins along with both teams. They stood hand-in-hand as the school anthem was played by the Eagle band.

Morgan raised his hand to quite the boisterous crowd and said, "We still have a task to complete. We have Galveston waiting for us this weekend. We are going to play in what is being billed as the greatest high school game in Maryland history. We know we will have your support over in College Park. Thank you and may God bless all our Golden Eagle Family."

As they were making their way back to the class room, Porter turned to Morgan and said, "You know you should go into politics, don't you? You spin a great line."

Morgan smiled and said, "You know you're not just a good basketball player, Lady, but you're mighty good looking, too." This statement it seems, had turned into his standard greatest compliment to his mother and best girl friend.

A shocked Porter feigned astonishment as she answered, "Why, Mister Morgan, that's about the nicest thing you ever said to me." They both laughed as she turned and entered the door to her home economics class.

Chapter Twenty-Six
The Rematch

The Maryland All-Classification Tournament was considered one of the premier high school events in America. Over the last 15 years the winner of the tourney had been crowned the National High School Champion eight times. Last year Galveston had won the honor. Currently the top two teams in America were the Salem Eagles and the Galveston Hawks.

The Class A champion Lloyd County Warriors would meet the AAAA State-Champion Salem Eagles in game one at 5:30 p.m. of the two-day tournament at College Park. The Class AAA Galveston Hawks would meet the class AA Martis Academy Red Devils in the 8:30 finale. Girls games were scheduled at 5:30 and 7:00 p.m.

College scouts and coaches from all over the nation would attend the game. It was televised statewide and on station WWLZ out of New York City.

The Vince Stevens story has been touched upon. While he was an exceptional player, he was just a cog in the whole scheme of things for the Galveston Hawks. At point guard for the Hawks, the only non-senior on the team had started since his freshman year. He was instrumental in helping them win their back-to-back class AAA titles and the last state all-class tournament. Jimmy Watts was an exceptional and unselfish basketball player.

The Galveston team was a team of All-State stars. Jerry Hall played guard opposite Vince Stevens in their 1-2-2 offense. He could literally fill the basket up from the outside. He was their second leading scorer with an 18.6 average per game.

Ron Eddy was a six-foot-five-inch center that was as physical as anyone in the country. He would literally climb the backboard to get a rebound. He was a ferocious defender with a soft touch on jump shots from around the perimeter. He averaged 14.5 points per game.

Butch Cobb had said after playing the Hawks earlier, "I had rather play against anyone in the state than Eddy. He takes everything I give and gives back double."

Mike Rison was a six-foot-four-inch forward that was a slasher and driver. He averaged around 10 points per game, but could score big if needed.

Of course, Vince Stevens and his 26-point average was what made the team go. He was rated as the best high school basketball player on the Eastern Seaboard and had over 80 colleges interested in offering him a scholarship.

Lloyd County had little hope against the Eagles. The Class A champs were a scrappy little team, but the bigger Eagles simply played volleyball on the backboards and kept tapping at the ball until it went in. At half time it was out of hand at 56 - 29. The final score was 108 - 74. Butch Cobb had his biggest game of the year with 22 points. Ellerson had 17 in a little over half the game. Mentz had 12 points while Morgan scored only 15. He took only four shots in the three quarters he played.

Galveston demolished Martis Academy, the AA champs by a 96 - 64 score. Stevens scored 31 in less than three quarters.

The stage was set.

Anticipation was high as the Eagles took the floor against the Hawks for the State of Maryland All-Classification Championship.

Galveston threw a surprise at the Eagles early when they came out in a tight man-to-man defense. Stevens was head-up on Morgan. It was some kind of battle in the open court. The super-quick Stevens was bothering Morgan with his swipes and touches of the ball as he tried to get the ball down the court. The referee's were letting them play a little more aggressively than usual. The game was being played all over the court. It was man-to-man from throw-in to possession completion. Neither team could get much of a rhythm going. Galveston was also deploying some stall tactics on offense. They were playing for completely open jump shots or lay-ups. At the end of the first quarter the score was Galveston 9 and the Eagles 8.

Morgan had scored only two points on two shots.

Stevens had four points for Galveston.

The second quarter opened up a little as Morgan began to assert his height on the shorter Stevens. He would pull up at the mid-court line and give the ball to Hogan, who easily beat Watts to almost any spot on the court.

Coach Breyer called time out with 4 minutes left in the half.

"All right guys, time to let her rip," said the Salem head coach. "Morgan, move to the foul line, Ellerson, take the right wing. Mentz and Cobb on the low post. Hogan, bring the ball down and go inside ---- first to Morgan or Mentz, then work outside to Ellerson for the drive or jumper."

In four minutes Morgan lit up the nets for 12 points on turn-around jumpers and added two assists to Mentz for lay-ups.

The score at the half was Salem 33 and Galveston 29.

The second half became more of a run 'n' gun as Morgan continued to light it up around the basket. He would take the pass from Hogan, spin and jump high into the air. He would either pass off to a breaking teammate or pop the jumper before coming back to the floor. His hang-time was astounding. He scored 11 of the Eagles 15 points in the third period.

The score at the end of he third period was Salem 48 and Galveston 45.

Stevens had 21 of the Hawks points.

Morgan had 25 for the Eagles.

The fourth quarter saw a flurry of action as both teams went to a quick-strike attack with quick shots on both ends of the court. Ellerson broke loose for six points in the quarter, while Morgan also scored six. Mentz had four and Cobb two in the quarter with 2:02 left to play.

Salem led 63 - 58.

Coach Breyer called time out.

"Great job, guys," exhorted the excited coach, "now lets put the ball in Morgan's hands for the next couple of minutes. We want foul shots. Lets do it."

The Eagles brought the ball down and went into a semi-freeze. With 1:39 left, Morgan drew the foul. He made two fouls shots to make the score 65 - 58. Stevens tossed in a set shot from 18 feet and quickly fouled Morgan as he went high for the throw in. You could see it in the eyes of the Hawk players. They knew Morgan was not likely to miss from the foul line and he jumped so high they could not prevent the throw in to him. They were literally between the rock and the hard place.

With 1:21 left, Morgan hit his two foul shots to make it 67 - 60. On the throw in three Hawks encircled Morgan and forced him to throw the ball long to Hogan who was fouled with 0:59 left in the game.

Hogan missed the front end of the one-and-one.

Eddy grabbed the rebound for the Hawks. The outlet pass went to Stevens. He drove hard to the basket. He went up for the shot as Morgan went high for the block. The Galveston star was able to spin in the air and get the shot off as Morgan came down on his arm just after the shot had been released. Stevens went to the line to complete the three-point play.

Morgan gazed at the Hawks star from the top of the circle and said, "good move, Stevens!"

Stevens nodded and made the foul shot.

It was 67 - 63 with 0:41 left in the game when Watts fouled a high-flying Morgan on the Hawks foul line. After the walk to the other end the Eagle guard made the two foul shots to stretch the lead back to 69 - 63.

The Hawks coach used his last time out.

With 0:36 left in the game, the Eagles picked up defensive intensity. Hall took a 15-foot shot with 0:22 left in the game, missed and Butch Cobb came down with the rebound. He was fouled by Eddy with 0:18 left to play.

After an Eagle timeout, Cobb missed the front of his one-and-one.

Eddy got the rebound and fired the ball to Stevens with 0:06 seconds left. The smooth Hawk guard pulled up on the far left angle and swished a 20-foot jump shot with 0:02 seconds left.

The Eagles lead was 69 - 65.

Hogan grabbed the ball and stepped out of bounds to throw in the ball. Time expired. The Salem Eagles had won the game 69 to 65.

Kyle Morgan sought out Vince Stevens. He extended his hand and told him, "You're tough, Stevens, good luck."

Stevens shook his hand and said, "You're unbelievable, Man. Good luck to yourself."

They parted company with a great deal of respect for each others immense talents.

It was a tired Eagle team in the dressing room. Morgan had scored 37 points, Ellerson had 11, Mentz had nine, Cobb and Hogan had scored six each.

Vince Stevens had scored 34 points for Galveston.

Morgan's parents, Porter and her parents and just about everyone Morgan knew stood outside the door as the team left the dressing room to head for the team bus. The team had finished at 31 wins and one loss.

Jack Ellerson had averaged 30.38 points and nine rebounds per game, Morgan had averaged 28.37, Mentz 17.81, Cobb 8.31 with 11 rebounds per game and Hogan 5.75 and seven assists per game.. The starting team had average over 90 points per game. Morgan had hit 71 percent from the field and 99.3 percent from the charity stripe. Ellerson had shot at 55.2 percent for the year and Mentz came in at 54.7 percent. The Salem Eagles were an extraordinary team. What made it even more amazing was that all the starters would return next season.

The Eagles were declared the mythical national champions by all the publications and newspapers that list such things. Some would argue that they possibly could have been the best team, college or high school in America. Not one college coach that saw him play would argue against Kyle Morgan being the best high school basketball guard in America. He would be named the National High School Player of the Year by The National High School Association Sporting News out of Indianapolis. Teammate Jack Ellerson and Galveston guard Vince Stevens were also on the team.

Coach David Breyer was named the Maryland High School Coach of the Year. He was runner-up for the national honor. Morgan, Ellerson and Mentz were all named to the ten-man All-State squad with Morgan selected as the Maryland Player of the Year.

Misty Porter was named to the girls high school All-America team by the Indianapolis publication. She was runner-up for the National Player of the Year. The dazzling junior was the Maryland Player of the Year and received the Marilyn Maxwell Academic Athletic Award for having the best scholastic average for a high school female basketball player in the state. Kyle Morgan received the Billy Hanson Academic Athletic Award for the best scholastic award by a male basketball player.

It was to be several weeks of honors for the Salem teams concluding a dream season on the hardwood.

With Porter back to lead the girls and the entire starting unit returning for the boys, it could only be imagined that next season could be a virtual replay of the past season.

Chapter Twenty-Seven
The Spring Season

There would be about a month off between the end of basketball season and the start of the baseball and track seasons at Salem High school. Morgan had several dates set aside to appear on various teen programs on National Television to promote his records and a new record album scheduled to be released in early July. He wanted to conclude this within the next two weeks and start getting into shape for track.

Probably the best sport for Kyle Morgan might have been track. He had always been able to run faster than anyone he went up against. The previous year he had ran a startling 12.91 - 120-yard high hurdle time in the state track meet in Georgia. He had also posted a 17.04 time in the 180-yard low hurdles that broke a state record that had stood for 28 years. His speed along with his tremendous coordination enabled him to skim a hurdle by mere fractions of an inch as he glided along in his three steps and over high-hurdle style. He had vaulted over 15 feet on numerous occasions and was looking to go 17 feet this season. He also ran a 9.22 - 100-yard dash during the season. He was an exceptional track performer that loved the sport.

He and Porter were spending a lot of time working out on the basketball court every evening. He believed she could increase her leaping ability by about six-to-eight inches with the proper exercise. He even told her that if she would work hard at it she could possible be able to dunk a volleyball by the start of the next basketball season. Spring basketball was slated to begin the second week in June just before the end of the school year.

Morgan was tossing a baseball around with James Mentz just about every day after school. He was also going over to the track and jogging two-to-three miles every afternoon around 7:00 p.m. He was also working on short sprints and form on the high hurdles every night while at the track. He planned on starting to work on the vaulting pit the following week.

The first day of baseball practice saw 44 potential players report on the first day of practice. The varsity squad would number 24 players. The balance would play B-team. The Eagles expected to battle for the region title even before Morgan, Mentz and Ellerson showed up at the school. Now with these three it appeared they would probably easily win the title. Van Greer was expected to be one of the better pitchers in AAAA this season. The previous year he had won seven games as a freshman. He threw in the low nineties and had a wicked slider that completely handcuffed opposing batters.

The first day was mostly fielding and some batting practice. It was evident after watching Morgan hit three "tape-measure home runs" he was not just an average baseball player.

Coach Reece Arnold walked over to Morgan and asked him, "Do you always hit the ball like that?"

Morgan grinned and answered, "It'll take me a few practices to get my timing down."

Coach Arnold shook his head and walked away.

Jack Ellerson was a first base candidate and James Mentz was working out at shortstop. A six-foot-seven shortstop. Coach Arnold was not surprised at anything he saw as he watched his tall trio hitting the ball all over the field.

The next day Morgan took some batting practice and again hit five balls out of the park in only 12 swings. He also showed his pitching ability in a 20-pitch audition in which he threw the ball at speeds of up to 100-miles per hour.

Coach Arnold just watched and wondered just how good his team may be this season.

That evening Kyle Morgan made his Salem debut on the track.

Coach Shaw watched in awe as the 16-year-old track phenom bolted from the starting blocks. After the first step it appeared he was going wide open.

He ran two 100s' in less than 10.0 seconds and stepped through a 13.32 --- 120-yard high hurdles. He went over to the vaulting pit and after about 15 minutes of pole carrying sprints to the pit box he placed the bar up and cleared 15 feet on three consecutive vaults.

He had cleared the height easily. Coach Shaw wondered just how high this boy could go if pushed. One thing he was sure of ~ Morgan was something to behold on the track.

It was two weeks later that Salem opened its baseball season with Murphy. The out-classed Murphy team was never in the game. When Morgan came up for his first at bat with Saye and Mentz on base, there was an eerie silence. It was as if the Salem fans were waiting for the inevitable to happen. Morgan took two outside pitches. The next pitch was about belt high on the outer half of the plate. The ball was almost past him when he swung and drove the ball to the opposite field for his first home run for the Salem Eagles. It was hit well over 450 feet. He hit another home run in the fourth inning as Salem closed out the game in four innings with an easy 18 - 0 win. Greer pitched a two-hitter. Morgan went 5 for 5 at the plate with two long home runs.

Three days later the Eagle track team entered the Carlton Relays over at Carlton County. There had been a feature story about Morgan in the Baltimore Gazette the previous day. It reviewed his amazing track performance in Georgia the previous year. The stadium was packed with anticipation of seeing several new state records from the spectacular track sensation.

Morgan did not disappoint them on this day. He easily won the 120-yard high hurdles in 13.14. He was never pushed. He ran an 18.10 ~ 180-yard low hurdles and pole vaulted sixteen-feet-five-inches. A vault of 17 feet was getting closer. He also anchored the 440-yard relay team to a school record 39.24 time and he ran the anchor leg on the mile-relay team that ran a sizzling 3.18.40 ~ a new school record. Both hurdle times and the vault were better than the existing state records. He had missed twice at 16'9" in the pole vault and called it a day.

Kyle Morgan was an incredible track athlete. He was without a doubt the best Coach Tom Shaw had seen in his 25 years of coaching track in Maryland.

It was in 1956 when an 11-year-old Morgan had first watched a track meet at his local high school in Georgia. He also tuned into the summer Olympics on television and literally fell in love with the pole vault event. To Kyle Morgan, the pole vault was the most fun of anything he had ever done. He had built a vaulting pit and placed some slats in the ground for standards. These homemade standards had nails about six-inches apart all the way up the back side. He cut a cross pole from the cane growing along the bank of the lake on the back of the Morgan property. He chopped down a three-inch in circumference bamboo pole and used it as a vaulting pole. By the time he was 12 he could vault over 10 feet. He also made some high hurdles and practiced them daily. It was not out of the ordinary for young Morgan to shoot a basketball for two hours everyday during the summer and then work for two more hours on his vaulting and hurdling.

Mr. Morgan watched his son work at his track ventures from afar. He was beginning to see an amazing potential in the track and field arena for his young son.

Misty Porter sat beside Mr. and Mrs. Morgan. She turned to Mr. Morgan as Kyle crossed the finish line in the mile relay and asked, "How in God's name does he do all these remarkable things?"

Mr. Morgan laughed out loud as he said, "Misty, we have been asking ourselves that for years. He sure didn't get his ability from us or anyone in our family that we know of."

Morgan would lower his high-hurdle time to 12.91 the following week in the Ashford Academy Relays. He ran an 18.03 ~ low-hurdle time and pole vaulted 16'8." All were Maryland state records.

In practice that week he had ran a 9.18 in the 100-yard dash. It was his first head to head race against Bobby Winkler. He was three steps ahead of him at the finish. Winkler was pushed to a 9.68, beating the state record by over a second. Morgan's time was the fastest time ever ran by a high school boy in the United States.

The second baseball game of the season for the Eagles was against old rival Galveston at Eagle Stadium. It was packed.

Jerry Hall, an All-State guard on the basketball team was pitching for the Hawks. Vince Stevens, the all-star guard was at short-stop. The Hawks were a good team. They were favorites to win their side of their region.

Coach Tom Shaw sat with Galveston football coach Bill Bridges off to the side of the home grandstand in lounge chairs. Coach Bridges asked, "You have any idea where that kid is going to school ?"

"None what-so-ever," replied Shaw, "he just doesn't give you much indication as to what his plans are."

His first pitching outing for the Eagles was a one-hit shut-out against his old basketball rival. He went 4 for 5 with two more home runs. He drove in 7 runs in the 12 - 0 win. It was in the second inning that Morgan established his legacy as the best hitter in Maryland high school circles.

His first time to the plate he had hit a frozen-rope liner into right field for a single.

As he approached the batters box for his second at-bat, the large crowd gave him a standing ovation. All eyes were on the super-slugger as he stepped into the batters box.

Hall came on the outside corner with two curve balls that Morgan took for a ball and called strike. The next pitch was on the outside of the plate, but too much in the strike zone for a hitter of the magnitude of Kyle Morgan. He swung and the ball left his bat in a high trajectory, headed for the tennis courts over 550 feet from home plate. It was measured later by Coach Arnold at 620 feet from home plate. The power of the young slugger was unbelievable as he hit another long home run in the fifth inning.

In his first eight games for the Eagles he had 31 hits in 37 at-bats with 12 home runs. He pitched in four games and had not surrendered a run. Two of the four wins were no-hitters with a one-hitter and a two-hitter on his stats. Two of the three hits against him were bunt singles.

Morgan consistently threw around 99 to 100-miles per hour with an occasional 101- mile per hour pitch thrown in. His curve ball would break a foot in either direction and his slider would look like it dropped off a table. He was simply not hittable to the high school players in the Maryland high school circles. At bat, he would literally knock the cover off the ball. He hit the ball so hard on almost every occasion that fielding it was not possible. It was more of a get out of the way type reaction from many of the Salem opponents.

The baseball team was solid all the way through the lineup with Ellerson at first base, Walt Hogan at second base, Bobby Saye at third base, Mentz at shortstop, Van Greer in left field when he was not pitching, Morgan in center field when not on the mound and Jeremy Price in right field. Billy Maxwell was usually an outfield starter when one of the outfielders was pitching. At catcher it was Daniel North, the football captain. Paul Bramblette was a spot pitcher as was Joey Bates. It was a good solid team.

Saturday was the Salem Relays. It would bring together the best track teams in the state. After this meet, it would be possible to chart just where Coach Shaw felt his charges could finish in the state meet later in the season.

At this point Bobby Winkler had the states best times in the 100 and 220-yard dash. Butch Cobb had the best discus throw and the second best shot put distance. Morgan had far away the best time in the hurdles and the top height in the pole vault. Both Eagle relay teams had state best times. It was a solid track team that was going to run away with the state title if things continued along the present course. They were also expecting points from Shealey in the long jump, Carter in the 440-yard dash and Mentz in the high jump.

Saturday was a beautiful day for a track meet. It was in the low 80s' with a clear sky.

The Salem 440-yard relay team opened the meet and won easily with Carter, Shealey, Winkler and Morgan running a sizzling 38.16 race.

Bobby Winkler had a solid 100-yard dash win in 9.73. This time was the best ever ran in competition in the state of Maryland. Winkler would later run a 21.36 in the 220 that was also the fastest time ever ran in Maryland.

Morgan zipped through the high hurdles in 12.79. Another record.

James Mentz went 6'10" in the high jump to win the event on fewer misses.

Carter and Shealey finished third and fifth in the broad jump with leaps of 21'8" and 21'4" respectively.

Cobb won the discus with a toss of 168'11". He threw the shot put 58'4", but was beaten by his old football nemesis Jerry Clinton of District-Heights, who had a throw of 59'8".

Morgan sailed 16'10" in the pole vault and narrowly missed on his final attempt at 17 feet. He felt he was closing in on the mark and would get it before the region meet with one more tri-meet and the Richmond Relays still on the regular season schedule for the Eagles.

Billy Watkins had finished third in the mile-run with a 4.22.31 time.

Carter won the 440-yard dash with a 48.41 time. The third best in the state at the time.

The Eagle mile-relay team of Bales, Carter, Winkler and Morgan won the last event of the day with a time of 3.09.23. Another state record.

It was an awesome display by the Eagle track team. They had scored 112 points in the meet. They were the odds-on favorite to capture the state AAAA championship.

Coach Tom and Martha Shaw sat and chatted that night.

"Tom, what I see on that track is impossible. No one can do the things that boy does. He's setting world records and he's only a junior in high school. What'll he do his senior year?"

Coach Shaw answered, "Martha, I don't have an answer to that question, but I can tell you this. Kyle Morgan is far superior to all other high school athletes I have ever seen. The Lord has endowed him with abilities to rise to unparalleled levels on athletic fields of competition. Did I tell you that I now have over 85 requests for interviews from various colleges at my office. Every school in the nation wants to offer this kid a scholarship. Next year when he opens this thing back up, he'll be inundated with interview requests and contacts. They want him for football, basketball, track, baseball and even academics. I honestly believe it'll be the biggest recruiting drive for a kid in the history of college sports."

Martha Shaw replied, "Well, you helped create this monster, so you need to be there for him when all this pops up. He'll need someone to help his father get all this mess sorted out."

"Yes, he will, Martha, and I will be there. All of us will be there. We owe it to him. He has certainly made all of us coaches at Salem look far better than we really are. We can never forget that."

Chapter Twenty-Eight
The Breaking of a Hero

Morgan and Porter had been planning on going to the movie to see the latest Elvis Presley film, Kid Galahad, for weeks. Both were big Elvis fans. Morgan had briefly met the singing super-star about two months earlier at a recording session at Landau Recording Studios in Philadelphia.

They planned on attending the matinee session on Monday evening at 6:00 p.m., but baseball practice had delayed him getting home until around 7:00 p.m. He and Misty had arrived at the theater around 8:25 p.m. for the 8:30 p.m. presentation.

It was after 10:30 p.m. when they left the theater and walked slowly toward his car. Misty said, "It was pretty good, Kyle, but I don't think I would pay to see it again."

Morgan replied, "I don't know. I just like Elvis. I think I've seen every movie he has ever made."

Very suddenly it happened. Four young men stepped from a van parked to the right of Morgan's car.

He quickly accessed the situation, at least two of the men had knives and it appeared that two had handguns.

Time stopped for Kyle Morgan. His thoughts flashed back to when he was 6-years-old. It was his third lesson in Tae-Kwan-Do at the Billings Academy in Collinsville, New York. His father was

214

undergoing training in the advanced marital-arts class as part of his Central Intelligence Agency training. He had decided to let his young son take this same training. A larger man had managed to get young Morgan prone on the floor with several well-placed kicks that took his breath away. It was almost a year before he was able to hold his own with the experienced marital-arts participants in the class.

His mind came back to the present. The young thugs surrounded the couple as one gunman stepped forward. The words that initiated immediate action were then spoken. "We want the girl to come with us," a gunman said. He told his two knife-wielding associates, "take her to the van."

The gunman demanded, "Give me your wallet, rich boy." He appeared to be the ringleader of the group. As Morgan reached for his wallet, he sprang into action.

A kick with his right foot to the gun hand of the assailant disarmed him. Morgan spun, grabbed the disarmed gunman, and pulled him in front of him as a human shield. The second gunman opened fire, hitting his partner in crime at least three times.

Morgan literally threw the mortally wounded gunman back onto the second gunman. He charged forward, brought his right hand down to the back of the would-be assailants neck. There was a crushing, cracking sound as the young man fell to the ground. His neck was broken. Morgan's blazing speed enabled him to quickly catch up with the two young men forcing Porter toward the van.

He grabbed the shoulder of one knife-wielding assailant, spun him around and delivered a thrust punch to his chest that left him sprawled on the ground stunned and breathless. The second knife-wielding assailant thrust his knife at him. He easily used a turning stance move to avoid the knife, then used a backward kick to the groin area of the assailant to bring him to the ground writhing in agony.

Porter began to scream for help. The two thugs struggled to their feet and tried to make their way to the van. Morgan turned his attention back to Misty. He started walking back toward her.

Neither Porter or Morgan had noticed that a fifth member of the gang was behind the wheel of the van. He climbed from the vehicle and aimed a gun at Morgan. It happened quickly. One shot and the high school super-star went down with a bullet in his back.

Screams from Porter had brought several bystanders toward the scene. Misty saw the gun pointed at Kyle. She had screamed, "Kyle, look out!"

It was too late! Morgan managed two steps toward Porter, then fell to the parking lot pavement. The three perpetrators were able to scramble into the van.

It quickly sped away.

One assailant was killed by the bullets of his partner in crime, while another suffered a broken neck that would leave him paralyzed from the neck down for the remainder of his life.

"Oh God, Kyle, No!" Porter screamed as he lay on his side on the cold parking lot pavement.

It was around 11:15 p.m. when Ken Morgan received word that his son was at Keller Memorial Hospital in critical condition. On the way to the hospital there was little conversation between the elder Morgan and Kyle's mother. Both were immersed in thought and praying in their mind that their only child would survive this terrible ordeal.

Porter and her parents met the Morgan's in the hospital lobby. A doctor came over to the couple and told them, "Your son is on the operating table at this time. He has a bullet lodged extremely close to his spinal cord. We are going to have to be extremely careful not to exacerbate the injury during the removal of the bullet process. We don't know as of yet if there is spinal cord damage. Your son has not regained consciousness since the shooting."

As Misty Porter related the story of what had occurred in the movie parking lot ----- Ken Morgan thought back to the first time he had asked Kyle to join him in martial arts training.

He had said, "Dad, I don't want to know how to break any bodies neck and beat them up, What's the sense in that?" Now, that training had apparently created a situation where his son had saved his young friend from terrible crimes against her, but may have cost him his life.

For over eight hours the families sat and waited for word from the operating staff. At 6:15 a.m., a doctor approached the Morgan's.

The green-clad physician said, "Mr. and Mrs. Morgan, your son is out of surgery."

Mr. Morgan quickly asked, "Can we see him?"

The doctor told them that he was heavily sedated and still in a critical condition room at the time. It would probably be eight-to-ten hours before he would awaken. He went on to say that they did not see any damage to the spinal cord, but this type of injury had been known to create instances of temporary paralysis and in some cases had created permanent paralysis.

The distraught parents agreed that it may be best to wait until he was awake before going into the room.

Misty Porter continued to cry as her parents sought to console her from the agony they knew she was suffering at this time.

She said to no one in particular, "You know he was just trying to protect me. I could see it in his eyes. I knew he was going to do something the minute they said they were going to take me with them. I was scared, but I didn't want anything to happen to Kyle." She looked at his parents and said, "I know I'm just a 16-year-old kid, but I know now that I do love Kyle. I don't want him to die."

There was silence as Mr. Morgan walked over to Misty and placed his arms around her. He said softly and calmly, "We know how you feel about Kyle, Misty, and while he probably hasn't ever come right out and said it, I think he loves you about as much as anyone can love someone at his age." The elder Morgan continued, "There was no way he would have let them take you with them. That is just not his way. He knew what he was doing and the risks involved. He thought you were important enough to him to take those risks. We don't blame you in any way for what happened tonight. We're proud of our son for his courage and bravery. We will get through this, Misty. Everything will work out. His fate is in the hands of God. His faith and the support of those that love him will carry him through this thing."

Porter and her parents moved into a conference room where she was asked to relate the incident to the police in exact detail.

Mrs. Morgan sat silently while Kyle's father paced the floor of the waiting room at the hospital. Her mind drifted back to a time when her crying four-year-old son stood before her with a badly-skinned elbow he had received after a fall from a tree he liked to climb in the families back-yard residence.

He had asked, "Mama, am I going to die?"

She had pulled him close and said, "Of course not son, it's not a serious injury. You'll be as good as new in a day or two." Her thoughts were now on whether or not she would be able to again look her son in the eyes and say in all honesty, "No, you're not going to die. It's not a serious injury. You'll be as good as new before you know it."

Mrs. Morgan broke down at this point. Only the comforting arms of her husband enabled her to regain any measure of composure.

The hours dragged by. At 4:30 p.m., a nurse came in and told the anxious parents that their son was awake and they could visit with him. They were told that Doctor Mark Broadhouse wanted to talk with them before they went into the room.

It was about ten minutes later when the doctor entered the room. He quickly got to the point. "Your son has paralysis in his right arm down through his right leg. It is too early to tell if it is permanent or temporary. The odds are that after a complete healing and stabilizing of the damage area, he could very well be normal in all regards. We'll just have to wait and see if that's the case."

When the Morgan's entered the room, a light went on in the face of the younger Morgan. He was still heavily sedated, but seemed coherent in his communications. After a few moments of conversation, he asked, "Is Misty okay?"

"Yes, she's fine son," Mrs. Morgan replied, "and she wants to see you very much. She'll be in a little later."

For over an hour the family talked.

At 5:30 p.m. Misty Porter entered the room. She hugged Kyle and kissed him gently on the cheek. Tears flowed between both youngsters as they talked about various nonsensical things over the next several moments.

At 6:00 p.m. a nurse asked that they leave for now to allow Morgan to get some natural rest. His sleep for the last 24 hours had been from the trauma of his injury and heavy sedation.

The possibility of paralysis had not been discussed with their son. On the way home, Lucille Morgan asked her husband, "Ken, what if he is paralyzed. What will we do?"

Ken Morgan answered in a low voice, "If it is the Will of God, there's not anything we can do. We just have to pray and put our faith in the Lord."

The story of the attack on the high school athlete and singing sensation was all over the evening news. Calls were coming in from around the country. A prayer meeting was held the next night at the Westside Baptist Church with over twelve-hundred people in attendance.

Morgan lay in his hospital bed alone in his thoughts. He knew he could barely move many parts of his body and could not move other limbs at all. He had purposely not asked about any possible paralysis. He didn't want to think of it as possible for the time being. He thought back to the incident and one thing really troubled him. He had underestimated the intelligence of the crime perpetrators in having a person left in the van to cover their backs. It was a mental error his CIA father would never have made. He made a mental note that he never would underestimate a potential dangerous situation again.

Morgan had planned to play American-Legion Baseball during the summer and enter several track meets as he pursued the magical 17-foot mark in the pole vault. He wanted to be the first person, high school, college or track club to clear 17 feet. Now all those hopes and dreams were shattered by the senseless act of a person he didn't know or had ever harmed in any way shooting him at almost point-blank range. Kyle Morgan cried himself to sleep that day.

Misty Porter would spend several hours each day with Kyle over the next week as he regained his strength and began to eat normally. They had obviously been brought closer together during this ordeal.

Morgan found himself wanting to touch her more and for the first time sex with the beautiful young lady even entered his thoughts. He was awakening to the realization of a maturation process that he hoped he would be able to nurture as he went forward with his life.

Porter was very positive in all her comments and actions with Kyle. She maintained an upbeat personality when with him. At night in her bed, she cried herself to sleep with the thoughts that the fabulous high school super-star may be unable to ever participate in sports again. One thing was certain, she would always be there for him as long as he wanted her to be. She had made a commitment to try and be a major part of the life of Kyle Morgan.

His parents and various guests would enter throughout visiting hours each day until the on-duty nurse had to virtually lock the door to keep them out.

Twelve days after the shooting incident ~ Morgan went home from the hospital. He was paralyzed in his right arm and right leg down to his ankle. He walked stiff-legged with a cane and could not bend his right arm at the elbow or raise his arm higher than his shoulder.

He attended several baseball practices over the next week. At baseball practice he would just sit and watch the team while chatting with well-wishers that always seemed to be dropping by. He displayed an upbeat demeanor that would act as the ice-breaker when words would be so hard to come by when talking with him. His actions made it clear that pity was not an option to the current Morgan calamity.

Morgan was in a three-days per week rehabilitation program at the hospital. He had no intention of giving up at this point. He still had his amazing intelligence and reasoning ability.

The Salem Eagle baseball team would finish second in the region and go out in the third round of the state playoffs. They had made the final four without their super-star.

Morgan attended the playoffs with Porter and other friends. He cheered for the Eagles until the very end.

The Eagle track team would finish second in the state meet. District-Heights had finished first in AAAA. Coach Shaw would add a possible 30 lost points from Morgan with firsts in the high and low hurdles, the pole vault, and two relay firsts and see the possibility of where the team could have finished if Morgan had been able to compete. They would have won the state by 20 points.

School would be out in three weeks. Morgan spent a great deal of time working on agility drills and on the various rehab machines at the hospital. Now he was on an every other day work-out program.

Morgan didn't know if he would ever play sports again, but one thing was for sure. His junior year was now over. He had to put the past behind him.

It was several weeks earlier around 7:00 p.m. when Morgan and Porter entered the track meet at Memorial Stadium. The petite Porter no longer discouraged any notion that she and Kyle Morgan were two young people that loved each other very much. You could see it in her eyes as she looked at the young man slowly making his way to a seat midway down to the track.

The meet had started at 6:00 p.m. Kyle would stay through the end of the meet. He said virtually nothing as he watched the running events and occasionally glanced at the pole vault area. An occasional air-punch or clapping of the hands were the only emotions noticeable to any onlookers.

One thing that everyone expressed amazement at was his upbeat attitude. He didn't mope around and feel sorry for himself. He visited the Mentz Pharmacy with regularity and attended the various school functions. He attended church every Sunday and enjoyed watching sporting events on television. He had been able to maintain a seemingly normal life path despite the tragedy that had occurred. He refused to shut anyone out of his life.

At the conclusion of the meet Butch Cobb, James Mentz, Bobby Winkler and other teammates gathered around him in a valiant effort to make him feel he was still an integral part of the Eagle family.

Coach Shaw walked over to him and said, "I'll be glad when you get back, Kyle. We miss you."

Morgan managed a weak grin, then answered, "I'll be back Coach, you can count on it." It was a short time later that Morgan and Porter walked from the stadium and climbed into his car. His thoughts were now on what was going to happen next in the life of the high school super-star during his senior year.

Chapter Twenty-Nine
The Battle Back

It had been two months since Kyle Morgan was seriously wounded in the parking lot incident. He had been regularly attending rehab sessions at the Wilson Clinic. There was not any improvement in his condition as far as he could tell. His doctor's could still not determine why all his tests showed negative as to potential causes for his right side of the body paralysis.

Morgan started visiting the medical library at Wilson a week after his rehabilitation sessions started. He had read many medical precedents for his condition, but none were a fit for his exact symptoms. He had virtually no feeling in his right arm from his wrist to his shoulder and he was numb from his right hip down to his right calf. He could not bend either his right arm at the elbow or his knee at the knee-cap.

One thing he had noticed. While lying quietly, he could feel some kind of twinge of pain or a burning sensation in his back. It would always be noticeable when he was in a totally relaxed mode or as he awoke during the night. Every test known to the medical profession was performed on him without any possible reason diagnosed for his medical condition.

It was on a Friday morning when Kyle approached his father in the living room. "Dad," he said, "I want to see if Dr. Jacob Jennings of the Chicago Medical Center will see me. He is the most renown surgeon out there as far as blood transport diseases." Kyle continued, " There is something not right inside me. I can feel it. I know my own body."

Kyle's father said, "Son, if that's what you want, you know we'll do it. We just don't want you to place all your hopes on this one person being able to come in, diagnose your problem, and get it corrected overnight."

Kyle quickly replied, "Dad, that's exactly what I do expect. I have a hypothesis I want to run by you and see what your thoughts are." He continued, "What if during my surgery something was not done properly. Could there be some damaged capillaries or some artery damage that was overlooked during surgery that can be repaired? I honestly believe the pain I feel from time to time is some kind of warning signal, telling me to look into this further"

His father clasped his hands in thought. He knew his son didn't make far-fetched, outlandish statements or irrational decisions. He then proceeded to the phone and started the wheels rolling to get in touch with Dr. Jacob Jennings.

It was almost a week later that Mr. Morgan received a call from Dr. Jennings. After explaining the situation to him, Dr. Jennings agreed to see Kyle in Chicago the first Monday in August.

The decision was now made. Kyle Morgan would go back under the knife. It was the Tuesday before leaving for Chicago on Thursday that he and Misty Porter sat in her den talking.

She asked softly, "Kyle, are you sure you want to do this?"

He looked into her tearful blue eyes and answered, "I've got to do it, Misty. I can't go through the rest of my life as a cripple. There is an answer. I won't be satisfied until I find that answer."

She asked, "What if you don't find the answer to your problem in Chicago?"

An emotional Morgan answered, "I'll move in another direction, with another doctor. It can be corrected. I can feel it. I know my body, Misty. My instinct tells me something is not right. I can feel it at this moment."

Porter said, "Kyle, I just want you to know that I'll be here waiting for you when you get back. I want to be a part of your life if you'll let me."

Morgan took her hand and said, "Misty, you are a part of my life. You have become a big part of my life. I don't know what lies ahead for me at this point. I care a great deal for you, but I can't make any promises to you because my life goal at this time is to overcome this paralysis problem. It's consuming me. I can't eat, I can't sleep. I've got to get it fixed."

He looked into Misty's eyes and said, "Every night I dream of being back on a football field or basketball court. You are always there cheering me on from the stands. I see your smiling, cheerful face that I saw all this past year. Then I wake up and have to struggle to get up and go the bathroom. I want to see that same smiling face again while participating in sports. I just can't live this way, Misty. I don't want pity from my friends and family. I have got to get this thing corrected. It can be corrected. I believe this with all my heart."

Porter placed her arms around him and spoke softly, "If you were playing a basketball game and it was close at the end of the game, I'd want you to take that last shot. I would know that you would probably make it. Well, I know you well enough to know that you'll work this thing out, too! I believe in you, Kyle Morgan. I'll pray for you. Please come back to me!"

Kyle Morgan would never forget that first kiss from Misty Porter as he held her in his arms.

It was a beautiful Thursday evening in August of 1963 when Misty Porter and her family watched from the concourse as the Morgan's boarded a plane for the trip to Chicago.

For over four hours Dr. Jennings examined Morgan literally from head to toe. He went over every x-ray and machine scan known to medical science at the time. He found nothing that should cause a paralysis condition. His only thought was it could be some nerve damage or even a psychological problem of some type.

Morgan then told the doctor what he wanted done. "Dr. Jennings, I want you to do a complete exploratory surgery along the path of the bullet. Expand outward three-to-four inches along that path. I am convinced that you will find something that was overlooked during the original surgery."

Dr. Jennings said, "Kyle, an exploratory surgery can be dangerous, especially if we have to get close to the spinal cord again."

He replied, "I understand that, but I am going to have it done, either by you or someone else."

Dr. Jennings knew the history of Kyle Morgan. He knew of his intellectual brilliance. He replied, "I'll do as you ask, but you have to understand, the odds of what you are thinking are less than one percent in several million that some poor repair was done inside that wound."

Morgan answered without hesitation, "I feel it, Dr. Jennings, I know it's there."

On Wednesday of August 6, Morgan went under the knife. The operation was expected to take up to six hours. The Morgan's sat quietly outside the operating room as the ordeal began.

It was almost seven hours later that Dr. Jennings walked out of the operating room and stopped in front of Ken Morgan. He asked the parents to step into a conference room just off the operating room.

He told the Morgan's that what he had to relate to them was the most unbelievable thing he had seen in over 35 years of medical practice.

He started his explanation. "Your son is not a normal young man by any means. We have found what appears to be mutated or "auxiliary" capillaries and nerve endings along the wound route. These are tiny, almost microscopic extensions that are coming off the normal capillaries and veins found in the body. It is my belief that these unique attributes are what enables your son to have incredible coordination, stamina and potentially greater strength than most boys. His great speed is a result of the more widespread blood and oxygen expansion throughout his body. It is my belief he can probably run miles and miles without getting tired and that he can run these distances at an incredible speed. This explains his remarkable speed at the shorter distances. His coordination and extraordinary intelligence is a symptom of increased brain cells and the greater flexibility within his body caused by the additional oxygen and flow of blood to his brain. He is not likely to become winded or experience normal feelings of simple tiredness. He could very well run 20 miles without any shortness of breath. His mind reacts at a far greater speed to tell his body what it needs to do than normal people. This enables his body to follow a sequence of brain commands a split second faster than most people. An example is his pole vaulting ability. His mind is able to react much quicker to muscle demands from his brain than the normal athlete, allowing for greater body and limb control."

Mrs. Morgan said, "Doctor, are you saying our son is some kind of X-Man. That he is a mutant?"

Dr. Jennings smiled as he answered, "It is true that your son has mutated genes in his body. They grew the extra veins, capillaries and arteries, but they are not something that changes the general philosophy of him being an average 16-year-old boy. It's like the child that has the extra toe, or when Siamese twins are born. His gifts are a blessing and not an aberration. Something along the way caused these things to happen. We just don't know all the circumstances to explain just what in a particular case."

He continued, "We have found several small nerve endings and capillaries that were left unattached during the previous surgery," explained Dr. Jennings. "We also found several microscopic muscles about two-inches off the wound path that had snapped as the bullet tore through his body. He has muscle attachments like we have never seen before. These tiny muscles had contracted away from the wound path. They are literally muscles attached to muscles. Very rare, I'm sure. I've certainly never seen anything like it or heard of anything like it before. I honestly don't feel anyone can be held accountable for this happening, because no one knew to look for extra physiological attributes during the surgery. I can assure you we doctors don't see any cadavers like Kyle Morgan's body during our medical school training classes."

Mr. Morgan quickly asked, "Do you believe this is what is causing the paralysis?"

Dr. Jennings placed his hand to his chin in thought as he answered, "Yes, I believe it is very likely the source of the problem. The muscles have been reattached already. I believe he'll be completely normal ~ or as normal as someone like him can be ~ once the healing from the surgery is complete. Now if you'll excuse me, I need to return to the operating room to assure that all loose ends are tied up." He smiled as made the in jest comment.

Tears came to Ken Morgan's eyes.

Lucille Morgan cried openly. They were tears of joy. She asked, "Dr. Jennings, how can we thank you?"

He took her hand and answered, "Just working with someone like your son has been payment enough." He then jokingly said, "but I'm still going to send you a bill."

It was eight days later when Kyle Morgan and his family walked out of the Chicago Medical Center. Morgan was still stiff and somewhat sore, but he had full movement of all body limbs. He moved slowly toward the car, paused and took a last look back at a smiling Dr. Jacob Jennings standing beside the main entrance. He waved goodbye, nodded slightly and climbed into the back seat of his father's rented automobile.

Morgan was on his way back to Ridgeview. He bowed his head and uttered a small prayer during the trip to the airport. He had not been told about the amazing abnormalities within his body as of yet. But then again, he had always known he was different from the other kids.

When his parents told him what had been discovered and the theory as to why he was able to do many of the amazing things he could do, he sat in deep thought for several moments. He bowed his head and prayed. He felt he had indeed been blessed.

Four days after his arrival back in Ridgeview, the Morgan's gave a "By Invitation" dinner to all of his many friends at their Eastside Restaurant. All his high school teammates from the various sports were there along with their parents. The Porters were seated with the Morgan's. His pastor and all the church members, all his teachers, the city council and Board of Commissioners were in attendance.

Coach Shaw stood before the group and announced that it would be about the fourth week of the football season, but that Kyle Morgan would return to the team when given an official doctor's release. He then awarded Kyle the Best All-Around Athlete Award for the previous high school year.

Two weeks later in mid-August of 1963, Kyle Morgan and Misty Porter sat on his front porch, watching some neighborhood children shooting baskets across the street.

Misty was amused as he heard one of the youngsters say, "Watch this shot, I'm Kyle Morgan."

She turned her attention back to Kyle and asked, " Are you ready, big guy?"

He looked at her, took her hand, and grinned as he answered, "I'm ready, Lady. I feel as if I could run all day."

Even though it was only two weeks after returning from his Chicago surgery ⁓ Morgan had been given a doctor's release to begin light workouts and slow jogging. As he and Porter started their jog down the street, the Morgan parents stood at the front door. They looked at each other, smiled and walked back inside their house.

The high school super-star was on his way back. They wondered what would destiny hold for their remarkable son his senior year.

Made in United States
Orlando, FL
26 March 2022

16163359R00146